THE TITAN TRAP

CHRISTINE POPE

DARK VALENTINE PRESS

THE TITAN TRAP

978-0692330074

Copyright © 2014 by Christine Pope

Published by Dark Valentine Press

Cover design and interior layout by Indie Author Services

Visit www.christinepope.com for more information
or to contact the author.

THE TITAN TRAP

ONE

CASSIDY EVANS WATCHED THE APPROACHING YELLOW-ish-orange sphere and thought, not for the first time, *I really need to get a better gig.*

All right, so she hadn't actually chosen to make the monthly supply run to the maximum-security prison on Titan. No, she'd inherited the contract, along with the aging freighter she now piloted, and since she didn't have many alternatives, she hadn't deviated from the sched-ule, had kept making the loop from the supply depot on the Moon to Titan and back again. It was tedious...okay, mind-numbingly dull...but it paid the bills. Mostly. The *Avalon,* which her father had named because of a maud-lin longing for his family's homeland of Wales (never mind that he'd never set foot there), was now older than Cassidy herself, and thirty years could put a lot of wear and tear on a girl.

Don't I know it.

Lately it seemed that most of her income went straight back into the ship, paying for the repairs to keep it limping along so it could continue to earn even the meager rates the Consortium's corrections division was willing to offer. Every once in a while she contemplated selling the aging freighter and using the money to buy her passage to one of the colonies the Gaian Exploration Commission was continually opening up, just so she could start over, but she wasn't sure the Avalon would even fetch that much. Never mind that the GEC didn't much care for single colonists. It preferred families so all those husbands and wives could keep producing more children to populate all those new worlds.

Yes, she knew there were shady organizations out there that, for a fee, would match up singletons such as herself so they could have quickie weddings and then apply for expedited colonist status, but Cassidy wasn't quite that desperate.

Yet.

The comm beeped, and she pushed the button to accept the incoming call.

A man's face filled the small screen mounted in the console. Expression stern, he said, "Freighter *Avalon*, this is Titan MaxSec Logistics. Proceed to Xanadu Station, Hangar 12."

Cassidy nodded. "MaxSec Logistics, proceeding to Xanadu Station, Hangar 12."

Protocol satisfied, the man relaxed into a smile, then continued, in a much warmer tone, "Welcome back, Cassidy. You ever going to let me buy you that drink?"

"Now, Dale, you know I never mix business and pleasure."

"I keep hoping maybe I can get you to change your mind about that."

"Not until you can offer something better than the depot on Hyperion."

Titan itself housed the prison facility and nothing else; all support personnel and their families lived in the domed outpost on Hyperion Base, which didn't have much to offer beyond breathable air, a lackluster commissary, and an even worse cafeteria-slash-pub. Dale had been flirting with her ever since her first solo run here, and she did find him moderately attractive, but her current desperation wasn't quite overwhelming enough to allow her to settle for a drab existence on Hyperion, where she'd be lucky to share a conjugal visit every ten days, since that was how often personnel were cycled in and out of the MaxSec facility to get their Consortium-mandated three-day break.

"Wish I could, beautiful, but I'm not seeing the inner worlds for another two years. Not until my contract's up."

"Then I'll take a rain check, and you can ask me again in two years."

He laughed, although Cassidy thought she heard something hollow in it. They'd been doing this same song and dance for the past three years, and nothing had changed. It was fine. The flirtation at least helped to break up the monotony, even though she knew nothing would come of it.

"All right, Captain Evans, we have you on final approach. Protocol Alpha."

"Copy that, Logistics. I'll be there before you know it."

"Protocol Alpha" simply meant that she would approach her designated hangar, dock, and wait for the automated carts to trundle into her cargo hold and remove the food, clothing, weapons, ammo, and any other items corrections had mandated be transported on this supply run. Xanadu Station was a supply depot and nothing more; the actual prison was located some twenty kilometers away. It was set up that way on purpose, as the corrections department wanted to make sure that the supply depots and the ships that docked there regularly could not be a tempting target, a means of escape.

Of course, no one had ever escaped the MaxSec facility, let alone managed to cross twenty kilometers of some mighty inhospitable territory, methane lakes and all, so Cassidy thought the whole setup was overkill at its finest. Not that anyone would ask for her opinion.

She'd done this so often that she really didn't have to think about it anymore—come in slowly, slicing through the moon's thick atmosphere, letting the beacons guide the ship in for the final leg until it came to a rest in a hangar. No point in making the hangar livable, as she—or anyone else—wasn't expected to set foot outside the ship, and the automated carts certainly didn't need to breathe.

Maybe that was the worst of it, that she came all the way here, ten days in, ten days back to the Moon, ten days' rest there, and never saw one single solitary person face to face. Her interactions with Dale, or, more rarely, Pablo or Roy, were always over the comm. She'd never met them in person, didn't know if they were short or tall or something in between. They were just disembodied faces on a screen.

So when she heard footsteps coming down the *Avalon*'s short central hallway, and a tall figure in an environmental suit burst into the cockpit, she thought she could be forgiven for letting out the beginnings of a scream before she managed to get hold of herself enough to stand up and say, "What the hell?"

The man pulled a shimmering titanium badge off the belt of his suit. "Security, ma'am. A prisoner managed to escape and was spotted coming toward Xanadu Station. We're searching all ships."

Escape? No, that didn't sound right. It was impossible to escape the MaxSec, let alone cross Titan's frigid landscape in order to get to the one place that would allow a prisoner to get off-planet.

"I-I didn't hear anything—Dale...that is, Sergeant Givens...would have contacted me."

"We went into immediate lockdown, ma'am. That means no comms contact as well, in case the fugitive somehow managed to monitor our transmissions." The stranger had made no attempt to remove his helmet, and Cassidy could see only shadowy glimpses of the features beneath the gold-filmed duraplast. "I came in through your cargo hold, inspected it, and then sealed it, but I also need to search the interior."

"Go ahead," she told him, since she knew there wasn't anything she could do to stop him. At the same time she hoped she'd remembered to make up her bunk this morning, and that she hadn't left any panties or other unmentionables lying around. After all, she certainly hadn't expected to have any visitors today.

After giving her a perfunctory nod, he went back out into the corridor. She could hear him moving around her cabin, and then the other, smaller one that used to be hers before she inherited the ship. Other than that, there was only the galley and the tiny alcove with its two built-in benches and small round table that functioned as the eating area. A Sirocco-class luxury transport the *Avalon* was not.

The guard's inspection barely took two minutes. Really, you couldn't hide a mouse in the crew compartments in this boat, let alone an escaped prisoner. Cassidy waited in the pilot's seat, nerves jangling, although she told herself she had nothing to worry about, that the officer had already checked the cargo hold, so of course there couldn't be some murderous fugitive lurking any-where on board.

The man returned. "All clear," he told her, which was what she'd been expecting to hear. Even so, she sucked in a relieved little breath and waited for him to go so she could let the unloading continue and then get on her way.

But he didn't. Instead, she could practically feel his gaze sweep over her from behind the helmet's visor, and he said, "I need you to take off. Now."

"What?" she blurted, sure she hadn't heard him clearly.

"The prisoner isn't here, but that doesn't mean he couldn't still come aboard. As long as this ship is docked, it represents a possible escape route."

"The unloading isn't even half done—"

"That doesn't matter. Take off…immediately."

"I'm going to need to get clearance to take off—"

"I'm giving you the clearance. Do it."

Something in his stance told her that she'd better do as she was directed. Muttering a curse under her breath, she turned back to the console, checked the security camera feed in the cargo hold to make sure she wasn't going to crush an automated cargo cart when she buttoned everything up, then flipped the switch. The cargo bay doors began to close slowly.

"You'll have to go out through the hatch," she said, pointing with her free hand in the direction of the corridor. "It's the door between the smaller cabin and the sanitary facilities."

In response, he widened his stance, effectively blocking the hallway. "I'm staying onboard."

"Excuse me?"

"Corrections Statute 197A, Paragraph 102 states that in the case of an escape, it's a corrections officer's duty to make sure any ships get off the planet's surface safely. You can drop me at Hyperion on your way out of the system."

This was insane. Completely insane. More arguments rose to Cassidy's lips, but she saw the way the officer's hand rested on the pulse pistol at his hip and decided discretion was definitely the better part of valor here. Yes, jogging over to Hyperion would slow her down, as she'd have to recalculate her route, but she could file a claim for the extra fuel expenditure. That didn't mean it would actually ever be paid, since Corrections was slow as hell to pay anything that was actually in her contract, let alone something so far outside it. Even so, she'd feel better for making the attempt.

The calculations for liftoff had already been entered in the computer, so she only had to make a few hurried adjustments for leaving several hours earlier than she had planned. The *Avalon*'s atmospheric engines rumbled on, and she engaged the thrusters, the ship lifting from the hangar floor and moving slowly out into the thick air, yellow and toxic as the Cloud that had swept across half of Gaia's surface and killed so many billions.

At the same time, the comm squawked to life, Dale's face strained and pale. "*Avalon,* report. Explain your early departure!"

Frowning, she replied, "Under orders from one of your officers, Sergeant Givens."

"No such orders have been relayed to me, *Avalon.* Abort takeoff immediately and await the arrival of a security team."

Horror swept over her, even as the man in the environmental suit leaned forward and smashed the comm screen with the butt of his pistol. Then he leveled the gun at her and said softly, "Disregard that order and continue on your current course."

Even though she wanted to protest, to do something to show he wasn't in control here, Cassidy knew she didn't have any other options. There was nothing she could do but comply.

So many things could have gone wrong. Even now, as Derek Tagawa watched the hazy surface of Titan drop away beneath them, he couldn't quite believe that he'd managed to pull it off.

Well, mostly. He would have preferred to have an escape vehicle that wasn't quite as old and poky as this freighter, but the one weakness of the MaxSec facility—the one he and his compatriots had managed to exploit—was that its defenses all depended on prisoners never getting out. It wasn't like some GDF base, fully stocked with fighter craft, ready to go on the attack. A shuttle came in once a week to rotate out personnel to and from Hyperion Base, and the ships brought in prisoners at erratic intervals, when there were enough of them lined up to justify the expense of hauling them all the way out here.

So the chink in the armor was the supply vessels, which dropped off their supplies twice each month. His intelligence had told him there were two ships assigned the contract, the *Avalon* and the *Orestes*. He'd hoped it would be the *Orestes* that was delivering supplies when the opportunity came to make his escape, but no, it was the much slower and older *Avalon*. Unfortunately, beggars couldn't be choosers…and neither could escaped convicts. At least he didn't have to worry much about pursuit. Not yet, anyway. Of course the security personnel would be contacting the GDF station on Ganymede, and they'd be scrambling fighters to intercept the *Avalon*. But that would take some time, and he already had a plan in place to make sure this hijacked piece of junk was never found.

Since he'd known very little about the *Avalon*, save that it probably should have been scuttled years ago, he'd been shocked to see that the pilot was a woman. He hadn't been expecting that. He also hadn't expected her to be so young and attractive. All right, bordering on beautiful, with features too delicate to be paired with the beat-up coveralls she was wearing, and her dark hair pulled up in a messy twist on the back of her head, as if she'd allowed herself roughly two minutes to get ready at the start of her day.

He told himself that the pilot's sex didn't matter, that as long as she was competent and did as she was told, she'd escape this whole thing with the sort of story that would get her free drinks for the rest of her life. Not that she probably had any trouble getting free drinks now, actually. She'd turn heads pretty much anywhere she went, let alone in the far more limited pool of available women on the Moon or in the outer worlds.

For a second or two, he contemplated telling her that she had nothing to worry about, that he had no plans to harm her in any way, then realized that probably wasn't a very good idea. He didn't like the fear in her wide hazel eyes, but he'd use it to his advantage now. Anyway, he had a feeling she wouldn't believe him if he told her the truth, that he'd never hurt anyone in his life and certainly wasn't about to start now.

After all, if he wasn't a murderer, a criminal of the very worst sort, what in the world was he doing in the MaxSec on Titan?

He knew she'd never believe *that* story.

TWO

HANDS SHAKING, CASSIDY MANEUVERED THE *AVALON* through Titan's turbulent upper atmosphere until at last they broke through to the cool black of space. "Where to now?" she asked, forcing her voice to sound calm, unconcerned. The whole time the pistol had remained trained on her, and she didn't want to make any sudden movements, do anything that might set off this madman.

"Europa," he replied.

All right, now she knew he was crazy. She'd guessed at his plan, that he was counting on there not being any real pursuit from the MaxSec. There wasn't supposed to be any way out of the prison facility, let alone off the planet, and yet he'd managed to pull off that supposedly impossible feat. All right, fine…the cavalry wasn't going to come bail her out. But on Ganymede, sister moon to Europa, there was a full GDF squadron, and she was sure they'd already been alerted to the hijacking of the Avalon and were scrambling fighters to intercept her ship. The Jovian system was the very last place they should be heading if this escaped convict wanted to stay escaped.

Not that she thought they had any real chance of evading pursuit, no matter what they did, but it seemed as if her hijacker wasn't even bothering to put much effort into it.

Even though she knew she should keep her mouth shut and do what he said, she couldn't helping asking, "Seriously? Wouldn't it be easier for me to turn around and let them capture you here on Titan so we wouldn't have to waste all that fuel?"

"Just head to Europa."

Cassidy shrugged and began laying in the new course. Taking the planets' current respective positions into account, it would take them approximately two standard days to reach Europa. What the hell she was supposed to do with this madman in her lap for two days, she had no idea.

Cheer up, she told herself, as she fed the new data into the computer and let it churn away at setting their course. *Those GDF fighters travel way faster than the* Avalon. *They'll catch up with us in a day, tops.*

She heard a rustling behind her, and shifted in her seat so she could see what her kidnapper was up to. Not that she moved very much—she didn't want to be too obvious—but if he was planning on shooting her in the back of the head once the course was set, she'd kind of like to have some advance warning.

That didn't seem to be his current plan. The rustling sound was coming from the enviro suit as he was undoing its fastenings and climbing out of it. She couldn't blame him for that; the suit was intended for Titan's bitterly cold temperatures, and although it could be adjusted somewhat, it probably felt achingly hot in the *Avalon*'s cabin, which always seemed on the warm side of comfortable no matter what she did to calibrate the climate-control system.

Underneath the suit he wore dark gray prison garb—a pullover shirt and baggy pants. And when he reached up to remove the helmet, Cassidy had to bite her lip from letting out a shocked gasp.

Yes, he was an escaped convict, probably a mass murderer or a serial killer or something equally vile, and he'd hijacked her ship and pointed a gun at her head… but he was also gorgeous. The kind of gorgeous that would have definitely intimidated her if she'd encountered him in a bar or a club, and somehow seemed even more impressive in close quarters like this. Regular features, full lips…and some Asian mixed in there, judging by the dark almond eyes and sharp cheekbones.

Then she realized she was staring, when she'd meant to only catch a quick glimpse out of the corner of her eye. She turned back to the controls and pretended to be absorbed in the schematics displayed on the console's scratched screen.

He approached her then, taking a seat in the copilot's chair. After transferring the pulse pistol to his other hand, he held out his right one to her. "Derek Tagawa."

Since when did hijackers introduce themselves like they were attending some sort of meet-and-greet? Cassidy looked at him blankly, and did not extend her own hand. "Captain Evans."

"Captain's an interesting name for a woman."

Oh, so now he was trying to be charming. It had probably worked for him in the past, with a face like that. Maybe that was how he seduced his victims, by letting them think he was some outrageously good-looking, funny, sweet guy who then turned out to be an axe murderer. Wait, did people even use axes anymore? Since she'd never actually set foot on Gaia, had spent her entire life on the Moon or shuttling around the Solar System's colonized planets, she was a little fuzzy on some of the finer points of life on her "home" world.

Fine. She'd play along. It really didn't matter if he knew her name or not. "Cassidy."

"Thank you," he said quietly.

She really didn't get him at all. Were convicts generally this polite? And the way his gaze kept flicking toward her, then moving away, as if he wanted to stare at her but knew it would be rude. It wasn't lascivious at all, which she'd halfway expect from someone who'd been locked up in MaxSec for years and hadn't seen a woman in all that time. No, it was more…admiring? But that couldn't be right. She didn't have on a speck of makeup, and her hair probably looked like it had been combed by one of the atmospheric thrusters.

For a second or two she didn't say anything, but only returned her attention to the readouts in front of her. Calculating exactly how long it was going to take to get to Europa was more difficult than she'd first thought, as she had data for how the ship handled when fully loaded and again when it was empty, and not so much for its current state, which was with a cargo hold a little less than half full.

Then she asked, "Why Europa?"

"I'll be getting some assistance there."

Assistance. "Was that how you broke out of MaxSec?"

The faintest ghost of a grim smile touched his mouth. "You could say it was a group effort."

Stranger and stranger. An undertaking of that sort would require a lot of planning and resources. Who was this guy? "All that trouble to get a murderer out of prison?"

Abruptly, the smile disappeared. "I'm not a murderer."

"Oh?" Her gaze flicked to the pistol, which he'd returned to his right hand. "Then you don't really need that, do you?"

He hesitated, then pressed the button to engage the safety and shoved the gun into his waistband. "Better?"

"Much." She swiveled her chair so she was more or less facing him. "So what does a person have to do to get sentenced to MaxSec if it's not murder? Political kidnapping?" That did happen from time to time, mostly with execs from one of the mega-corps, like MonAg or Hallbrecht. Most of the time the ransoms were paid, but the perpetrators usually didn't get much of a chance to enjoy their ill-gotten wealth before the authorities caught up with them. No capital punishment on Gaia any longer—the Eridanis had expressed their distaste for the practice and made sure it was abolished before they signed any treaties with the Gaians—but Cassidy had a feeling that life imprisonment, especially on Titan, wasn't much of a trade-off.

"No," Derek Tagawa replied. His expression remained grim. "Let's just say the Consortium likes to use MaxSec as its own personal oubliette."

"Oubliette?" she repeated, rolling the unfamiliar syllables around in her mouth. She'd never heard the term before. "What's that?"

"Back in the day, it was an overlooked cell in a dungeon, the sort of place you put someone you wanted the world to forget. Well, Gaia's kind of short on dungeons, but MaxSec does well enough in a pinch."

"So why would they want the world to forget about you?" Not that she really believed anything he was telling her, but if she kept him talking, then at least he wouldn't get any funny ideas. Or so she hoped.

"That's a long story."

"It's a long way to Europa," she pointed out.

He didn't reply, only stared out the window, at the brilliant starfield that surrounded them, broken here and there by a pale disk that Cassidy knew was one of Saturn's moons, even if she couldn't identify any of them in particular, not at this distance. At last he replied, "You'd never believe me."

That was true—he hadn't even started talking yet, and already she was pretty sure she couldn't allow herself to trust a single thing that came out of his mouth. But he didn't have to know that. "Try me."

Another weighty silence. She waited, listening to the soft hum of the climate-control system, the myriad little creaks and pops the ship made. The freighter had been her home for so long that she was accustomed to all of its sounds, knew which ones were normal and which ones were telling her that she had repairs she really couldn't afford ahead of her.

At last he said, "I'm not a murderer."

"You told me that already."

"Or a kidnapper. Or a serial rapist."

"Environmental terrorist?" she suggested.

His lips twitched. "No, not that, either, although I guess you could say it's a little closer to the mark. I'm a scientist. I was working for GARP."

A terrible name for something that was supposed to be doing a great deal of good. The Greater Asian Reclamation Project had been going full force for some ten years now, as the Consortium government sent its best scientists and engineers to the ravaged Asian continent on Gaia, burying the countless billions who had died during the Cloud, cleansing the land and the air so it might again support a human population. It was grim work, and the personnel engaged in it were generally respected for their efforts. So what Derek Tagawa had managed to do that was so heinous, it ended up with him being sent to MaxSec, Cassidy couldn't begin to guess.

"That doesn't sound like a punishable offense," she said, and settled back in her seat, waiting to hear what sorts of excuses he planned to make.

"No, as long as you don't go digging where the government doesn't want you to."

She didn't reply, only lifted an eyebrow and crossed her arms. Great, another conspiracy theorist convinced that the big bad Consortium was evil incarnate. She'd heard it all, from seedy bars in Luna City to the waiting rooms of understaffed medical clinics, and although she was the first to admit that the Consortium wasn't perfect, she also didn't think it was quite as awful as some wanted to believe. Mercenary, yes. Grasping, certainly. Actively malevolent? Probably not.

And really, if anyone should be holding a grudge against the government and its policies, it should be her, considering it was those very policies that had prevented her father from getting the medical attention he needed, resulting in his death. Now, some would argue that it was Owen Evans' fault in the first place, for getting stuck through the ribs during a barroom brawl gone horribly wrong, but even so, his injuries weren't so life-threatening that the medics couldn't have patched him up and sent him on his way. Everyone knew there wasn't much modern medicine couldn't fix. No, the real problem was that his insurance didn't include the expense of the open-heart surgery those injuries required, and so all the doctors could do was make her father comfortable while he slowly bled to death inside.

Cassidy had fought the hospital bureaucracy, but their hands were tied, too. Even attempting to throw more money at the insurance company hadn't worked, as its reps had only informed her that the new coverage wouldn't be effective for an illness or injury incurred before said coverage went into effect. So she'd sat and watched her father die for no good reason, and had to pick up the pieces afterward. But that didn't mean the government and its policies were actively evil, merely mercenary. Although she supposed there were some people who would argue they were one and the same.

At length she asked, "So where did you go digging?"

He leaned forward slightly, hands placed flat on his knees. "I really didn't intend to be digging at all. I was there to monitor the air processors—they're similar to what we use in terraforming, although on a smaller scale, since we're only cleaning the air, not trying to alter its actual chemical composition."

She nodded.

"I'd just been transferred to Hunan Province, which was one of the worst-hit areas. The air processors had been chewing away at it for decades, and we were told that it was finally safe enough to get boots on the ground and obtain some readings that way." A pause, and he seemed to stare down at his hands. The golden-brown skin was crisscrossed with scars, some of them old and pale, some raw and half-healed. Cassidy couldn't help wondering how he'd gotten them.

"Anyway, I knew that a military team had been there before us, but I didn't think much of it. Just SOP, to make sure the area was safe enough to bring in a bunch of civilians. When I really started analyzing the data, however, it seemed…off. Strange concentrations of potassium and some other heavy metals, things that should've been scrubbed out by the air processors."

"What was it?" Cassidy asked, despite her inner vow not to seem too interested in his story.

His fingers tightened on his knees, and she noticed he wouldn't look at her directly. "I asked for permission to go out and personally inspect the processors, since I was worried that something had gone wrong with their programming or their calibration. That permission was denied."

"By whom?"

"The whole operation is under the control of a GEC officer named Colonel Marquez."

"GEC?" she echoed, surprised. Why would the Gaian Exploration Commission be in control of an operation on its home planet's surface? Wasn't its entire mission to discover and exploit new worlds, rather than Gaia itself?

"The rationale was that the GEC has far more experience with terraforming and the equipment associated with it, so that's why its personnel were put in charge."

"Ah." It still didn't make a lot of sense to her, but then again, she'd sort of stopped trying to figure out why the Consortium did half the things it did.

Derek Tagawa went on, "I asked Colonel Marquez to explain the problems with the readings, and he said he couldn't risk a valuable member of the team on a mission like that, but that he'd send one of his own engineers to look into it. I didn't like it, but I decided to let it go. But the readings kept getting worse, and so it seemed obvious to me that his people were burying the data, or at the very least, not interpreting it correctly. In the end, I talked to one of the team's programmers, Theo Karras, and he agreed to come with me to check things out."

"Even though you'd been told not to."

The dark eyes glinted at her as he looked up suddenly and seemed to pin her in place with his stare. "Do you always do what you're told, Captain Evans?"

Generally, no, but she wasn't about to tell him that. "If it means saving my own skin, then yeah, most of the time I'll let my self-interest do the talking."

He shook his head. "Well, I guess my scientific curiosity overrode my sense of self-preservation. So Karras and I borrowed a vehicle—"

"Stole," she broke in.

"Commandeered," he amended, and despite the overall serious cast to his features, she thought she detected a small twitch at the corner of his mouth. "And we headed out to the nearest air processor. When we ran the diagnostics, everything seemed to be working fine. I don't know if you've ever seen one, but they're big, about five meters square, and we were careful to park our vehicle so it couldn't be seen from the road." His expression sobered abruptly. "Funny thing, that road. You've probably seen the images, how every street and highway and footpath was choked with people fleeing the Cloud. People died where they stood. And yet that road was so empty we could've gone two hundred kilometers an hour on it."

"Maybe the advance team cleared it off so your people wouldn't have to worry about access to the air processors," Cassidy suggested. It seemed obvious enough to her. What was the point in bringing in a team if they couldn't navigate anywhere?

"That's what Karras said. And I was willing to go along with him…until I saw the convoy going by."

"Convoy?"

"Military vehicles flanking a long line of open-bed haulers." He took in a breath, gaze seemingly fixed on her, but Cassidy got the feeling he wasn't looking at her at all, was instead seeing the desolation that used to be the most populated country on the planet. "And in those haulers were bodies. Hundreds…no, thousands… of bodies."

"But—" She broke off, mind flailing at the wrongness of what he'd just told her. Everything that had been written about GARP and its objectives said the goal was to dispose of all those bodies humanely, to treat them with the reverence they deserved. Being told that the remains of the Cloud's victims had been piled up like so much cordwood was just…wrong.

"I know," he said grimly. "Neither of us could believe it. So we waited until the convoy passed, then followed them. I don't think they paid us any attention because, after all, we were driving a vehicle with clear GEC markings. They probably thought we were with them."

"So where were they going?"

"Some sort of processing facility. We didn't stick around long enough to get the particulars. It was enough that it existed. Anyway, Karras said he'd investigate on his end, that it would be a lot more efficient for him to do some discreet hacking and find out what was going on that way, rather than trying to sneak around and play detective, and probably get caught."

But you got caught anyway, she thought, although she didn't bother to say the words out loud. "So I'm guessing he found something."

"You could say that." Derek Tagawa slumped back in his seat, shoulders drooping. "What they were processing in that facility was the corpses."

"Wait…what?" That couldn't be right. This Theo Karras person must have made some mistake.

He gave her a mirthless smile. "That was my first reaction. That is, we knew the government was performing salvage operations, collecting valuables as it remediated the area. Payment for the work being done, and not that many people have ever protested because, after all, in general there aren't a lot of relatives left around to protest. But this was something else. What Theo found was that anything of value in the bodies was being extracted—gold teeth, titanium joint replacements, that sort of thing. And then the corpses were being ground down to nothing. You know all those new terrace farms the government's been touting, saying they've upped production on a massive scale?"

Cassidy could only tilt her head slightly. She didn't want to say anything, because a sick feeling in the pit of her stomach told her what was coming next.

"Well, guess where they're getting all the phosphorous for their fertilizer?"

"That can't be true," she said. Actually, it came out more as a whisper.

"I'm afraid it is."

Her stomach lurched, and she gripped the edge of her seat and told herself that she was not going to throw up. She just wasn't. The roiling settled down somewhat, but she still felt like someone had just punched her in the gut.

"So…what happened?" In a way, she hated herself for asking the question. At the beginning of this, hadn't she vowed that she wouldn't believe a word he said? For some reason, it was hard to not believe him. She wouldn't call herself an expert on human nature or anything, but something in the way he told the story seemed to ring true. If he were really a criminal, wouldn't he have come up with a far less elaborate lie to prove his innocence? Her father had always said, "If you're going to lie, make it a simple one, or you'll end up losing track of the facts."

Maybe not the sort of thing that parenting experts would advise a father to tell his daughter, but she couldn't deny that Owen Evans had been right about that one thing at least.

Derek Tagawa sighed. It wasn't an exaggerated thing, heaved to garner pity, but a quiet exhalation of his breath, as if he needed clean air in his lungs to tell her what was coming next. "We got caught. Or rather, someone noticed Karras poking around. He figured it out, too, realized things were getting hot and that he needed to get out of there. His husband Liam was on the team as well, and I think they were both planning to leave, although I'm pretty sure Liam didn't know exactly why Theo wanted to get out of there. Not that it got that far. A GDF security detail showed up, and they shot Theo."

"Just like that?" she asked, appalled.

"Basically. I was standing there in shock, waiting for them to kill me next, and then the commander shoved the gun in my hand, made sure my prints were all over it. After that, I was hauled away and charged with Theo's murder. It was publicized as a lover's quarrel." He grimaced, running a hand through his short-cropped dark hair. "Theo and Liam were both very good men, and I admired them, but I don't play for that team. Not that anyone cared much about the truth by then. They just needed a scapegoat."

Cassidy had already gotten the impression that Derek was thoroughly hetero, but she still experienced an odd flicker of relief at his words. Then she wanted to shake her head at herself. What the hell difference did it make whether Derek Tagawa was gay, straight, or somewhere in between?

"What happened to Liam?"

"Nothing. That is, he'd never been involved with or had known anything about the hacking Theo was doing—Theo made sure of that, to keep him safe—so although Liam was questioned, he was never held for anything. Anyway, I had the impression that Liam's parents are pretty far up the food chain in the local government on Ganymede, and I think his younger sister just married an exec with MonAg. So Liam had some pretty highly placed people to speak for him. Also, swearing that he was going to kill me himself probably didn't hurt his cause, either."

"So he really thought you killed Theo?" That seemed difficult to believe. After all, what would've been Derek's motive, if Liam knew his husband wasn't actually having an affair?

Derek's face went blank. "He did…I mean, he does. And nobody's bothered to disabuse him of that notion."

She wasn't sure how to react to that. Something didn't feel as if it was adding up, but she wasn't sure which questions to ask. "So they shipped you off to MaxSec."

"Two years, five months, and eight days ago. Yes."

"Why not kill you, too?"

"They probably thought about it. But they wanted to cover up Theo's death more, and they probably figured I wasn't going to be much of a threat locked up on Titan. After all, everyone in there is innocent, or claims to be. I could tell everyone within earshot that I didn't do kill Theo Karras, and it wouldn't matter a damn bit. The ironic thing is, I know for a fact that a couple of us prisoners actually are innocent."

He got up from the copilot's seat and gave a quick glance around. "What kind of food do you have on this boat? Escaping from MaxSec works up a hell of an appetite, and it's a long way to Europa."

For a second or two, she only stared at him, jarred by the sudden change in topic. She got the feeling, though, that he was done talking for the moment. So she stood up as well, then said, "I'll show you."

THREE

HE COULDN'T BE POSITIVE, BUT DEREK THOUGHT
Cassidy Evans believed him, or at least she was beginning to. In the grand scheme of things, it really didn't
matter whether she thought he was telling the truth or
lying his ass off...but something in him wanted her to
believe his story, to understand that he was no criminal.
The criminals were the people desecrating those bodies
in Hunan Province, the man who had shot Theo point-
blank between the eyes.

All other considerations put aside, Derek was pretty
sure he couldn't have hit any kind of target with that
sort of accuracy, let alone a human skull. He'd had some
basic firearms training before being sent into the field,
but he knew he was no marksman. The soldier who'd
leveled his gun at Theo?

It was pretty clear that he knew what he was doing.

"It's not exactly gourmet," Cassidy was saying, going to the refrigeration unit and pulling out a few packets of food.

"It'll be better than what I got in MaxSec," he told her, and the tight set of her features relaxed into a reluctant smile. It seemed to light up her face, give a glow to those hazel eyes, and he hoped he'd get to see that smile a few more times before he had to leave her. There had never been much time in his life for women, and right now he was beginning to regret all those busy, barren years.

"You're probably right about that." She set the food packets in the infrared heating unit, then turned back toward him. "So…Europa. You want to explain that to me, now that we're being all cozy? Because I still don't get it."

He knew that, on the surface, the plan seemed crazy. But everything up until this point had been planned with mathematical precision, and he knew the Europa element was a calculated risk. Telling Cassidy was not necessary, and in fact might hurt her. The less she knew, the better.

"I'm not at liberty to discuss that," he replied. "I told you about what happened to me in China because I wanted you to know that I wasn't a murderer, and have no intention of harming you. But if you don't know anything, then the GDF security personnel won't be able to get it out of you. They'll question you, sure, and inspect your ship. They won't find anything, though, so they should let you go with a minimum of fuss." He added, since her expression was more than a little dubious, "You can tell them I held you at gunpoint the whole time."

At that remark, she let out a short, humorless laugh. "You really think that's going to make a difference? If by some miracle you do manage to get away, they're still going to impound this ship while they question me. They'll go over every inch of the *Avalon,* looking for anything that'll help to track you down. And when they're done, you think they're going to let me have her back? If I'm really lucky, they'll charge me some ridiculous impound fee that I can't afford. But more likely they'll claim the ship as seized assets and leave me out in the cold on my ass."

Derek almost replied, They wouldn't do that, and then he realized that yes, they would. Not because Cassidy Evans was guilty of anything except some extreme bad luck, but because they'd want to make an example of her. They'd say she should've fought back or resisted somehow, done something to keep him from getting off Titan. And their words would make her guilty, and then they'd take her ship, just because they could.

"I'm sorry," he said at length. "I wasn't thinking of the consequences to you, and I apologize for that."

Surprise flickered in those hazel eyes. "I'd say it was all right, but it really isn't." She pulled the heated food packets out of the infrared, and busied herself with opening them and dumping their contents on a couple of plates that she'd gotten from the minuscule cupboard.

Despite her warnings to the contrary, the food did smell good. After picking up the plates, she went over to the equally cramped table and set them down, then pulled two pouches of water out of the refrigeration unit and put them by the plates. "So I think the least you can do is tell me why we're headed toward Europa instead of out to Triton, where we might be able to trade in this boat and get passage out of the system."

Her casual reference to the smugglers' paradise on Neptune's moon startled him somewhat, but not as much as the comment that they'd be able to sell her ship in return for safe passage on a vessel traveling far away from Gaia. "'We'?" he said delicately.

A look of irritation passed over her features, although it seemed more directed at herself than at him. "Oh, well, I just told you that I've basically got no future here in the Gaian system, thanks to your little escape plan. Right now the only asset I have is this ship, but it's not going to do me any good if the authorities get their hands on it. So heading to Triton seems a lot smarter than running to Europa, when you know a GDF squadron is going to intercept us sooner rather than later if we maintain this course."

He'd spent so much time dealing with abstracts, with the cool precision of numbers and formulas, that her hard-headed practicality startled him somewhat. To cover his confusion, he sat down on one of the built-in benches at the table. After a brief hesitation, she did so as well, seating herself with a thump he felt rather than heard, her gaze still fixed on him.

"I have…contacts…in the GDF squadron stationed on Europa," he told her, after guessing she would keep staring at him like that until he provided some answers to her questions. "Or rather, my contacts have contacts. The story's starting to get around, and those who've been working secretly against the government are stepping up their efforts, knowing this may be the impetus they need to sway public opinion."

"You mean the underground is real?" she asked. Her tone sounded skeptical, to say the least.

"Yes. Real, and growing. The Consortium's policies have won them a lot of enemies. They're still operating from a position of strength, but how long will that last when the general public realizes its own government is processing the Cloud's dead, the people who were supposed to be given proper burials, looting their bodies and grinding the rest into fertilizer?"

She winced, then glanced down at the food on her plate as if the very sight of it made her sick.

"Sorry," Derek said, although he wasn't. Not really. "I'd never had any contact with any of the underground until my trial…such as it was. My state-appointed attorney was a joke, but that didn't matter, because the clerk handling my case had a direct pipeline to underground personnel who'd taken an interest in me. Their network is larger than you can imagine." Finally, he picked up his fork and took a mouthful of what looked like ramen and chicken, although he guessed the "chicken" was some sort of soy substitute. Even so, it tasted worlds better than the slop he'd been given at MaxSec.

"So big it reaches all the way to Titan?" she inquired, not sounding terribly convinced.

He couldn't blame her. The personnel at the prison facility were vetted back and forth and up and down and sideways from Sunday, but even the most rigorous filtering process wasn't infallible. Slip in one or two agents whose motivations weren't exactly in line with Consortium policy, and it became easier to escape than one would think. He knew he could never have done it without their help, and he could only hope that the people who'd assisted him would manage to escape detection. If their treachery was ever discovered, he knew they wouldn't survive long enough to be imprisoned. The Eridanis couldn't protest violence they never found out about.

"Yes," he replied shortly, before eating another mouthful of ramen. It was salty, so he reached out and picked up the water pouch Cassidy had set out for him.

"If it's so big, how come everyone thinks it's a myth?" At last she picked up her own fork and ate a bite of her food, although he could tell she wasn't too interested in it.

"Who controls the media?" he asked in return.

She wasn't stupid. A nod, and she said, "So of course the underground is a myth, and nothing for all us good citizens to worry our pretty little heads about."

"Exactly."

Another silence as she seemed to chew that concept at the same time she chewed her food. Derek continued to eat, partly to give her time to think, and partly because he really was hungry; they never fed the prisoners quite enough at the MaxSec, and besides, breaking out of a maximum-security prison did tend to work up an appetite.

"So…your 'friends' in the squadron," she said after a long pause. "Are they going to fire on their comrades, or do they have some other plan in mind?"

"I don't know," Derek admitted. "They didn't give me all the details. I was told to secure the freighter that was currently making its supply run, then rendezvous at Europa. Or at least, en route to Europa. As you said, the squadron is a lot faster than this ship. They should intercept us in another eighteen standard hours or so."

With her free hand, she was tracing circles on the scratched plastic of the tabletop. A nervous gesture? Maybe, although she didn't seem the nervous type. Possibly it was something she did while pondering a particularly difficult problem.

"Well, the proximity sensors will give us some warning, although of course they're not as good as what you'd find on a newer ship. Maybe twenty minutes if we're lucky." She set down her fork and seemed to contemplate him, head tilting to one side in a gesture he was already beginning to recognize. "Do your friends have any way of contacting you?"

"They have the comm code for this ship."

"The comm you smashed," she corrected him, brows drawing together, as if she'd just remembered the damage he caused when he first came on board.

"But that's not your only comm unit, is it?" he asked, and her frown deepened.

"How did you know about that?"

"My contacts know a lot of things."

The look of consternation that crossed her delicate features might have been amusing under different circumstances. "All right, you caught me. I guess it's a good thing you knew that particular tidbit, but the authorities on Titan somehow didn't."

"Well, to be fair, they weren't hanging out in dive bars trying to get intel on the people who manned the supply shuttle. From the sound of it, my contacts had to do some digging to get that much." He paused, wondering if she was going to probe any more deeply as to the sources who'd provided that "tidbit." Funny how the mechanics who worked on starships were only too willing to offer up all kinds of information, if the price offered was right.

But she only appeared resigned, instead saying, "So, okay, so your people have the access code to the secondary comm. I assume they'll contact us in advance?"

"Probably not by much. Those channels are monitored closely, so if they send a transmission too early, they're going to end up tipping their hand." Only one bite of ramen remained on his plate, so he scooped it up with his fork and chewed the noodles slowly, wishing there had been more. Actually, it looked as if Cassidy didn't intend to finish her dinner, but he knew better than to ask if he could have it. After wiping his mouth with the rough recycled paper napkin that was sitting next to his plate, he asked, "So where's this comm unit?"

Her expression of resignation only deepened. "In my quarters."

It felt so very odd to have a strange man in the tiny chamber where she slept. No, scratch that. It felt odd to have a man in there, period, whether he was a stranger or not. Her last encounter with a member of the male species had been so long ago that she actually had to stop and do a quick calculation in her head. Fourteen standard months. Some slick talker in Luna City on business. He'd had an expense account and a fancy suite at the Selene Towers. A misnomer, since the whole thing was built underground, but it was fairly lavish. Way above her pay grade, but it had been nice to spend an evening drinking champagne and eating huge strawberries grown in the hydroponics farms just outside Luna City.

Her rule had always been: Never bring men back to the ship. They weren't so thick on the ground that she had to enforce that rule very often, but she'd stuck to it. This place was her only sanctuary, and she'd never had a relationship so serious that she wanted the man in question to come with her to the *Avalon,* and that was even after her father died and she had the freighter to herself.

Now, though, Derek Tagawa seemed to fill the cramped little chamber, his head almost touching the ceiling. Strange, because he hadn't seemed that tall before. And thank God she actually had tidied up this morning, a little ritual she practiced whenever she made planetfall, like actually putting on makeup before she ventured out into Luna City during her layovers there.

"The comm's here," she said, pointing at the small console, which—thank God again—was set into the wall opposite the bed, instead of above it. Her father had never adequately explained why he had a second comm system, although she guessed it was because he'd been involved in a few shady dealings before he'd somehow managed to secure the Titan contract.

That had been a long time ago, back when her mother was still around. Actually, although Owen had never given Cassidy the particulars, she had the impression that it was the very Titan contract which had broken up their marriage, that her mother had walked because she didn't want to be an absentee wife to a man who was only around ten days out of every thirty.

Of course, that didn't explain why she hadn't taken Cassidy with her.

Shaking her thoughts loose from the unpleasant past, she went on, "I suppose you'll need to be back here to monitor the comm, so I'll just stay up in the cockpit."

That suggestion made Derek frown. "You have to sleep sometime, don't you?"

"Oh, I sleep in the pilot's chair all the time," she replied with a casual wave of one hand. "It's no trouble." *And I doubt I'll sleep a wink while you're on board my ship anyway, so it doesn't really matter where I am, whether it's back here or up in the cockpit.*

"Even so—"

"It's fine. And really, it's going to be a while before we meet up with them, so you might as well get some rest. I'll just need to change the bedclothes for you."

The thought of him sleeping in her bed disturbed her, but there wasn't much she could do about it. She couldn't move the comm, and it was no use to put him in the smaller sleeping chamber across the hall, the one that had been hers until she inherited the ship and the larger captain's quarters—not that they were anything to write home about, being three meters square and mostly filled by the bed and the console that contained the comm.

Derek didn't say anything for a few seconds, only watched her with narrowed eyes, as if attempting to discover what she was really up to. At length he gave the smallest of shrugs, then said, "Thank you. I'll admit I could use some sleep. But make sure to wake me if anything changes."

What exactly he expected to change, when they were out in the middle of the Solar System's equivalent of nowhere, she wasn't sure. Rather than argue, though, she replied, "Sure. Let me take care of that bed for you."

So she knelt and pulled out one of the storage drawers under the bed, extracting a set of fresh sheets, and went to work stripping the old ones off the bed and putting on the fresh set. They really hadn't been due for changing, as she'd swapped them out only a little more than a week ago, but no way was she going to have him lying on sheets she'd already slept on.

During this procedure he lingered in the doorway, as there really wasn't enough space in the chamber for him to be there while she worked. "Thank you," he said again, as she twitched the thin synth-cotton coverlet in place, then stepped away.

"It's nothing." She had to walk past him to get out of the room and into the equally cramped corridor, and something about being that physically close to him as she squeezed past made her want to hold her breath, as if she thought he would reach out to touch her. That was stupid, though. Except for that one admiring glance, which she'd probably imagined, he'd been completely neutral, completely correct, with her.

His mouth opened, as if he'd meant to say something else, but then he closed it again, instead giving her a nod. Once she was out in the corridor, he pushed the button to shut the door.

So much for him being hot for your body, she chided herself, grimly taking the few strides it required for her to get back to the cockpit, after which she settled down in the captain's chair and stared out into the darkness. Everything seemed calm and still, their speed not great enough to show the stars actually moving, although they were still traveling at many thousands of miles per hour. Realspace, of course; the *Avalon,* being an intra-system ship, wasn't even equipped with a subspace drive. She'd often wondered what it would be like to pilot a real ship, one that could take her far away from Gaian space so she could see worlds she'd read about but had never visited: Eridani, Nova Angeles, even dry, dusty Iradia.

The chances of her getting to any of those places were probably a lot lower than her chances of ending up in a Consortium prison somewhere, and she sighed. Unlike Derek's former associate back on Gaia, she certainly didn't have friends and family in high places who could bail her out. She had no one at all.

Those were the sorts of thoughts she generally wouldn't allow herself to entertain, as she knew they weren't at all productive. But now, with an escaped convict sleeping in her room, and a GDF squadron hastening to intercept them—whether or not said squadron really did have members of the underground sprinkled among its ranks—she thought she'd earned some good old self-pity. Really, she still hadn't quite determined why the universe apparently had it out for her, but even the most impartial of observers would be hard-pressed to deny that her whole life had been one spectacular run of bad luck after another.

Cassidy pulled in a breath, then another. Okay, sure, things had never been easy, but so far she'd survived everything thrown at her, and she'd survive this, too, no matter what happened. Anyway, she was sick of the Titan run, sick of the endless weeks with no company other than the "entertainment" the Consortium beamed out to every planet, station, and ship in the system. Trying to lull the population with a steady stream of carefully edited news, interplanetary sports, vapid "reality" shows, ongoing serials with plot lines so improbable she couldn't believe anyone took them seriously? That was about the size of it. So maybe having the *Avalon* impounded would be just the kick in the pants she needed to change things, to get out of here and start over fresh.

Very brave, she told herself. *If dumping the supply gig and hooking up with some random guy so you could get set up with a homestead on a colony far away from here is so great, why haven't you done it before this?*

Inertia. Entropy. The irrational fear that the shade of her father would rise up and chastise her for getting rid of the *Avalon,* the only thing he'd ever seemed to care about all that much?

Who knew? In the end, it really didn't matter, because she was here now, and she would have to deal with the situation one way or another. At this point, about the most she could probably hope for was not getting vaporized when the GDF squadron finally did show up. Its pilots weren't really known for their restraint.

She didn't know how long she sat there, brooding, until her eyelids drooped and she fell asleep, the blackness of space and the darkness behind her eyelids blending and becoming one. All she did know was that she dreamed fitfully, nightmarish images of hands coming out of the dark and grabbing her, and behind it an incessant, low-pitched *chug-chug-chug* sound, which her mind told her was the processing plant, chewing up bodies, and the hands were reaching for her because they were going to throw her down into the blackness to be processed with all the other corpses. Their fingers were cold because they actually belonged to the dead, and she tried to scream, tried to claw herself free, but they were too strong—

"Cassidy!"

A male voice, one she didn't recognize at first. She blinked and saw Derek Tagawa peering down at her, brow creased with concern.

"Are you all right?"

Was she? She reached up and touched a hand to her forehead, which felt clammy with cold sweat. "I—I'm fine. Just a bad dream."

He continued to stare at her. "Now I really feel guilty for taking your bed."

"Don't," she said. "I probably would've had bad dreams no matter where I was sleeping, after those stories you told me." To change the subject, she went on, "Have you heard anything?"

He shook his head. "No, but it's only been about six hours. As I said, they're going to wait until they're almost in range before they try reaching out."

"Then you should've slept a little longer."

"No point." Although she hadn't invited him, he sat down in the copilot's chair as casually as if it belonged to him. "That's about all I can manage on a good day anyway. But maybe you should get some real rest."

And leave him up here unattended? No way. "I'm fine."

Those dark eyes, such a dark brown they were almost black, scanned her face. Looking for a lie? Maybe. "I wouldn't do anything to your ship."

"Did I say you would?"

"You didn't have to." He leaned forward then, staring into the darkness. Why, she wasn't sure, as there wasn't anything to be seen out there. Just millions of miles of empty space. Somewhere in that space was a squadron of GDF fighters hastening toward them, but those ships weren't all that big—the sensors would pick them up long before they could be detected by the naked eye. Then he turned back toward her. "What do you do to keep yourself amused out here?"

She blinked at him. That wasn't some kind of oblique come-on, was it? No, of course it wasn't. With a shrug, she replied, "Watch vids. Read. There's not much else to do. Well, yoga."

"Yoga?" he repeated, one eyebrow going up in apparent amusement.

"What's so funny about that?" she said with some asperity. "I have to do something to stay in shape, and you might have noticed that there really isn't room for a track or a weight room in here."

"Sorry, I didn't mean to offend you. It's just that you don't seem much like the 'inner peace' type."

Was it that obvious? Probably. She doubted she came off as very zen to anyone who met her. "I'm not. To tell the truth, I probably couldn't even name the positions correctly, since I learned them from watching vids. But the exercises are very effective."

"True."

Her imagination must have decided to play with her mind a bit more, because she could have sworn that his gaze traveled swiftly over her, as if seeing the shape of her body under the baggy coveralls she was wearing. But that, she thought, was flattering herself. She looked like complete ass right now, and she knew it. Her meager wardrobe did contain a few nice gowns and one tailored skirt suit for when she had to do something official, like go to the Consortium's Division of Shipping to renew her transport license, but she certainly wasn't going to waste time getting dolled up when she was only sitting on her ship with no one to look at her.

Well, there was someone here now. And she was almost positive he had been looking at her, although his attention flicked back to the window quickly enough as her own gaze sharpened on him.

"Anyway," she said, deciding to let it go for now, "there's an entertainment console in the smaller bedroom. I use it as my study now. All the books are on my handheld, and I'd rather not loan that out, if you don't mind."

"No, of course not," he told her. It was never polite to point-blank ask to use someone's handheld, as they generally contained a good deal of personal information. "I'll check out the console."

She realized then that his clothes were sleep-rumpled, his hair mussed. Since they had plenty of time, he might as well take the opportunity to freshen up a bit. "Go ahead and take a shower. It's steam only, but it's better than nothing. And there's still some of my dad's old stuff folded away under the bed in the second bedchamber. He was about the same height as you, so it'll kind of fit, although it'll probably be baggy. But at least it's clean."

"Thank you," Derek said, and it sounded like he meant it. Well, he was probably aching for a chance to wash the dirt of that prison off his body.

And she'd just have to do her best not to think about what that body might look like, once it was out of its baggy prison garb....

FOUR

A STEAM BATH WAS STILL HEAVEN COMPARED TO THE luke-cold two-minute showers he'd been allowed once a week back on Titan. Derek stood in the tiny compartment, so cramped he could feel his bare ass touch one metal wall, and let the hot steam scrub off the stink of the MaxSec, a mixture of male sweat, greasy hair, and desperation. Even here he couldn't luxuriate for as long as he liked, since the shower unit had a timer set to a precise seven and a half minutes, but it was worlds better than anything else he'd had in years.

When he was done, he took one of the thin towels from its rack on the wall and wrapped it around himself, then shot a quick glance down the corridor. The back of Cassidy's head was to him; it appeared that she was looking down at something on the console, so it seemed safe enough to slip out of the shower unit and into the second bedroom. This one was even smaller than the one he'd slept in, just a narrow bed with more storage drawers underneath it, and, as she had said, a screen built into the wall opposite the bed. The remote was still sitting there on top of the thin blue coverlet, so he picked it up and turned on the vid.

He'd never had much time for watching shows, so most of what he scrolled through as he flipped past the channels would have been foreign to him anyway. But it seemed even more alien and strange after being away from Gaia for so long, after seeing only the faces of the guards and his fellow prisoners. The clothing seemed overly structured and uncomfortable, the women's faces so painted they didn't quite appear human anymore. Was that a new fashion, or had they always looked like that?

In contrast, Cassidy's face flashed into his mind, the wide hazel eyes, the full, pretty mouth. If she wore any cosmetics at all, they certainly weren't obvious. He liked that. He liked that he knew what she really looked like, and not what she wanted him to think she looked like, which appeared to be the intent of the women on the screen before him.

He found what purported to be a news program, although it didn't seem to him as if any of the news being reported bore much resemblance to the truth. Yes, he'd been locked away for two years, and had no idea of what sorts of events might have transpired in his absence, but he did know that the report on the regrowth of the polar ice caps was dead wrong. After years of heavy lifting, the ice caps weren't melting anymore, but that was not quite the same thing as saying that the ice was "re-establishing itself at an encouraging rate of two percent each year." And the report on the Asian rehabilitation project was absolute bullshit from beginning to end, but he supposed he shouldn't have expected anything else.

He changed the channel in disgust, searching for something—anything—of substance, but there wasn't much to be found. At last he came to a film he'd loved as a kid, about a group of misfits working as asteroid miners. Highly embellished and bearing only a passing resemblance to the truth, but the actors were good, and listening to dialogue he hadn't heard for more than twenty years made a rush of nostalgia go over him. Since Cassidy had made it clear that he should be entertaining himself and not expecting her to do it, he settled in to watch the film. At least it would take up a few hours, and it meant they'd be that much closer to the rendezvous with the GDF squadron from Ganymede.

He couldn't help the shiver of anticipation that went over him then. Everything so far had gone more or less according to plan, but in this he was trusting the contacts of his contacts to make sure he got through the encounter unscathed. No reason why they shouldn't, but still....

He'd be very glad when it was over.

Even from the cockpit she could hear the comm beeping in her bedroom, as Derek hadn't shut the door when he came out. She wanted to curse at him for not answering it, but she realized that was partially her fault. After all, she had told him to go and entertain himself with the vid, like some kid she didn't want underfoot.

Okay, he certainly wasn't a kid. But he made her nervous…not because of anything he'd said or done, but because of the way she seemed to react to him. She'd admit she wasn't all that experienced with men. Even so, she could handle herself in normal situations, like in a bar or a club. That was easy. Her expectations had never been any higher than an hour or two of fun with someone she'd never see again, and even those were few and far between. Still, it was a regular sort of transaction. A few drinks, maybe dinner, and then she'd be in his hotel room, and then she'd leave and come back to the *Avalon*. Simple.

Now, though, with probably the best-looking man she'd ever met trapped in this freighter with her, she didn't know what to do. She still wasn't sure she believed every aspect of his story, but then again, if he'd really been a cold-blooded killer, he would have gotten rid of her once their course was set and they had nothing else to do but twiddle their thumbs until they got to the rendezvous point. And even if he wasn't a killer, he was much bigger than she was, taller than she by almost a foot, and probably massing at least thirty kilos more than she did. If he'd had any need to scratch a biological itch after more than two years in the MaxSec, he could have taken her, and she couldn't have done much about it.

But he'd done none of those things, had acted like a gentleman, and so of course she'd made sure to send him away so she wouldn't have to deal with him.

Smooth, Cassidy.

She got up out of the captain's chair and hurried back to her room. The comm kept beeping away, and she knew it wouldn't stop until she answered it, as this one had never been set up with an automated response system.

Pushing down the button to open the line, she said, "This is Freighter *Avalon*."

A brief hesitation. "*Avalon*, permission to speak to your passenger."

No names. Well, that made sense if, as Derek had said, there was a good chance their transmissions might be monitored. "One moment," she replied, and pressed the "hold" button.

The door to the second bedroom was ajar, so she wondered how he couldn't have heard the comm going off across the hall. She had her answer when she peeked inside, ready to give him a ration of crap for not answering the call he'd been waiting for.

Although the vid was still blathering away, he'd fallen asleep on the meager little bed, long legs half hanging off the edge, head smashed into one of the flat pillows. He looked so oddly adorable like that, Cassidy hesitated to wake him up. But then she realized he'd probably be more than a little irritated if she told him later that she'd allowed him to miss the call just because she wanted to let him sleep.

So she stepped into the cabin, laid a gentle hand on his shoulder. "Derek."

He started awake immediately, eyes wide and staring, until he seemed to realize where he was, who was shaking him. "What is it?"

"Your call." She jerked a finger toward the captain's cabin.

No reply except a hurried nod, and then he was on his feet, moving quickly to the other room. She waited in the corridor; it wasn't as if he was so far away that she couldn't hear what he was saying.

"Tagawa." A pause, and then he said, "Understood. We'll be ready."

And that seemed to be it, because after that he came to the doorway and stood in it, looking down at her. "We're set."

"Set for what?"

"For the rendezvous. We're to continue on our current course. Intercept should be in about two hours."

"That fast?" She'd underestimated the speed of the squadron. Then again, it wasn't as if she was exactly privy to all the latest upgrades and improvements in the Consortium's defense fleet.

"That fast," he replied, and a certain twinkle danced in those dark, dark eyes. "Are you ready for this?"

She had a stock answer for that question, and she handed it to him now. "Honey, I was born ready."

They both sat in the cockpit, the atmosphere so tense Derek could practically feel it crackling around them. True, Cassidy had said she was ready for anything, and the way she'd handled his presence here told him she wasn't lying. But as he himself didn't know precisely what to expect, he had little to say to her. They stared out into the darkness, waiting, not speaking.

A harsh whining noise blared from the speakers, and he started. At once Cassidy reached forward and modulated the volume somewhat, although the sound still grated on his ears.

"Proximity alert," she told him. "That means they're twenty minutes out at the most. Probably a little closer, judging by how quickly they got here." Her voice was calm, controlled, as if she'd faced this sort of situation a thousand times before.

"Got it," he replied. Right then he wished his contacts had been able to give him more details, although he understood why they'd been hampered in doing so. At least he knew they planned to knock out the ships that posed a threat, and form some kind of escort to get the *Avalon* safely away. Away to where, he had no idea. The system was so heavily policed that he found it difficult to believe it would be anyplace close by. But although he wanted nothing more than to get back to Gaia, to confront the people who'd stolen the last two and a half years of his life, he understood his personal vengeance might have to wait.

Especially if it meant doing anything that would endanger the woman who now sat only a few feet away from him.

Her profile was to him, sent into sharp relief by the starfield behind it. Her attention remained fixed on the console, and so he guessed she didn't realize he was looking at her now. Not for too long, just enough to remind himself that she'd been dragged into this whole mess unwillingly, and that he needed to make sure she got out in one piece, no matter what happened.

"There," she said, pointing at the display on the console. A cluster of pale blue sparks appeared there, representing the ships now moving toward them. "I count twelve."

Twelve ships, to bring back one prisoner? It seemed the GDF wasn't taking any chances. But he only nodded. "They'll probably wait until they're closer before they make a move."

"Let's hope they don't wait too long, or this could get real interesting." Cassidy paused then, slender brows pulling together as she stared at the screen. "What the hell?"

"What is it?" he asked, something in her tone tightening the knot of worry that seemed to have balled itself up somewhere in his sternum.

"Look!" She tapped the screen, where the group of twelve blue sparks seemed to have multiplied, the new dots smaller and moving more quickly than the main group. "The bastards just fired on us!"

"What?" He launched himself out of his seat, then stared down at the display in consternation. "They were supposed to be firing on each other!"

"Well, I guess someone didn't get the memo." Already the fingers of her right hand were dancing across the controls, while she reached out with the left and grasped the handle of what appeared to be the ship's thrusters. At once the *Avalon* seemed to drop straight downward, and Derek stumbled, grabbing the arm of the copilot's seat so he wouldn't fall over completely.

"What're you doing?" he asked.

"Taking evasive action. Not that I think this crate can do a lot to evade a group of Heron missiles, but I'm sure as shit not going to just sit here and wait for them to hit us."

Her jaw was set, her hand on the thruster controls white-knuckled. Derek said, "Anything I can do to help?"

"Do you know how to pilot a starship?"

"Unfortunately, no."

"Then hang on and shut up."

The *Avalon* jerked to the right, then dropped again. He guessed she was trying to keep their movements erratic enough that the missiles wouldn't be able to get a lock on them, but he wasn't sure how well that would work. His area of specialty was not weapons mechanics, but he knew that the Herons were guided by an A.I. that not only locked on heat signatures, but minute changes in the chemical composition of a certain region of space. In laymen's terms, it meant they went sniffing for spent fuel, and could calculate in a millisecond where a ship might be headed based on where it had been.

Cassidy was muttering something that sounded like *shit, shit, shit* under her breath, but since her words obviously weren't directed at him, he decided the best thing to do was hold on to the lumpy chair where he sat and not say anything. The ship rocked upward, jinking to the right in a movement he wouldn't have believed the creaky old freighter was capable of. Then again, the *Avalon* had clearly been Cassidy's home for most of her life. She probably could coax more out of it than even its designers would have believed.

Maybe it wasn't smart to hope, but he had to believe she could get them out of this. Better to think of that, hold on to that idea, than stop to wonder why they'd been fired on at all. Something had gone horribly wrong, and that meant only one thing. The conspiracy had been discovered, and now the people he'd been counting on to help him were probably already dead.

Then it felt as if a giant's fist had punched the stern of the freighter. Despite himself, Derek let out a startled gasp, and Cassidy dispensed with the muttered "shit"s and growled, "Fuck!"

"What?"

"What do you think? They hit us!" Her eyes were scanning the controls, and by the way she scowled, he guessed that what she saw was not good news. "Not a full hit—we'd be vaped if that had happened—but they still knocked out the rear thrusters, and we're losing air. I can't maneuver worth a damn, and we're going to be breathing space in about five minutes."

"No need to soften things—how bad is it really?"

She shot him a look that seemed half irritated, half amused. "Pretty bad. Scratch that. *Really* bad. And since they're shooting at us, I'm pretty sure they're not going to send out a rescue party."

"I don't know…maybe they're trying to take me alive."

"What, so they can execute you properly later?"

"Gaia doesn't have capital punishment," he reminded her.

"Yeah, well, all that's going to be moot in about four minutes and thirty seconds." She paused, mouth pursed, as she appeared to think rapidly. "Okay, I think we've got about one shot at surviving this. Come on."

She pushed herself out of her seat and Derek did the same, even as he asked, "Where are we going?"

Without looking back at him, she hurried down the corridor, then paused at a locker he'd noticed earlier but hadn't seen her ever use. She fumbled with the latch, then opened it. Inside were two spacesuits, one slightly larger than the other. "Here," she said, pulling the bigger of the two out of the locker and thrusting it at him. "That was my dad's. It'll fit well enough. Mine was my eighteenth-birthday present. Sweet, don't you think? I suppose, if nothing else, it was a good way of making sure I stayed at fighting weight."

Derek undid the fasteners and began to climb into the suit. It was a little roomy, just as the borrowed clothes he wore beneath it were, but this was certainly no time for complaints. "I'm surprised you have them at all."

"They're necessary," she replied, pulling her own suit on with practiced movements, seeming to squish the coveralls she wore into it with little effort. "Ships always need minor repairs, patching, that sort of thing. Most of the time it's stuff you've gotta do on the outside on the hull. So it's just part of the equipment you need, although they're damn expensive." She latched her suit shut while Derek was still fumbling with the closures on his. With the slightest roll of her eyes, she reached out and expertly closed him up, then tugged on his gloves. She did the same with her own, finally reaching for the helmet that went with his suit and slapping it on his head. As soon as it was latched in place, he heard a faint hiss and realized it was the oxygen mix automatically cycling into the helmet.

At the same time she was closing up her own suit. She pushed a button on the small control unit on her wrist, then said, "Follow me."

They went to a hatch in the floor, one that opened up into the cargo bay. There was a ladder attached to the bulkhead, one she climbed down without waiting for him. Fine; she knew where she was going, and he didn't. The ship rocked again, and this time the missile must have hit the cockpit, killing the controls, as all around him was plunged into darkness. A series of red emergency lights switched on immediately, but something about their illumination was faint and wavering, and Derek guessed they weren't long for this world, either.

He grabbed the ladder and let himself drop—or at least, he attempted to. His stomach seemed to swim up into his throat as he found himself floating. That last hit must have killed the artificial-gravity generators.

"Here," came Cassidy's voice through the speaker embedded in his helmet, and he felt her gloved fingers touch his, yank him away from the ladder. He was glad of her touch, glad to hear her speaking, because those things helped to center him somewhat, to make him feel as if he wasn't spinning through an unending darkness. Her grip was stronger than he'd imagined it would be, given her somewhat fragile appearance, tight and unyielding. "You okay?"

"Yes," he said, although he wasn't sure how accurate that assessment actually was. Nothing in his life had prepared him for this. He'd been to the Moon several times, but that was the limit of his experience with space travel, save the trip to Titan, when he'd been drugged within an inch of his life to keep him from putting up any sort of a struggle. His interests had always been focused on Gaia, on making the planet beautiful and livable again.

"Good," Cassidy replied, although something in her tone told him she didn't really believe his answer. "Hang on—I need to get two of the spare oxygen tanks. And after that I'm going to open the cargo bay doors."

The first part of that sounded sensible enough. The rest? "You're going to *what?*"

"One more direct hit, and the ship is gone. So we need to be gone, too."

"Where exactly do you plan to go?"

A low chuckle came over the speaker. "You'll see."

He didn't know how to answer that, so he remained silent as they bumped along a wall, then stopped at the locker. Her gloved fingers fumbled with the latch—the process made even more difficult because she didn't let go of him with her other hand—and then she had it open, was pulling out two long, silvery cylinders before handing one to him.

"Hang on to that like your life depends on it," she instructed. "Because it probably does."

Tucking the cylinder under one arm seemed the best solution, so he did that while she grasped the second one. They bumped along the wall, feeling the ship shudder under them once again.

She muttered, "Dead in space, and they're still firing on us. Bastards." But she didn't stop, continued to keep them moving through the cargo bay, until she paused at a control panel that had a flashing red light mounted on top of it.

Not sure exactly what she was planning, Derek watched as she briefly slipped the cylinder she carried under one arm so she had a hand free to reach out, grasp the lever, and pull it down. Immediately, a set of large doors began to retract into the ship's hull, showing a vast panoply of winking stars. There was no rush of air being sucked into the vacuum of space, as the cargo bay had never been pressurized in the first place.

Cassidy paused there, staring out into the blackness, and then he saw her give a brief nod. "Got you, you fucker."

"Got whom?" he asked.

"Hang on," she answered, which wasn't an answer at all. Taking the cylinder from under her arm, she fiddled with the valve on top. Immediately afterward, air began to stream from it, propelling them out of the protection of the ship and into open space.

"What the hell are you doing?" he shouted into the mic. "We need that air!"

"All the air in the world isn't going to do us any good if we don't have some way of getting out of here. Look." She couldn't point, as one hand was occupied with the cylinder, using it as a sort of miniature propulsion unit, while the other was still clinging to him with a death grip, but she did sort of incline her head into the blackness.

Maybe there was a faint glint of something there… or maybe he was just imagining things. "What is it?"

"One of our friends. Usually, when a ship is disabled, they leave pickets like this, keeping an eye on things, while the others in the squadron go in for a closer look. That means he's separated from the others, and a target."

"A target?" Derek repeated. His head was spinning slightly, and he didn't think it was just because of the over-oxygenated air mixture he was currently breathing.

"How can he be a target when we don't have anything to target him with?"

"We have ourselves," she said calmly, still propelling them forward, heading toward that faint glint, the one that now was resolving itself into the shape of a sleek two-man fighter.

And while he attempted to puzzle that one out, the GDF ship grew closer and closer. Now Derek could see she was coming up from behind, out of the pilot's visual range.

"Don't they have sensors that could pick us up?" he asked in a murmur, worried that the GDF pilots might somehow be able to scan their communications.

"Not likely. These fighter craft aren't built to scan for lifeforms, just ships and objects above a certain size. We're below that threshold."

That sounded encouraging. At the same time, he couldn't help wondering how Cassidy Evans, pilot of one of the system's more rundown freighters, was privy to this sort of information. "And you know all this how?"

Another one of those low, grim chuckles. "About five years ago I dated a fighter pilot whose squadron was stationed at the base at Luna City. He liked to talk a big game, but since his main duty seemed to be providing escort duty to diplomats and muckety-mucks getting ferried back and forth from Gaia, I doubt he ever saw any real combat. But, as I said, he liked to talk, and I liked to listen. Yeah, he was telling me things that could've gotten him court-martialed if anyone ever found out, but I didn't share any of it, and he bought my big-eyed 'gee whiz' act. Anyway, you never know when you might pick up something valuable that could help you later on."

That was for damn sure. "So what's the plan?"

She closed the valve on the oxygen cylinder and let it drift away, its work done. They were now still moving slowly toward the ship and would continue to do so, now that they'd been set in motion. "All these ships have an external emergency release for the cockpit canopy. You access it from a panel directly behind the gunner. I'll pop it, and then we'll yank those bastards out of their comfy padded seats and let them find out how fun it is to breathe space."

"Surely they have flight suits—"

"Yes, they do. Rated for exactly three minutes of exposure to vacuum. So maybe their friends will come along and rescue them before then, but I kind of doubt it."

This whole plan sounded like it was predicated on any number of "ifs," and Derek didn't find any of it very appealing. But they were committed now. It was the lives of the two men in that ship, or his and Cassidy's. And considering that the members of that squadron hadn't shown any compunction about firing on an unarmed vessel, he decided he'd probably better put aside his squeamishness.

Now the ship was only a few meters away. He held his breath, thinking that surely its occupants must see them, must realize they weren't alone out here. But he and Cassidy were approaching in what was effectively a blind spot, so maybe she'd been right. All he could do was hope the ship wouldn't get some kind of signal from its compatriots and switch on its thrusters, or the two of them would be instantly incinerated.

The little ship seemed to drift there in the empty space between worlds, though, not moving, doing as Cassidy had said, which was keeping watch while the others did their dirty work. From behind him, he caught a brilliant orange flare at the very edges of his peripheral vision, and he realized the *Avalon* must have been fired on again, this time being utterly destroyed.

Maybe there was the faintest of sighs coming from the helmet speaker. He realized then that Cassidy had just lost her home, the only one she'd ever known. The barest of pauses, and she said, "Let's do this. I'll get the emergency release, then take care of the pilot, since I need to be flying this thing. You get the gunner."

She made it sound so easy, as if the whole thing required no more effort than pulling on a pair of pants. No going back now, though, so he replied, "Got it."

"On my mark. One...two...three!"

And her gloved fingers were on the surface of the ship, pulling herself along, while Derek did the same, moving on the opposite side of the vessel from her so she could access the emergency release and then pull herself forward unimpeded. A second, then two, and the canopy flipped backward, revealing two men wearing zero-g suits and helmets, but not the heavy spacesuits he and Cassidy had on. The helmeted heads swiveled around, trying to see what had caused the malfunction, and Derek yanked himself upward, grasped the buckle of the man's harness and undid it, even as the gunner swung his hand at Derek's helmet, attempting to crack the duraplast visor.

A wave of fury went over him, and he returned the favor, only with more success, as the gunner's helmet wasn't latched as firmly to his suit as Derek's own was. The black helmet went tumbling out into space, the man's eyes widening in fear as Derek pulled him free from his harness and kicked him in the stomach, sending him hurtling into the dark.

He looked forward, thinking he would need to assist Cassidy, but she'd had much the same thought, had torn the helmet from the pilot's head and taken advantage of his shock to undo his harness and push him out of the cockpit.

"Get in!" she shouted, and he managed to squeeze himself into the gunner's seat, although the bulky spacesuit was making the procedure more difficult than he would have liked. But somehow he managed to accomplish the task, and the canopy dropped over their heads just as he was buckling the harness over his chest.

The fighter craft leaped forward, moving away from the remains of the *Avalon*. All around him readouts were blinking, but he couldn't decipher the information they were attempting to relay.

"Hang on," Cassidy said as the ship continued to accelerate. "I think our friends' buddies just realized something went wrong with their picket ship. We've got to outrun them."

"How can we outrun them if they're flying the same kind of ship?"

"Because we have a head start."

He'd never had this experience of speed in any other ship he'd been on, not the shuttles that had taken him back and forth to the Moon, and certainly not in the sluggish *Avalon*. It almost sounded as if the engines were whining, which he knew was impossible, since sound didn't carry in vacuum.

It was impossible to look back, so he had to trust Cassidy, trust that she knew what she was doing.

And hope like hell that she knew what she was doing.

FIVE

SHE'D NEVER FLOWN A SHIP LIKE THIS BEFORE. IF IT weren't for their current dire circumstances, in that first moment of acceleration, she would have thrown her head back and laughed out of pure joy.

This thing was fast. So fast, so sleek and responsive. She had no doubt the personnel in the other fighter craft were desperately trying to contact her, but since they were all on a different frequency from the one her suit and Derek's shared, she heard nothing. Only blessed silence.

The readouts told her the other eleven ships were regrouping and coming after them. So much for attempting to rescue their stranded comrades. Although the enormity of what she had just done would probably catch up with her later, right now she wouldn't let herself think too much about that, especially not when it was either those two GDF pilots or her and Derek. Not much of a choice.

"Deploying countermeasures," she said, falling into the no-nonsense delivery of a military pilot, even though she doubted her companion cared about protocols. In that moment, it seemed it would help to keep her head on straight if she did everything by the book…even if it was a book she'd never actually read.

Derek's voice came through the helmet speaker. "Countermeasures?"

"Basically, drones that carry traces of fuel, designed to clutter up the space between us and an enemy, fool their missiles." She touched the button on the screen, and at once the cluster of countermeasure devices fell behind them and began to spread out, confusing the signal they were leaving behind and, hopefully, mucking with any missiles the remaining GDF ships might fire at them.

That task done, she began scanning the other read-outs, seeing where they were in terms of fuel and oxygen. Yes, they'd blown a whole lot of atmosphere into space when they popped the canopy, but the backup oxygen tanks had already kicked in. There was plenty left, at least a good twenty hours' worth, and they still each had a few hours of air left in the tanks attached to their spacesuits as well.

Fuel levels were also good. These ships were system craft, and so they didn't possess the subspace engines necessary to propel a vessel the unimaginable distances between the stars. No, their propulsion systems wouldn't have seemed too strange to engineers from several hundred years in the past, although they were far more efficient, capable of reaching speeds no long-ago shuttle or probe could have hoped to match.

The best thing to do would be to push the little starship to the utter limit of what it could manage. Yes, if their pursuers were dedicated—and crazy—enough, they might do the same, but then they'd risk stranding themselves among the outer worlds. Titan was the last outpost of civilization, except for the one place she was pretty sure a bunch of GDF ships really wouldn't want to go…which meant it was the perfect destination for her and Derek.

Cassidy poured on the power, watching in satisfaction as the red blips indicating their pursuers began to drop behind. Smaller blips emerged from those moving dots, and she knew they must have fired. Missiles were faster than ships, but they still had to find their target.

And there she saw it—the smaller red blips flashing and then disappearing, meaning they'd exploded harmlessly against the countermeasures she'd deployed. Nothing like using the Consortium's own technology against its pilots.

To be safe, she arced away in a trajectory that would make it look as if they were about to head sunward, toward the inner planets. She couldn't burn too long in this direction, but she wanted to do what she could to put them off the scent…not that they'd probably be all that interested in following it, once they figured out what she was doing. The readouts showed they were still giving chase, but falling behind. Even better.

Her fingers danced over the keys to the nav-computer. Thank God that navigational systems were all more or less alike, although this one was far faster and more responsive than the computer that had just gotten blown up on the *Avalon*. A whole lot else had just gotten blown up, too, but she couldn't let herself think about that right now.

Derek spoke again. "So what's the plan?"

"Working on it." There. By some great good luck, their destination was on approach to Saturn, and not on the far side of the sun. That would've doubled their flight time. At their current speed, they should reach their destination in about fifteen hours. That was roughly fourteen hours longer than she wanted to spend in a spacesuit, but at least it was manageable. The suits would handle any annoying bodily functions in the meantime, although they'd want to find a hostel at the earliest opportunity and get cleaned up.

As she worked, Derek remained silent, but finally he asked, "Where are we going?"

Cassidy settled back against the padded seat and let out a long breath. "Triton."

At first he wasn't sure he'd heard her right. Triton? That den of thieves…and worse…on Neptune's moon? His brain tried to work at the question from several directions, but in the end he could only say, "I beg your pardon?"

"It's the only place in the system where the GDF has no real jurisdiction. Sure, they could go in there swinging their dicks if they wanted to, but that would make a whole lot of people mad, people the Consortium really doesn't want to mess with right now." There was a rustling sound over the speaker, as if she'd shifted in her seat. "Besides, this fighter is worth a lot of units. We can sell it, get what we can out of it, and then buy a different ship or passage on a transport that'll get us out of the system."

He had his own thoughts on that subject, but he knew better than to voice them now, especially since Cassidy had just managed the impossible and had saved them both from the doomed *Avalon*. "Okay," he said at last. No use arguing with her; she was in control of the ship, and anyway, going back and forth on the subject would use up too much precious oxygen. Instead, he asked, "How long?"

"Approximately fifteen hours." She paused, adding, "Go ahead and shut down the oxygen in your suit and crack your helmet, but don't take it off. We're using the backup air on the ship, but it should be enough to get us to Triton. If we end up having to switch over at the end, I'll let you know. In the meantime, you might as well make yourself comfortable back there."

It crossed his mind to ask her if she was joking, but he knew she wasn't. Actually, to get from the orbit of

Saturn's outermost moon to Triton in fifteen hours was a not-inconsiderable feat, and he guessed she must be pushing the fighter craft as hard as she could, not worrying about saving any fuel, as she obviously intended this to be a one-way trip.

One-way to Triton.

He didn't exactly sigh, but he did let out the smallest of breaths, then said, "Will do."

Shifting in his bulky spacesuit, he attempted to find a more comfortable position in the cramped seat. He wasn't sure if he was entirely successful, but at least it gave him the appearance of having some control over his surroundings. Then he reached up and cracked his helmet, taking in a breath of the fighter craft's air. It did smell and taste fresher than what he'd been breathing through the spacesuit.

Then, since he didn't have anything else he could do, he leaned his head back against the headrest and shut his eyes.

By the time they were approaching Triton, Cassidy was so tired she could barely keep her eyes open. For a while, pure adrenaline had kept her going, but as the hours ticked by and she lost all sight of her pursuers, she could feel her body wanting to shut down, to lose itself in a few hours of oblivious sleep. If the faint snores she heard from time to time through the helmet speaker were any indication, Derek was doing that very thing.

At first it had irritated her, that he was getting rest while she was sitting in the pilot's chair, eyes glued to the readouts, scanning for any signs of hostile activity. But she told herself he really had nothing else he could be doing, and at least one of them might as well be alert and in control when they reached the outpost moon of Neptune. She supposed she should count herself lucky that, even in the heart of the Gaian Consortium, traffic in the outer reaches of the Solar System was not so heavy that they ran much risk of discovery.

No, the hard part would be when they reached Triton.

When they were approximately a hundred thousand kilometers out from Neptune, the fighter's comm squawked to life. "GDF ship, this is Triton Control. You are approaching interdicted space. You are directed to turn around at once or be fired upon."

Go ahead, she thought. At least then I'd get some rest. But since that was her exhaustion talking, she ignored that inner voice, pushed the button on the comm to open a channel, and replied, "Triton Control, this is a GDF ship, but I am not a GDF pilot. Permission to stay on course."

If silence could be startled, that was what the ensuing pause sounded like. Then, "Uh…come again, GDF ship?"

"Again, this ship is not under the control of GDF personnel. My name is Cassidy Evans, and I used to pilot a freighter called the *Avalon*."

Another silence. Cassidy guessed whoever was on the other end of the line was hurriedly looking up the *Avalon* in the Consortium's ship registry. She waited, wondering if they had come all this way, only to be shot down.

Then the voice said, "Welcome to Triton, Captain Evans. We're not sure how you got your hands on that ship, but…kudos."

She let out a rusty chuckle. "Thanks, Triton Control. Let me know where I can land this thing…and also where a girl can find a place to lay her head."

"Rolling out the welcome mat, Captain Evans. We're sending coordinates now."

Numbers danced across the screen, and she plugged them into the nav-computer, allowing herself a relieved sigh when she saw they were now less than a half hour away from landing on terra firma. It might be solid methane ice, rather than actual rock, but at this point she'd take what she could get.

"Hey, sleeping beauty," she said into her suit's mic. "Wakey, wakey. We're almost there."

"Almost…wha?" came Derek's voice, so groggy she had to smile.

"Almost to Triton. And it sounds like they're going to send out the welcome wagon. I guess making off with a GDF starfighter earns you some points with the crew that calls Triton home."

"Well, that's something."

She grinned. It wasn't anything she would have believed if she hadn't been here to see it for herself, but it seemed as if they might survive this place after all.

They landed in a small hangar on the outskirts of the enormous complex of domes that made up the main settlement on Triton. Derek had never thought he'd see this place in person, so he had to force himself to keep from gawking like some rube who'd never left the surface of Gaia in his entire life. Maybe at one point this had been an orderly scientific outpost, but the less savory elements of Gaian society had taken it over more than a hundred years earlier, and now it was a hodgepodge of rundown housing, shops, bars, strip joints, cafes, and commissaries.

Although her eyes were shadowed with exhaustion, Cassidy walked briskly enough beside him, her chin up. Where they were headed, he had no idea, as neither of them had any cash or vouchers, and this didn't look like the sort of place that exactly extended credit to unlucky travelers.

"Do you know where you're going?" he murmured to her, making sure he couldn't be overheard by any of the sentient flotsam and jetsam, Gaian and otherwise, that crowded the byways of the domed settlement.

A quick nod. "My friends at Triton Control gave me an address, said there was someone here who'd be interested in taking the ship off our hands."

So she was still on that kick. "Cassidy, if we get rid of the ship, we're stranded here."

She didn't look over at him, but he could see her jaw tighten. "We're stranded either way, since there's no way we can take that thing anywhere near Gaia itself, and it's only a system craft and won't get us anyplace else. So we might as well get some money out of it."

"And what's to stop them from killing us and taking the ship anyway?"

"Nothing."

That's reassuring. He didn't say anything, though, only strode along beside her, hoping he looked tougher than he felt. Probably not, in the ill-fitting borrowed clothes Cassidy had given him, his face rough with stubble.

What she really needed here was some muscle, not an atmospheric scientist who couldn't even handle a gun properly. Not that guns were allowed here…not openly, anyway. There were signs in the hangar where they'd disembarked, and posted on every ersatz street corner, and they'd had to walk through a full-body scanner when they exited the hangar complex. Made sense, he supposed; one pulse bolt through a dome, and everyone was in a world of trouble. Also, maybe it kept violence to a personal level, and not the whole-scale nightmare it might otherwise be in a place whose population was composed almost entirely of criminals.

"Here," she said, turning into a dubious-looking prefab building with an animated holo sign that proclaimed it to be the Pink Elephant. The trunk of the aforementioned elephant moved up and down jerkily, showing that its programming had begun to deteriorate. Something about it was vaguely nausea-inducing, so Derek shifted his attention from the sign to the interior of the bar that now surrounded him.

It wasn't much of an improvement. Shabby, worn plastic tables and chairs, the bar itself seeming to be made of extruded aluminum, every inch marred by the initials and other graffiti that had been carved into it. The place smelled of stale beer and sweat, and the indefinable humid aftertaste of a well-used locker room.

Apparently undeterred by all that, Cassidy paused in the middle of the seedy room, eyes scanning the few occupants. None of them seemed to match the description of the person she was looking for, as she planted her hands on her hips and frowned.

Then a scruffy-looking man who appeared to be in his late fifties emerged through the door behind the bar, a door that probably led to a storeroom or possibly a kitchen, although Derek couldn't imagine actually eating any of the food served here. The man paused behind the bar, gave Cassidy one raking look from head to toe, then said, "You the one with the ship?"

An expression of relief passed over her face, one Derek could tell she was trying to hide. She nodded and moved closer to the bar, taking a seat on one of the worn plastic barstools. He followed her, not wanting her to get too far away, although he didn't know exactly what he could do to protect her if things really went south.

"You interested?" she asked.

"Yeah, I'm interested." The man's flat gray gaze traveled to Derek, paused briefly, then moved back to Cassidy. "I know some people who'd like to open her up and see what makes her tick."

"What're you offering?" Her tone was casual, but Derek could see the muscles in her throat move as she swallowed, and he knew she was far more on edge than she wanted to let on. Then again, he was amazed at how functional she was. How many hours straight had she been up now? Forty-eight?

The man grinned, revealing yellowed teeth that had never seen the benefit of cosmetic dentistry. "Relax, sweetheart. You earned some points, swiping that ship from those GDF assholes. I can't give you full market price, of course, but my contacts are willing to do a quarter-mil."

A quarter-million units. Just like that. It would buy them a replacement ship—if they could find one—or passage out of here. Hell, it could buy them just about anything they wanted.

Save, possibly, their freedom.

"That works," Cassidy said, voice calm, as if she hadn't just been handed their ticket out of this night-mare. "Voucher?"

"Of course. And some cash. A lot of the places around here don't take anything else."

She nodded. "It's a deal."

The man spat on his palm and extended his hand, and Cassidy did the same, unruffled as if she engaged in this sort of unsanitary transaction every day. Obviously, she had some experience with it, whereas Derek felt as if he were an anthropologist observing the rituals of a far more primitive race. Well, it was already fairly clear to him that he and Cassidy had come from very different worlds.

"Give me a minute," the man said. "In the meantime, drinks're on the house. What'll you have?"

Drinking anything here didn't seem all that appealing. On the other hand, refusing would seem downright rude. "Gin and tonic," Derek replied, wishing the remark hadn't ended on an upward inflection, as if he wasn't certain of what he'd requested.

"I can do gin without the tonic," the man said, one eye twitching. Maybe it was supposed to be a wink.

"Sounds great," Cassidy put in, and the bartender reached out to the shelf behind him and poured them a couple of shots. After that, he disappeared through the door again, leaving Derek and Cassidy alone.

"Are you sure about this?" he asked.

"Too late for second thoughts now. Besides, a quarter-mil? We'll be set." She sipped from the shot glass and winced. "Holy shit, that's nasty. I bet he makes it himself in the back room there."

Derek wondered briefly when he and Cassidy had become "we," but he decided not to mention it. In a way, it felt good. Actually, it felt damn good, although he didn't want to ascribe too much meaning to what most likely was just a slip of the tongue. After all, she was probably running on fumes right now. Since he'd already been dubious about the gin, he ignored the shot glass. Not that he couldn't use a drink right about now, but he figured he could wait to get something from a more reputable source. If, of course, there was such a thing here on Triton.

The bartender returned, holding a translucent credit voucher in one hand and a bag that jingled faintly in the other. The cash, Derek supposed.

After pushing the voucher and the bag across the counter toward Cassidy, the man said, "Five thousand cash, the rest on the voucher. The ship?"

"Just a sec," she replied, digging in a pocket of her coveralls and producing her handheld. "I'm sure you won't mind if I check this?"

"Not at all," the bartender said with a yellow-toothed grin.

She passed the voucher over the screen and waited briefly. Although Derek couldn't see exactly what it said because of the angle at which she was holding it, he assumed she was pleased with what she saw, as she nodded.

"It all looks good. I appreciate doing business with you."

"Our pleasure," he replied. "I'd recommend the Trident, if you're staying over."

"Thanks for the rec," she said, and downed the rest of her gin. Derek was surprised she could still stand upright after that, but she hopped off her barstool in a surprising show of dexterity, adding, "Let's get going. I could use some sleep."

That, he thought, was probably the understatement of the century. But he nodded and got off the stool where he'd been sitting.

"Hang a right as you leave the bar, then another right at the next intersection, then a left. You can't miss it."

Cassidy gave the barkeep a thumbs-up and headed in the direction he'd indicated, Derek a pace behind. She'd slipped the voucher in the same pocket as her handheld and put the bag of units in another, where it made something of a bulge against her thigh. Not much, not enough that you'd notice if you weren't looking, but it still made him uneasy. The people they passed on the street looked like they'd mug a person for a lot less than a quarter-million units.

But maybe the word had gone out, or maybe he and Cassidy appeared rumpled and poor enough to not merit a second glance. In either case, they made it to the Trident unmolested. Surprisingly, it was almost respectable-looking, a two-story prefab building that at least was clean and whose interior was sleek and up-to-date, with dark laminate floors and pale gray walls. An angular crystal chandelier hung in the middle of the lobby. Derek could almost imagine he was back on Gaia in one of the modest establishments he'd frequented during his business travel. Environmental science wasn't exactly a field for those wishing to get rich quick, or who preferred more posh surroundings.

He wondered whether Cassidy would ask for one room or two. They weren't together in any sense of the word, but it seemed safer for them to stick close by one another. She appeared to have the same idea, as she asked if there were any suites available, and seemed to relax slightly when the clerk informed her there was a two-bedroom unit on the second floor.

"We'll take it," she said, not even bothering to ask the cost. Then again, it probably didn't matter all that much.

"Luggage?" the clerk asked.

"It, um…got lost," Cassidy replied. "We'll be going shopping later."

"Very good," the clerk, a young man in his early twenties, replied. How he'd managed to end up on Triton, when he appeared to be perfectly respectable, Derek wasn't sure. Maybe he'd been born here?

It didn't really matter one way or another. The important thing was that he stopped asking questions and pushed a key card across the countertop. No mention of a deposit, no request for their personal information for the hotel's database or anything like that. Well, it was entirely possible that they did things very differently on Triton.

Cassidy murmured a thank-you and scooped up the key card, then headed for the lifts. Once they were inside, she leaned back against the polished stainless-steel wall and let out a sigh. "I kept thinking for sure someone was going to jump us."

"You're not the only one."

"But we're safe now." She grimaced, shaking her head. "That is, it seems like we're safe now. They could still send someone to get that voucher back, but there's not much we can do about it. If I don't get some sleep, I'm going to fall over."

"Frankly, I'm surprised you haven't fallen over already."

She shot him a brief, weary grin. Then the elevator doors opened, and she got out, moving to the left, apparently following the signs. Their suite was at the end of the hall, and when they went inside, Derek was once again impressed by their surroundings. Muted cool tones of gray and deep red, soft carpet underfoot. No windows, but there wasn't much to see in this domed community. However, there were two huge vid screens on opposite walls, both of them currently set to show a spectacular vista of the Grand Canyon.

"What is that?" Cassidy asked.

He turned to her in surprise. "You've never seen it before?"

"Why would I? I've never been to Gaia."

As he'd grown up outside Tucson, Derek was more than familiar with the rugged beauty of Normerica's Southwest. "It's the Grand Canyon. You know, in Arizona?"

"Oh," she said. "It's beautiful." Then she yawned and shook her head. "I can't worry about geography right now. All I want is a shower and a bed."

"Looks like the bathroom's in there," he told her, pointing.

"Perfect."

Without further comment, she disappeared into the chamber in question, and a minute later, he heard the water turn on. Real water, not a steam shower. Luxury, indeed.

Since he had nothing else to do, he made a quick inspection of the suite. Two bedrooms, as advertised, one slightly larger than the other, but both with good-sized beds and their own vid screens. He took the smaller one and sat down on the bed, then turned on the vid. Most of the programming didn't interest him much, as it was the same pre-packaged crap beamed everywhere in the Gaian system. However, there were a few local channels, one of which seemed to advertise a service that would deliver pretty much anything you asked for to anyplace in the dome. And if you were staying at one of the local hotels, you could have the requested items added to your bill.

Tempting. He knew he needed some fresh clothes, and Cassidy as well. As to her size, well, she was slender. If things came in small, medium, and large, he'd guess that she was a small. And it would only be a few things. She could get the rest later.

He scrolled through the offerings, chose a few pairs of pants and some shirts for himself, a package of underwear, a jacket. The same for Cassidy, including a beautiful silky tunic in a deep crimson shade, with matching slim pants and flat shoes. He had no idea what her shoe size was, but if they didn't fit, he supposed she could exchange them. That outfit was one she probably didn't need, but for some reason he wanted to see her in something attractive and flattering, and not simply utilitarian.

The requested items were delivered with such alacrity that Cassidy was just stepping out of the shower, bundled in a gray robe she must have found in the bathroom, as Derek was closing the door and setting the package on the low table in the sitting area.

"What's that?" she inquired.

"A few changes of clothes. I don't know about you, but I don't think I could face getting back into these things after taking a shower."

Her face lit up, and she came into the sitting room, watching as he opened the packet and began making separate piles for the two of them. "That's amazing. You just ordered them?"

"For an outpost populated by thieves and smugglers, they do seem very efficient around here."

"Yeah, it's amazing what can get done when you don't have the Consortium bureaucracy getting in your way." She went to the pile of her own clothing, reached out to touch the silky crimson tunic. "It's beautiful."

"I had to guess at your size—"

"I'm sure it'll be fine. You're a scientist, right? I'm sure you have very keen powers of observation."

This last was said so wryly that he had to grin at her. She smiled back, but almost immediately the smile stretched into a yawn. "As much as I want to try this stuff on, I really need to get a few hours of sleep."

"I'd say more than a few hours." He tilted his head toward the larger of the two bedrooms. "Go ahead. Get as much sleep as you like."

"Okay. And after that, I'm buying you dinner." An almost comical frown pulled at her brows. "Or lunch, or breakfast. Whatever it ends up being."

"Sounds good." He was hungry now, but he'd see if they could send something up while she was sleeping. Something light, just to tide him over.

"'Night. Or morning. Or…whatever."

With that she drifted into the bedroom and shut the door behind her. Derek felt vaguely disappointed, as if he thought she should have left it open. No, that was foolish. She deserved her privacy, to sleep undisturbed as she got some well-deserved rest.

As for him…well, he was no fan of watching the vid, but that was what he'd do for now. Who knows…maybe he'd even find something of interest. Stranger things had been known to happen.

Such as escaping from MaxSec and evading a squadron of GDF fighters.

He shook his head at himself, and went to his own room.

SIX

ALTHOUGH SHE KNEW SHE'D ONLY HAD THE ONE SHOT of gin, Cassidy felt positively hung over when she finally opened her eyes and blinked up at the flat gray ceiling overhead. It was farther away than the low ceiling in her quarters, and so she knew she couldn't be on board the *Avalon*. And the bed was luxuriously soft, and large. She doubted the mattress could have even fit into her cabin.

No cabin left for it to fit into, she realized. The *Avalon* was gone, along with everything she owned. Her meager wardrobe. A few holo-portraits of her parents, among them the treasured one of the couple in front of a brand-new *Avalon,* her father beaming with pride, her mother wearing an oddly worried smile, as if she somehow knew the ship behind her was going to be the destruction of her marriage.

All of it now dust. Not even dust, really…more like blown to its constituent atoms. The thought felt oddly unreal, as if it was someone else's ship that had been lost. Probably hadn't sunk in yet.

She was on Triton, in a hotel there. Derek was somewhere in the suite, she supposed. She couldn't imagine him wandering around the settlement's streets unaccompanied. And then she remembered the money, shoved into a pocket of her coveralls.

They were lying draped across a chair, exactly where she'd left them before she collapsed into bed the night before. Or the day before. She hadn't really noted when they were according to local time. The chronometer next to the bed said it was almost nineteen hundred hours, but she had no frame of reference for that reading. Had she slept for five hours? Fifteen?

Well, she'd figure that out soon enough. First things first. She slid out of bed and went to the coveralls, let out a little gasp of relief when her fingers found the reassuring bulge of hard currency in one pocket. It didn't appear to have been touched.

All well and good, but since the chunk of their payout for the GDF fighter craft had gone on a credit voucher, they could still be up shit creek if their mysterious benefactors had decided to withdraw the units they'd assigned to it. A difficult transaction, but certainly not an impossible one.

She slipped her handheld out of her coveralls' pocket, then pulled out the voucher as well and passed it over the screen. Almost at once it displayed the reassuring number: 245,000.

So far, so good. Now she realized that the closet door was open, and hanging within it were several sets of clothes, all of which she recognized as the items Derek had ordered before she passed out the night before. And stacked on the shelf above the closet rack were packages of unopened underwear, as well as a small sterile bag that contained a toothbrush and toothpaste, face wash, a battery-powered disposable razor, colored lip balm… in fact, just about everything a girl might need to make herself feel more human.

All this had to be Derek's doing, of course, which meant he'd come in here while she was asleep and hung everything up. She paused for a second to decide whether she minded or not, then realized she didn't. It had been thoughtful of him to get all this stuff for her, even though she wasn't sure how he'd managed it, since all of their cash appeared untouched.

Well, she'd ask him in a minute. She'd showered before bed, so she didn't need to do that again, but it still felt wonderful to brush her teeth and wash her face, tidy her hair, apply some lip balm. Her hazel eyes stared back at her from the mirror, and by some miracle they didn't appear all that shadowed. Maybe she really had slept for fifteen hours.

There were two sets of practical-looking clothing: dark trousers and shirts, all of which appeared to be her size. But there was also that beautiful dark red tunic and matching pants. When was the last time she'd worn a color like that? Cassidy couldn't really remember, but she knew it had been a long time ago. And it was close to dinnertime. If the dome city on Triton had a hotel this decent, there had to be someplace they could eat that was up to snuff.

She pulled out the red outfit, opened the package of underwear, and got dressed. Amazing what a difference it could make to be clean, to have fresh new clothes and a nice chunk of sleep under your belt. Even the shoes more or less fit, although they seemed a little loose. That was fine, though…as long as they didn't have to end up running anyplace. Then it was one last pass of the brush through her hair, and she thought she was more or less ready to face the world.

Or at least face Derek Tagawa.

He was sitting on the sofa in the main living area of the suite when she emerged. His attention was focused on a new and shiny-looking handheld, and he was wearing a trim pair of black pants and matching jacket, so obviously he'd done a bit more shopping for himself while she was passed out. As soon as she entered the room, though, he set the handheld aside and offered her a polite smile. She could tell it was something of an act, though, as the smile couldn't hide the surprising look of admiration in his eyes.

Feeling absurdly pleased by that, she still managed to casually say, "Sorry I conked out for so long."

"You needed it. I slept some, too, but not as long, since I spent most of the trip here passed out."

True. He sounded sheepish, but she saw no reason for him to be. There hadn't been anything else for him to do on that long, long flight. "Been doing some more shopping, I see."

That remark made him look even more apologetic. "I suppose I should've waited to ask you if it was all right, but since we had absolutely no luggage, no personal items, I figured doing a bit of replenishing our supplies couldn't hurt too much."

"No, I appreciate it," she replied, one hand brushing against the silky fabric of her tunic. "And this is beautiful. Thank you. But how did you pay for everything?"

"Added it to our tab. The hotel management didn't have a problem with it. I get the distinct impression that we have some sort of fairy godmother watching over us."

His tone was half-joking, but the expression on his face told Cassidy that he was sincere. She wasn't sure she would've phrased it exactly the same way, but she had the distinct feeling someone was looking out for them. Why, she couldn't begin to guess, unless it was the way they'd managed to steal that starfighter literally from under its pilot's nose. She supposed that sort of stunt might earn them a few points with the people who ran Triton base. Fans of the Consortium, they were not.

"I'm willing to go with that for now," she said. "And if we're more or less safe here, I say we go get something to eat. I'm starving."

"As you should be. You were asleep for more than twelve hours."

Shit. She'd worried it was something like that. "I'm really sorry—"

"Don't be. I slept some, as I said, ordered up some halfway decent soup and a sandwich." The dark eyes were warm, watching her, and she could feel an uncharacteristic blush rise in her cheeks. "But I could definitely do with something a bit more substantial."

Cassidy nodded, saying, "I'll get the funds." As she retrieved the pouch of units and the credit voucher, along with her handheld, she realized she didn't have anyplace to put them. Neither the tunic nor the pants she wore had any pockets. And of course, being a man, Derek hadn't thought to get her a new bag to go along with her new clothes. Well, for the time being, she'd slip the voucher inside her bra, and Derek could carry the cash. She wasn't worried about him taking off with it—after all, where would he go? Five hundred units wasn't enough to get him anywhere.

Some part of her mind wanted to chide her for even entertaining such a thought. She knew deep down that he would never abandon her and take the money with him, even if the voucher represented a far larger portion of their current assets. Why she was so certain of that, when she'd known him for a total of approximately forty-eight hours, a good portion of which either one of them had been sleep, she wasn't sure, but something told her Derek Tagawa was an honorable man. Hell, even while she'd been passed out trying to catch up on her sleep, he'd done more to take care of her than her father ever had.

"Can you take these?" she asked, handing the pouch of units to Derek. "Love the outfit, but it's a little short in the pocket department."

"Of course," he replied immediately, and stowed the money in an inner pocket of his jacket. It bulged a little but didn't look too bad. And she could tell he was surprised and pleased that she'd trusted him with it at all. In an apparent attempt to cover that up, he added, "I did look up where we could eat around here. There's actually a fairly large hydroponics setup on the far side of the dome, so some of the food is fresh. But if you're a big meat eater, you're out of luck."

She shrugged. Most of the time she couldn't even afford real meat, and made do with soy substitutes. Going without now wouldn't be too much of a hardship. "That's not a problem."

His expression brightened. "Good. Then there's a place within walking distance that promises the best eggplant parmesan this side of Naples."

Having never eaten in Italy, Derek couldn't really vouch for the authenticity of the food, but it was surprisingly good…especially when you considered it was in a cramped establishment on a side street in Triton's dome city. There were only six tables, and five of them were occupied when he and Cassidy entered. The host, who also seemed to be the owner, smiled and led them to their seats, tapped a button, and left them to peruse the menu the table displayed on the wall next to them.

"They can't have real wine out here, can they?" she asked, inspecting the bill of fare with some incredulity. "I mean, the rotgut in that one bar was one thing, but…."

He shrugged. "I've never heard of anyone being successful with growing wine grapes hydroponically, but maybe they import it. The prices would suggest that." It was true, too; he didn't pretend to be any kind of connoisseur, but he'd gone out to eat in enough establishments on Gaia and on the Moon as well that he knew the owner here was charging approximately five times what a similar bottle would cost on one of the inner planets. "So we don't have to have any, if you think it's too much."

A flash of a grin, one that lit up her hazel eyes even in the dimly lit restaurant. "I'm feeling flush right now. And I think we've earned the right to a little celebration, don't you?"

That was an understatement. The two of them should be dead, but by some miracle they weren't. If Cassidy didn't mind being severely gouged for that celebratory bottle of chianti, far be it from him to protest. "Yes, I do think we've earned that."

The owner came back, and they asked for the wine, along with eggplant parmesan and vegetable lasagna. He seemed pleased with their choices…or maybe he was just thrilled someone had been a sucker enough to purchase that overpriced wine…and disappeared back into the kitchen.

"Who knew Triton would be so civilized?" Cassidy remarked, and Derek shook his head.

"Not I, that's for certain. Everything I'd heard made it sound like the worst of Iradia and the Detroit slums rolled into one."

"Have you been there?"

"Where? Iradia, or Detroit?"

"Either."

"Neither," he told her, realizing that he'd gone to the Moon and back multiple times, and back and forth from Normerica to the Asian continent, but he'd never gone farther east than the Colorado River. Had never really seen the point at the time—immersed in his studies at first, and then volunteering for GARP after he got his doctorate and realized he wanted to do something with it, rather than stay safely in Tucson, teaching bored undergraduates. "How about you?"

She made a face. "I told you—I've never even set foot on Gaia."

The wine made its appearance in that moment, and she fell silent while the owner uncorked the bottle at the table, then poured a measure each for them. After promising a basket of bread, he went back to the kitchen, and Derek lifted a glass, which of course was plastic and not actually glass.

"Well, here's to seeing new places, then," he said.

Cassidy raised her glass as well, and they both drank. To his surprise, the wine was good, so it appeared to have survived its journey to Triton unscathed. She nodded, then told him, "I'll drink to that. I'd just prefer those new places to be something exciting, like Nova Angeles or Paris."

Her remark sobered him a bit. They'd needed some time to take their bearings, but at some point they would have to decide what to do next, where to go. Or at least, she needed to make that decision. He knew he had to do something to clear his name, to prove he was no murderer. That meant going back to Gaia, an idea he was sure would find no favor with her.

And she looked so beautiful, sitting across the table from him, her dark hair loose over her shoulders, the deep red of the tunic making her skin look like cream and her hazel eyes almost green, that he was loath to say anything that would disturb their current cozy tête-à-tête. "I'm sure either one of those places must be fascinating."

Her eyes narrowed slightly. "But...."

"But nothing."

She wasn't buying it. Her fingers tightened around the stem of her wine glass, and she took a sip, but Derek could tell her thoughts were elsewhere. "But you don't have any intention of seeing the galaxy."

"Not at first," he admitted. Avoiding the subject was one thing, but he wouldn't lie to her.

"So what's your plan?"

Your plan. Apparently she was back to you and me, not us. Really, what else could it be? They were practically strangers. She'd saved his life, and somehow he'd figure out a way to repay her, but he was a fool for thinking even for a second that there might be anything else between them but that.

"I need to go back to Gaia, get some real legal representation, get this thing cleared up so I can go on with my life."

"Are you nuts?" This was delivered in a harsh whisper. Clearly she didn't want anyone overhearing their conversation, although no one else seemed to be paying much attention to the two of them, or what they were saying. "If you go back, they'll kill you."

He'd been expecting that response. The owner came by with the basket of bread at exactly that moment, so Derek couldn't do anything except smile his thanks, then wait for the man to go away. Cassidy was looking at him expectantly, so he knew he'd have to give her some kind of answer. "I guess that's a risk I'm willing to take."

Her eyes glittered with anger. "That's some thanks for saving your ass."

Oh, hell. "I didn't mean it that way. You think I don't know everything you've done for me? But I don't want to live my life on the run, always looking over my shoulder."

"It's still better than being shot on sight." Mouth tight, she took a piece of bread from the basket, broke off a tiny piece, and put it in her mouth without bothering to butter it. Not that the "butter" sitting on the dish in the middle of the table was actually the real thing.

He floundered for something to say. Confrontations had never been his forte, whether they were with his father or the few women he'd attempted to have relation-ships with over the years. "Maybe. But I guess I'm still enough of an idealist that I want to believe there's some way to set this right. Bring the guilty parties to justice. And I can't do that while hiding out in some far-flung section of the galaxy."

"You think you can take on the entire Consortium?" She didn't bother to hide the incredulity in her voice.

"No, of course not. But if I can meet up with the underground, utilize their resources—"

"Because that worked out so well the first time," she retorted. "In case you hadn't noticed, your friends blew up my ship and nearly took us with it. So I don't know who these 'contacts' of yours are, but you might want to reevaluate your relationship with them. I don't think it's working out."

He couldn't argue with her there. However, he was fairly certain that whoever had broken him out of MaxSec had been genuine, had wanted him to expose the scandal of what GARP was actually doing in Hunan Province. Somewhere along the way, there had been a leak, or the Consortium had managed to catch wind of the planned rendezvous near Europa. But just because that had all gone disastrously wrong, it didn't mean there weren't good people in the underground, people who would help him…if he could only get in touch with them.

"All right," he said, settling back in his seat and pick-ing up his glass of wine. "You think my plan's crazy. So what's yours?"

"Buy a ship," she said promptly. "With what we have, we could get a decent used passenger vessel. Not a Sirocco, of course, but something serviceable. And with that we could go anywhere we wanted."

"And then do what?"

Her brow creased. "What do you mean?"

"I mean, let's say we have a ship. And let's say I agree that it's nuts to try to fix things on Gaia. So we fly away and leave all this mess behind. What happens after that?"

Something in her expression hardened, although her tone was cool enough as she replied, "Whatever you want. You tell me where you want to go, and I'll drop you off. I'll even give you a little of what's left on this voucher to get yourself started. Probably the first thing to do would be to buy a new identity."

That wasn't what he'd meant. Or rather, maybe it was, but he hadn't intended for her to think that he'd want nothing more to do with her. Despite all the insanity that had surrounded them during their time together, he liked her, liked the way she thought on her feet and her hard-nosed way of looking at the galaxy. It was so refreshingly different from the women he'd known back on Gaia, all members of academia like him, all of them worried about their particular place on the professional totem pole, little birds scheming to knock someone else off their perch so they could move up another rung.

It would probably also have helped if she weren't so damn beautiful.

He cleared his throat. "I didn't mean to give that impression, Cassidy. I only meant—"

"Here we are!" broke in the owner, who approached their table, his hands laden with large white plates overflowing with food.

Despite his hunger earlier, Derek found he didn't have much of an appetite. He managed a smile, though, while Cassidy did the same, saying,

"It all smells great."

Luckily, the man didn't seem to notice the tension between the couple seated at the table…or, being a professional, chose to ignore it. Either way, he departed, leaving them alone again.

Cassidy picked up her fork and cut herself a bite of her eggplant parmesan. From the expression on her face, it seemed she suddenly wasn't all that hungry, either, but knew she needed to force something down.

"Look," Derek said, lowering his voice. "I know we're in…kind of a strange place."

"Triton?" she replied, her tone all innocence.

He stabbed a forkful of his lasagna. "And here I was just thinking one of the reasons I liked you was because you didn't play games."

That seemed to get to her. She paused, her gaze fixed on her plate, fork pushing into the food but not actually retrieving any. "Okay. No games. I don't know what to say, Derek. Part of me is thinking I shouldn't care, but part of me does." Another hesitation, and she added, "I mean, care about what happens to you. If you go back to Gaia, they're going to chew you up and spit you out. Some people would probably call me crazy for trusting you, but I do. I think everything you've told me is true, and it sucks, but I can't help thinking the galaxy would be a better place if you kept on breathing, even if you had to do it very far away from here and using a different name."

"Thank you," he said, and her eyebrows went up in surprise. "No, I mean it. Thank you for trusting me." He sounded a little rattled, even to himself, and he reached for his wine and took a sip in an attempt to regain his composure. It had been so very long since anyone had believed anything he said, had thought of him as anything except a murderer. Well, he supposed the people who'd been trying to kill him knew the truth, but that was cold comfort.

"So…can't you think it over for a bit? I'm not even sure how easy it's going to be to find a ship, so we might not be doing anything for a few days." Her eyes seemed to be pleading with him, and he gave a slow nod.

"I can do that," he replied, and although he didn't say the words aloud, for you echoed in his mind.

She seemed to pick up on that echo, because she nodded, then returned her attention to her meal.

In that moment, he wondered if he'd just made a promise he couldn't possibly keep.

SEVEN

So just how close had she come to giving herself away?

Way too close.

Maybe it had been the wine, the mood of cozy intimacy in the restaurant. Her surroundings made it too easy for her to relax, to not guard every word she was saying. Whatever it was, she'd almost admitted that she cared more than she wanted to admit. She didn't want him to go back to Gaia and get his damn fool ass killed. She wanted....

What *did* she want?

That was a question she'd stopped asking herself years ago. What did it matter what she wanted, when it was pretty clear she'd never actually get it? She hadn't wanted to be raised on that freighter, basically teaching herself to read and write, because even before he got the Titan gig, her father was shuttling cargo all over the

Gaian system, and there was no way she could go to a proper school. She hadn't wanted to be stuck with the *Avalon* and the MaxSec contract after her father died, but it was the only thing she knew, and she didn't know what else to do with herself.

And now her father was gone, and the *Avalon* was gone, and she really didn't know what she should do. Maybe she was clinging to Derek, trying to keep him from going back to Gaia, because then she would be alone, truly alone, and the spurious security of his presence was better than nothing.

No, she didn't want to believe that about herself. Hadn't she made it these last three years all on her own? She didn't need a man around, especially some crazy idealist like Derek Tagawa. The only reason she didn't want him to go was that she didn't want to think all of this—helping him get away from Titan, losing her ship—would end up meaning absolutely nothing in the end.

That sounded like a very good reason. Too bad it wasn't even close to the truth.

Attraction she could deal with. She'd met men over the years she was attracted to, and either things happened, or they didn't. With each of those men, though, she'd known there was no chance of a future, and most of the time it didn't bother her that much. They were people to spend a day or a weekend or—in a few very rare cases—a few weeks with, nothing more.

But Derek was so very different from all of them, in ways she couldn't begin to quantify. He was…decent. Thoughtful. Intelligent.

Way above your pay grade.

The remainder of their dinner had been conducted mainly in silence, with only a few comments on the food. He seemed to realize that she wanted to leave the subject alone, and, unlike most of the men she'd known, he'd respected her wishes, hadn't attempted to poke or prod any further. And then they'd walked back to the hotel, gone up to the suite, and retired to their respective sleeping quarters after taking turns in the restroom.

But she couldn't help thinking about how he was right there, just on the other side of the bathroom. Was he asleep already? Or was he as preoccupied as she was, lying awake when he should be getting his rest?

She rolled over once again, cursing her brain, which didn't seem to want to leave her alone. Maybe it had been a mistake to try to sleep, since she'd only been up for about three hours since that marathon twelve-hour coma. But the wine had made her feel tired, and she knew the best thing she could do for herself was get back on something of a normal schedule.

Normal. There was a joke.

After punching the pillow to get it to lie flatter, she let out a breath, then drew in another. That was it. Deep, soothing breaths, the kind that would bring the oblivion she craved. Her body needed sleep, her brain even more so. Breathe…breathe….

Her handheld beeped into the silence. Cassidy froze, mentally scrambling to figure out who in the world could be calling her. Derek? No, that was silly. He didn't even have her code, and besides, if he wanted to talk to her, he'd just come and knock on her door.

The beep came again. She knew it would automatically go to voicemail if she left it alone, but her curiosity got the better of her. Pushing back the covers, she climbed out of bed and picked up the device, then squinted at the screen.

No identifying image, no code. No nothing. Just five terrifying words.

We know where you are.

Derek had just drifted off into blessed blackness when he heard Cassidy's harsh whisper.

"Derek. Derek."

He sat up, blinking, and realized she stood in the open door of his bedroom, her figure vaguely outlined by the soft illumination of the one lamp he'd left on in the main sitting area. The second thought that struck him was that she wore only a sleep shirt, and her long, slim legs were visible from approximately mid-thigh down.

Somehow he managed to shift his attention away from those legs and up to her face. Now that his eyes were adjusting, he could see the strain in her features, how pale she was.

"What's the matter?"

Wordlessly, she crossed the room to him and extended her handheld. He took it from her, then froze as he read the words glowing pale blue against the dark gray of the screen.

His heartbeat sped up, but he made sure his voice remained calm as he asked, "When did you get this?"

"Just now. I heard it beep and wondered who it might be, since not many people have my code."

God damn it. He should have known this bit of breathing space couldn't possibly last.

"When you say 'not many people,' how many is that actually?"

She went over to a chair placed up against the wall and sank down into it. "I don't know—that is, of course it's in the Corrections system database, since I had a contract with them, and because I'm a contractor, I assume that any other government agency would have access to that information as well. So that's a pretty big pool to choose from. But other than that? Not many. The company that leases me hangar space on the Moon. The health clinic I go to. Things like that."

Shaking his head, Derek replied, "I doubt it's any of them. You just gave the finger to the GDF, and by extension the whole government, so I don't think we need to look any further than that."

After giving him a shaky smile, she said, "Well, my father always did say to go big or go home." She drummed her fingers on her bare knees. "The thing is, okay, they know where we are. But how likely are they to come after us here on Triton?"

He wasn't sure of the answer to that question. True, the outlaw outpost was not the sort of place for GDF troops to come swaggering in and waving their guns around, but that didn't mean the Consortium wouldn't send a different kind of agent to dispatch the two troublemakers. He had a feeling that sort of operation would be a lot more difficult for the powers-that-be on Triton—such as they were—to stop.

"Very likely," he said, not bothering to be politic in his reply. "It's not if, but when."

"That's what I was afraid of." She pushed her hair back, off her shoulders, then asked, "How soon?"

"I have no idea." While he was gratified that she thought he'd have some insight on the matter, the truth was that he really had no idea. Researching the methods of the Consortium's black ops personnel fell a little outside his particular field of expertise. She gave a grim nod, and he added, "I suppose it all depends on how close any agents they'd use for this job might be."

"They could still be on Gaia?" she asked in hopeful tones.

"Maybe. Or on Ganymede…or even embedded here on Triton."

"Thanks for that ray of sunshine."

Despite their current situation, he couldn't help cracking a grin. "Just trying to be practical." But since they'd already spent too much time talking, he pushed the bedclothes away and got up, heading toward the closet so he could get dressed. "We need to get ready, and we need to be prepared. Go ahead and pack your things."

"On it," she said, sounding resigned, and rose from the chair. "But Derek—where exactly are we going?"

"I don't know," he told her. "Anywhere but here."

Thank God for those twelve hours of sleep, because Cassidy had a feeling it might be a long time before she found a safe place to lay her head. No other messages had been forthcoming, even as she felt her gaze keep shifting to the dresser where she'd set down the handheld. Now she was dressed in the pants and jacket and long-sleeved knit shirt Derek had purchased for her, glad that the spacesuit she'd worn had been designed to go over clothes and footwear, and so she still had her favorite pair of flat boots, broken in and shabby and endlessly comfortable. She had a feeling she was going to be needing them real soon.

They had no luggage, but she fished the bags that the clothing and other items had been delivered in out of the trash, then packed everything as quickly as she could. Barely five minutes had passed since she'd alerted Derek to the unwelcome message, and yet it still felt as if they were taking too long, as if Consortium agents would be breaking down the door at any minute. No, that probably wasn't right. Any dirty work they planned to engage in would be done as quietly as possible to avoid any unwanted attention.

She felt a stir of triumph at being ready sooner than Derek. Then again, it wasn't as if he'd spent a lifetime learning how to travel light. But he emerged from his bedroom only a minute or so after she'd put her bag down on the coffee table to wait for him, so she couldn't really blame him for any delays.

"Do you have a plan?" she asked him, hoping he'd say yes and knowing he'd probably say no. It wasn't as if she'd come up with anything terribly constructive in the meantime. After all, they were stuck in a domed city. There weren't that many places they could go. She'd never bothered to read up on Triton, and anyway, any facts she might have gleaned from official sources were no doubt completely inaccurate. But she guessed, from the size of the dome and the density of the buildings it contained, that maybe six or seven thousand people lived here. It might be enough for them to get lost in.

Might.

"Other than keep moving, no, not really," he responded.

"Well, that's slightly better than 'stay here and wait for someone to come and kill us,' so I'm on board with that."

He shot her a sideways glance but didn't say anything, instead went to the door.

"Open it from the side," Cassidy told him, moving to flatten herself against the wall on his other side.

"Why?"

"Because it's easier to get shot if you're standing right in front as you open it."

"Ah." He flicked her another one of those sidelong looks. "Was that part of your training as a freighter captain?"

"No," she said easily. "It's just something I've seen on the cop vids I've watched over the years."

His pained expression told her exactly what he thought of using scripted vid shows as a basis for formulating a survival strategy. However, he did as she'd instructed, hugging the wall next to her. It was the first time he'd been this close, only a few inches away, and in that moment she realized how tall he was, how broad his shoulders. Maybe he'd been eating slop in the MaxSec for the past two years, but you'd never know it to look at him.

And that is exactly the last thing you should be thinking about right now. She held her breath as Derek pushed the controls for the door.

It slid open...and nothing.

No pulse bolts, no troop of heavily armed men running into the suite. Derek moved away from the wall an inch or two, just enough so he could peer through the doorway.

"Looks clear."

Cassidy slipped past him and looked as well. No one outside, no sign of movement at all—which made some sense, as it was now close to eleven hundred hours, not exactly peak time for people to be coming and going from their rooms. She wouldn't exactly allow herself a sigh of relief, but it did seem that they'd made it past the first hurdle.

The second was the stairway. They'd both looked at the lifts and, by mutual agreement, shook their heads and continued instead to the access stairs at the end of the hall. Yes, there was still a surveillance camera mounted in one corner, but at least it would be easier to make a break for it on the stairway than it would trapped in an elevator.

No one stopped them, though, and they emerged in the rear of the lobby, far enough away from the front desk that Cassidy thought they'd be able to slip out the back door without too much trouble. Then she looked down at the new clothes she was wearing and paused. The last thing she wanted to do was skip out on their bill.

"How much did all this stuff cost?" she asked Derek, pointing at his jacket.

"I—what?"

"How much? They put it on our tab, and now we're taking off without paying for any of it. Doesn't seem fair."

He frowned, appearing to do a quick mental calculation. "Maybe three hundred units?"

Well, that was doable at least. She took the pouch with their cash and removed a hundred units, then handed them to Derek. "You keep these. I'm going to leave the rest behind to pay for everything."

A look of surprise flitted over his features, followed by another one of those admiring glances. "Good idea. We wouldn't want to add petty theft to our long list of crimes."

Crimes that now did include murder, if you wanted to call the deaths of the two men in the starfighter murder. She preferred to think of what she'd done as self-defense, a clear-cut case of "us or them," but she could see why Consortium authorities might view the matter differently.

There was another security camera mounted right outside the entrance to the stairwell. Since Cassidy knew she'd already been seen on it, she made no attempt to hide her face, but only lifted the bag of money, jingled it twice, and then set it on the floor immediately next to the wall.

"Okay, that should do it…I hope."

He shrugged. "It's a gesture."

Opposite the stairwell was a door, one which probably led to an access corridor of some sort. By an unspoken agreement, they headed toward it, Derek moving through first, Cassidy immediately behind him. No one attempted to stop them, but that could've simply been because their attempt to make some sort of payment had been noticed, and the management at the hotel didn't see any reason to detain them further, if they really did want to take off in the dome community's equivalent of the middle of the night.

The corridor in which they found themselves was strictly utilitarian: gray walls, floor, and ceiling, punctuated here and there by doors that probably led to storage areas, laundry facilities, maybe the kitchens. Neither of them seemed inclined to stop and investigate. Instead, they hurried through the hallway until they emerged in a dingy-looking alleyway, piled high with packing crates, empty boxes, and the usual flotsam and jetsam any high-density populated area would produce.

"What now?" Derek asked.

Cassidy hesitated. She didn't know Triton well—all right, at all—but it seemed if they were going to put that credit voucher to good use, then they'd better head back toward the settlement's hangar complex, see if there was a ship to be had for love or money. Lots of money. Surely there had to be someone on this hunk of ice who was even more desperate than they were.

"Back to the hangars, I guess. I mean, I haven't seen any used spaceship lots around here, have you?"

He chuckled, although the laughter had a grim note to it. Something in his expression told her he wasn't expecting them to have much luck. Maybe they wouldn't be able to buy a ship at all, would end up paying too much for passage on a transport ship or, even worse, a freighter. She'd spent her whole life on one, so she knew exactly how lacking in creature comforts those types of vessels tended to be.

"I suppose that's best. And if we—" His words cut off abruptly as his handheld beeped. He fished it out of his pocket and stared down at it, brows drawn together.

An icy trail of fear inched its way down her back. After all, the last message she'd received on her handheld wasn't exactly reassuring. "What is it?"

In answer, he extended his hand to her so she could see the device's screen clearly. This communique, like the one she'd gotten, had absolutely no identifying code or name stamp. However, its contents were slightly more encouraging.

Go to Hangar 19G. A ship will be waiting for you there.

"What the—"

"I know," Derek said, cutting her off. "So…do we trust it?"

She hesitated. Surely it couldn't be that easy. "Smells like a trap to me."

"That's what I was thinking. But how much of a choice do we have?"

None at all. They couldn't really stand here forever, debating their choices. Either they'd decide to trust the message, or they wouldn't. And since they'd already determined it was the hangar complex or nothing, she thought they might as well head in that direction.

"We'll go over there. But we need to keep an eye out for anything unusual."

The lifted eyebrow he gave her seemed to indicate that he thought almost anything they saw on Triton would be unusual. Fair enough. A place like this wasn't exactly something your normal atmospheric scientist encountered, even one who'd spent a few years in MaxSec.

But he didn't argue, only gave a faint nod, and so they headed back to that quadrant of the dome. The hangar complex itself was technically outside the dome, as of course it couldn't exactly open and shut to allow ships to enter or exit. No, there was a long above-ground tunnel, one that connected the actual structures where vessels landed to the complex where they'd been checked for weapons less than a standard day ago.

Something about the thought of that tunnel made Cassidy nervous. She didn't communicate her unease to Derek, as she couldn't articulate exactly why the thought of it bothered her. It wasn't as if they hadn't gone through it without a hitch when they first arrived. Besides, although it felt like the middle of the night to her, there were still plenty of people coming and going on the dome's streets, especially as they got closer to the hangar complex. You arrived at a planet when you arrived. It wasn't as if shipping activity confined itself to "normal" working hours…whatever those might be.

They passed through the screening devices once more. The lights on the walk-through structure glowed green, indicating that they were not carrying any weapons that could damage the dome. Those devices strictly focused on pulse guns and the old-fashioned projectile weapons that preceded them, and Cassidy wondered what would happen if she tried to smuggle a knife or other bladed weapon through the screener. Maybe nothing. It wasn't as if you could drive a sword through the tough material of a dome, a super-composite that was impervious to most types of impact.

Despite her attempt to appear calm, it seemed as if some of her disquiet had communicated itself to Derek, as she noticed he walked so close beside her that their hands brushed against one another from time to time. Not that she minded too much; it felt good to have him next to her like that, even if she knew he probably couldn't do much to defend her if the worst happened. He looked big and capable, but come on—he was a scientist, someone who spent his life working on a computer or, at the most, going out in the field to take readings and observations. Having fended off an attack or two in some of Luna City's more questionable districts, Cassidy thought she was probably better equipped than he to take on any assailants who might come their way.

Even this late there was some foot traffic in the tunnel, people who didn't seem to pay her or Derek any mind, who moved briskly along, gazes focused on their destination, absorbed in their own thoughts. Most of them didn't look particularly seedy or menacing, but even in her short time here, Cassidy had come to realize that Triton's dome city wasn't exactly the seething hotbed of crime the Gaian authorities painted it to be. She had no doubt that a lot of the people here were operating outside the Consortium's playbook. However, that didn't

mean they were intent on blindly assaulting or otherwise defrauding every citizen they came across. Maybe
it was a simple matter of there being more honor among
thieves than she'd thought, but, either way, she'd take it.

The foot traffic ebbed, and the only people Cassidy
saw were a couple dressed in somewhat rumpled business clothing coming toward them, a man and woman,
maybe some ten years or so older than she and Derek.
They looked tired, and Cassidy wondered how long a
flight they'd taken to get here, and why this supposedly
outlaw world was the destination of such a respectable-
looking pair.

She didn't have to wonder for long, since, just as the
couple was passing by, they lunged at her and Derek,
knives glinting under the blue-white overhead lighting.
A startled little scream erupted from her throat, and
after that she wasn't sure exactly what happened.

Derek shoved her, pushing her out of harm's way,
even as he lashed out with one foot, catching both the
man and the woman behind their knees in a sweep
so fast Cassidy could barely keep her gaze focused on
it. They stumbled but regained their balance quickly,
descending on Derek, apparently leaving Cassidy to
be dealt with later. Once again the knives flashed, and
she was sure he was about to be skewered—but no, his
hand chopped against the woman's forearm, and even
from where she was crouched on the ground, Cassidy
could hear the bone break with a sickening crunch. The
knife went flying, clattering off the curved metal wall,

and she skittered toward it on her hands and knees, even as the woman let out a screech and then struck toward Derek with her left hand while her companion whirled, attempting to drive his knife right into Derek's midsection.

Somehow he whipped himself out of the way just in time, leaving the knife to whistle harmlessly through midair. The man cursed and lifted his arm to strike again, but Derek kicked out, catching him directly in the groin. At the same time, Cassidy felt her fingers wrap around the plastic handle of the knife, still warm from the female attacker's grasp. As the other assailant bent over, groaning from the impact of Derek's kick, Cassidy thrust herself to her feet and drove the knife into the woman's side while she was momentarily distracted by her companion's obvious distress.

The woman gasped, then reached back and jabbed an elbow into Cassidy's ribs. Luckily, it was a glancing blow, and so she didn't think any ribs were cracked, although she guessed she'd have a hell of a bruise later.

If there was a later.

Obviously, the woman wasn't one to be stopped by a simple knife wound, since she yanked the knife from her side and thrust backward with it. Somehow Cassidy managed to jerk herself out of the way at the last minute, although she heard rather than felt the blade cut through the fabric of her new shirt.

God damn it.

She threw a glance over her shoulder, saw Derek grab his assailant by the shoulders and yank him downward as he thrust up with one knee, catching the man in the nose. Blood sprayed everywhere, and the man staggered backward—bumping into his companion, who lost her balance for a split second. That seemed to be the only opening Derek needed, as he kicked out again, hitting her in the exact spot where Cassidy had stabbed her and throwing her back against the wall. She slid down it, blood pouring from her side. Even then she tried to push herself to her feet, knife still clutched in one hand.

In that same moment, a group of four men in dark, close-fitting clothing approached, and Cassidy felt her heart sink. Okay, Derek had done better than she could have imagined, but even with that, she didn't see how he could possibly take on four more men in addition to the one who'd assaulted them initially. That man was as bruised and bloodied as his companion, but clearly not down for the count just yet, since he was already starting to push himself to his feet.

As she braced herself, wondering if she had it in her to fight off two of the newcomers in addition to the bitch who wouldn't die, the four men swarmed their assailants. Cassidy couldn't see exactly what happened, but a few seconds later, both the man and the woman were passed out on the ground. Something glinted as one of the men slipped it into the pocket of his coveralls. Some kind of knockout drug?

Whatever it was, it obviously worked. One of the men turned toward her and Derek, saying, "Hope you don't mind us butting in. It looked like you were doing okay there, but we figured you could use a hand."

"It's no problem," Derek said, sounding a little breathless. He flicked a glance at Cassidy, frowning when he saw the tear in her shirt. "You okay?"

"I'm fine," she replied, noting that she sounded out of breath herself. "Just caught the shirt, not me." She turned her attention to their rescuer. "Who are you?"

He grinned. Under normal circumstances, she would've said he was fairly nondescript-looking—sandy hair, brown eyes, features regular but not particularly handsome. But something about the way he carried himself told her he was a pretty tough customer. "A friend."

"A friend, huh?"

"Thanks for the rescue," Derek put in, obviously less than thrilled by her skeptical tone.

"It's no problem. You can continue to Hangar 19G now."

So these guys were in league with whomever had sent that message? "What's in Hangar 19G?"

His brown eyes crinkled a bit at the corners as he shot her a grin. "Just what the message said. A ship. Or do you not want it anymore?"

"Oh, we want it," Derek said. "Don't we, Cassidy?"

She knew when to keep her mouth shut. "Absolutely. Thanks again."

The man's grin only widened, but she ignored it and went to Derek, looped her arm through his, and went on through the tunnel as if absolutely nothing untoward had happened. Once they were a few yards away from the scene of the attack, she murmured, "How the hell did you learn to fight like that?"

Derek didn't look at her, just kept walking. After a long pause, he said, "My father would never allow his son to bring dishonor on the Tagawa name by not knowing how to defend himself. I started training in martial arts when I was five years old."

Holy crap. And she thought her father had expected a lot of her. "Well, it sure came in handy."

No reply, only a grim nod. She got the hint that he really didn't want to talk about it, so she kept her mouth shut as they left the tunnel, then paused to inspect the holo-map of the hangar complex conveniently displayed on the wall opposite the tunnel's exit. From there they had to walk down a long corridor, then another, until at last they found the hangar bay designated as 19G. It was sealed with a biometric lock, and she looked over at Derek, perplexed.

"What now?"

His expression was unreadable. "Try it."

"What do you mean, 'try it'? I've never been before, so how can it be keyed to my print already?"

"Just try it."

Fine. She lifted her right hand and jabbed her thumb against the glass plate. To her surprise, the light above the lock glowed blue, and a second later the door slid smoothly open. "How did you know it would do that?"

"I didn't, but I'm guessing, considering that whoever is helping us got the code to my handheld even though no one in the galaxy should have it, and that they also knew to send those guys to bail us out, they probably lifted your prints from the hotel room and used them to key the lock here."

None of that was outside the bounds of possibility, but even so, the thought that someone had been watching them so closely made a chill creep up her neck. She didn't like it, even though so far their intentions seemed to have been completely beneficent.

All those misgivings were forgotten, though, as she stepped inside the hangar and saw the ship their unknown benefactors had left there for her and Derek. No, it wasn't a Sirocco, but the next best thing—a Zephyr-class personal transport, sleek and fast, capable of sublight travel, even if it didn't have the Sirocco's Gupta drive.

"Someone must really like you," she remarked, moving closer to the ship, seeing that the hatch was open, its steps descended.

"Or you," he returned, but Cassidy shook her head.

"I doubt that. The captain of a fifth-rate freighter doesn't warrant this kind of attention."

He seemed to consider her words, looking doubtful, but then said, "Either way, it's a good ship, right?"

"It's a great ship." In fact, she couldn't wait to take a peek inside. Trying to sound casual, she added, "I think I'd better go in and check things out."

The grim look evaporated from his face, and he even smiled slightly. "You do that."

This was the sort of ship she'd always dreamed of owning, the sort of vessel that could take her anywhere she wanted...especially if it was far, far away from that unholy route between the Moon and Titan.

Where their benefactor had gotten it from, Cassidy couldn't begin to guess. Technically, she knew even the newest Zephyr would now be a couple of years old, but this ship looked as if it had just been taken out of mothballs for their use. No signs of previous occupants, no scratches, no stains on the upholstery in the little dinette area. All the controls in the cockpit gleamed new and fresh, not smudged with fingerprints, and both the pilot's and copilot's chairs didn't appear to have ever been sat in.

She could hear Derek's footsteps behind her on the metal floor. "Everything up to spec?"

"And then some." She moved closer to the console, flipped a few switches. "Fully fueled for in-system flight, and the subspace drive has a complete charge as well. We're ready to go."

"Sounds good." He was holding both their bags of supplies in one hand. Cassidy didn't even remember him retrieving them from the scene of the fight. Then again, she'd been a little befuddled during the wrap-up.

She supposed she shouldn't be too surprised that she'd missed that one small detail.

"There should be three cabins," she told him. "Pick whichever one you like."

He brought one hand up to his brow in a mock salute. "I'll leave the largest one for you, Captain."

With that he turned and went back down the corridor, leaving Cassidy to take her seat in the pilot's chair, to flick her fingers over the controls, going through the routine, which was somehow exciting in this new and shiny ship. Artificial gravity generators…check. Oxygen supplies just as topped off as the fuel. The only thing she didn't know was where they were going. She found she really didn't want to ask. Odds were that Derek would make the case for heading to Gaia, and she was feeling just giddy enough at the prospect of flying this ship that she really didn't feel like getting into that argument right now.

Unfortunately, she knew that confrontation would come sooner rather than later.

EIGHT

DEREK WENT INTO ONE OF THE TWO SMALLER cabins, which were identical in size, and set the bags of their belongings down on the bed. He'd have to transfer Cassidy's things to her stateroom, but for now he wanted a chance to catch his breath, to try to figure out what was going on.

The cabin where he now stood had a single narrow bed, a low dresser with four drawers, and a half-moon-shaped table bolted to one wall, two small side chairs seeming to await a cozy breakfast or other meal. No industrial grays and beiges here; the covering on the bed was a deep, deep blue, the upholstery on the chairs blue and red and a soft wheat color. The ship clearly had been designed and outfitted for someone a hell of a lot higher up the food chain than Derek Tagawa.

Frowning, he wondered where the ship had come from, whether it had been obtained through legal means or whether the previous owner had been conveniently gotten rid of. That didn't feel right, if for no other reason than the vessel seemed the next thing to new, with no obvious signs of wear.

His handheld beeped, and he pulled it from his pocket. Good thing it hadn't gotten kicked or fallen on during the tussle with those two toughs. A new message glowed in pale blue on the screen.

How do you like the ship?

"It's…nice," he said, letting the handheld translate his speech to text.

Just nice?

"Okay, it's great. Cassidy seems thrilled with it." He paused, then decided he would ask the question anyway, even if he wasn't sure how it would be received. "Where did you get it?"

Through completely legal means. Its registry is clean. In the larger cabin, you'll find a small case with new identities for both of you, completely sanitized and untraceable.

What the hell was he supposed to say to that? This whole thing was so outside his experience that he wasn't sure how to deal with it. "Um…thank you."

You're welcome.

There was so much he wanted to know, but he didn't know the parameters of their relationship with whoever was managing things at the other end of these transactions. "Who are you?"

A friend.

"A friend? I don't know anyone who can pull the kinds of strings you've been pulling lately."

We've never met. Your case caught my attention. *That's all you need to know for now.*

More like, all this mysterious person wanted him to know. Pressing the issue might get him in trouble, but his whole life he'd been asking questions, and he didn't plan to stop now. "And what if we take this ship back to Gaia?"

You want to clear your name. That's understandable. Not particularly wise, but understandable.

"So you think I should run?"

You've been given a second chance, Dr. Tagawa, which isn't something that should be taken lightly. On the other hand, I can understand why you would want to restore your reputation. Only you can decide if that's worth taking on the entire government at this time.

He hated to ask the question, but he did so anyway. "And if we run into difficulty…can we count on any further help?"

No answer. The screen on his handheld remained blank and gray. It seemed clear enough that their benefactor was only willing to go so far.

He huffed out a breath and shoved the handheld back into his pocket. It wasn't as if he wasn't grateful for all the assistance he and Cassidy had received so far. They'd be dead if it weren't for the intervention of their mysterious sponsor. On the other hand, he doubted the person who'd been helping them understood what it meant for him to simply walk away…to give up everything he'd fought so hard to achieve. To never clear things up with his father.

Derek's mouth compressed, and he forced himself to back away from that particular line of thought. It wouldn't do him any good now, and besides, they had some hard decisions to make. Going to the bed, where he'd set down both his and Cassidy's meager belongings, he gathered up the bag with her things and left the cabin. He didn't want to have this discussion with her, but he knew he had to do it now.

Since she didn't want to wait in the hangar, just in case more thugs showed up, possibly with some kind of contraband armament that could do serious damage to the ship, Cassidy got lift-off permission from the control center and brought the vessel up into a long elliptical orbit that would take them away from Triton. At least that way they'd be clear of the moon, but not so far off that they couldn't slingshot back if necessary. Not that she wanted to go back. No, she wanted to be far, far from here…and as quickly as possible.

A soft tread behind her indicated that Derek was done with whatever had been occupying him for the past few minutes. She hadn't heard any protests about their taking off, but that could have meant he was okay with it, or that he'd been so busy he hadn't been paying any attention.

"Where are we headed?" he asked, settling himself into the copilot's seat.

"Nowhere in particular. I just figured it was better to put some distance between us and Triton in case any reinforcements decided to show up."

A slight nod, his gaze fixed on the twinkling starfield outside the forward windows. "Aren't you worried about wasting fuel?"

"Not particularly. With what we're carrying right now, we could criss-cross the system about five times before we'd need a refill. We're fine." Cassidy swiveled her chair so she was pointed toward him; now that the orbit had been set, she really didn't need to keep that close an eye on things. Their proximity alarms, much more finely tuned than those on the Avalon, would alert them to any ships that might cross their path. "But this does bring us to the point where we have to decide what we're going to do next."

His expression was blank. She didn't pretend to know him very well, but she thought he was doing that on purpose, trying to look as impassive as he could. Which probably meant he was about to say the one thing she really didn't want to hear.

"I know it's a lot to ask of you—"

She didn't need to hear any more. "But you want to go to Gaia," she cut in.

"Yes."

Although the temperature inside the cabin was pleasant, a perfect 22 degrees C, Cassidy felt a chill go over her body. Just because she'd known that was what he planned to say, that didn't make it any easier to hear. She pressed her lips together, then let out a gust of breath. "Then I need you to tell me why."

A hint of annoyance, quickly erased, passed over his features. "You know why."

Irritation flared in her as well. She clenched her hands on her knees and said, "No, I want to know the real reason why. I don't think you've told me everything."

"Because wanting to clear my name of a false murder charge isn't enough?"

His tone was mild enough as he spoke, but she could see the flash of anger in those dark, dark eyes. What, was she not entitled to pry? Just supposed to point the ship wherever he asked? True, she wasn't the one who'd saved him this last time—he looked like he was doing just fine without anyone's help, frankly—but she'd saved his ass twice already…and she had a feeling she'd only add to that tally if they ended up going to Gaia.

"No," she said slowly. "I don't think it is. This feels… personal…to me. Tell me I'm wrong. Tell me I have my head up my ass." Flinging that particular challenge at him seemed safe enough to her, as she knew Derek was not the type to say that sort of thing to anyone, let alone the woman he needed to shuttle him from planet to planet. She wasn't going to allow herself to think that he regarded her as anything more than that.

His gaze flickered away from hers, seeming to settle on the shimmering blackness that surrounded the ship. Mouth tightening, he replied, "No, you're not wrong."

"So what is it?"

She got the impression that he wanted to get up and pace around the cabin, that he often did that when he was attempting to sort through his thoughts. If asked, she couldn't have said exactly why, except all of him feel tensed, as if he wanted to launch himself from the copilot's seat. But since there wasn't enough room for that, he appeared to settle for leaning forward slightly, hands tight on the chair's armrests.

A second ticked by, then another, and another. At last he said, "I told you how the authorities put it out there that Theo's death was the result of a lover's quarrel, some love triangle gone wrong?"

Cassidy nodded but didn't say anything. Again she had the impression that this was very difficult for him, and she didn't want to interrupt or do anything that would keep him from speaking, from explaining to her why he was willing to head to the very last planet in the galaxy where he would be safe.

He smoothed his hands over the knees of his pants, a nervous gesture, probably the first she'd seen from him. "I'd had a falling out with my father anyway. He didn't see the point in my working on GARP when I could've had a cushy teaching position at the university in Tucson."

That didn't make much sense to her. Clearly, Derek had some Asian blood in him, judging by his features and his last name, so why would his father would be opposed to his son helping with the rehabilitation of the continent? "But you're…." she ventured, then broke off, since she didn't know the best way of putting it.

"Half Japanese?" he finished for her, his expression almost wry, as if he'd been asked that question more than once before.

"Well, yes."

"If GARP was focusing on Japan, it might've been different. But that's last on the list, you know? Not much usable land…at least not compared to China. It's ancient history to most people, but the Japanese and Chinese were never the best of friends, and my father still carries those…prejudices…with him." Derek's gaze had been focused on her through most of that speech, but once again it shifted to the dark, star-studded skies outside the window. "Of course he was born in Normerica, but his family retained as much of as its traditions as it could after the Relocation."

Cassidy nodded. The Cloud had wiped out countless billions, but there were survivors, of course, most of whom had relocated to the southwest region of the former United States. Although she wasn't sure how he'd respond to the question, she found herself compelled to ask, "But if he was such a traditionalist, then why…?"

The question seemed to trail off on its own, but Derek appeared to understand what she was asking. A grim smile on his lips, he said, "Then why would he marry someone who wasn't Japanese? I never had the guts to ask him. My mother is an extraordinary woman, a surgeon, who also teaches at the university. How it happened, I don't know for sure." Was it her imagination, or did Derek's gaze shift to her for a telling second or two before he added, "Trying to explain what happens between two people isn't always easy."

That was for sure. Cassidy was still trying to figure out what was going on between her and Derek…if anything. Leaving that aside for the moment, she said, "So were you speaking at all?"

"Not much." A shrug, but she could see some of the pain he was trying to hide. It showed in the narrowing of his eyes, the tightening of his fingers on the armrests of his chair. "Mostly messages passed through my mother. The whole situation bothered her, but she knew that trying to force my father to do something he didn't want to was like trying to shoot a rocket into orbit without any fuel. So she mostly let it go, probably telling herself that my contract was only for three years anyway, and at the end of my stint in Hunan Province, I'd come home and all would be forgiven."

"So would you?"

"Would I what?"

"Have gone back to Tucson?"

Another one of those hesitations. Then his shoulders lifted slightly. "Possibly. It would have depended on whether I thought I was making a difference. Before Theo and I discovered what was really going on, I thought maybe I was. The air is, to put it simply, getting better. I'm not saying it's going to be fit for people to live there permanently, not for at least another decade, but considering it's been dead for more than three hundred years, a decade or so shouldn't make that much of a difference in the grand scheme of things."

Cassidy tried to visualize being involved in an enterprise that required you to think in terms of decades, or even centuries, rather than the here and now. For most of her life, she'd trained herself to not look much further ahead than the next Titan run. But of course Derek's line of work was very different from hers. "So you would have stayed, then."

"I don't like to speculate on something that's never going to happen now. If I'd continued to see progress, then yes, I probably would have continued with my work. It wasn't as if I had anything much to bring me back to Tucson."

For some people, family might have been enough of a reason. She found that concept difficult to relate to, as it had only been her and her father for so long that she had no more idea of how a typical family was supposed to work than she did of what daily life was like for the reclusive cloaked and hooded Zhore. "Really?" she asked. "Nothing?" What she really wanted to ask was, *No one?*, but she wasn't quite that brave.

He seemed to pick up on her meaning, though, and his gaze sharpened on her. "Not really. I was always focused. My father taught me that, if nothing else."

Well, that and how to break someone's arm with one kick, Cassidy thought, but she remained silent.

"I did my undergraduate work in three years, got my doctorate in four. After that I did some traveling, training with some of the top minds in the atmospheric sciences, helping to fine-tune the atmospheric processors so they'd do the far more delicate work of cleaning the air rather than altering an alien atmosphere to Gaian standard." Another lift of his shoulders. "It didn't leave much room for a personal life."

"No, it doesn't sound like it," she agreed, in what she prayed would sound like convincingly casual tones. That was one good thing about this whole situation…at least it appeared as if Derek was blessedly free of any potentially messy connections with ex-wives or girlfriends. Or current wives or girlfriends, assuming any of them would've hung around after the false rumors of the gay love affair and subsequent murder made the rounds.

And then Cassidy wanted to kick herself, because, beyond a few glances that could've been admiring or could've simply been her flattering herself, she had no reason to think Derek was interested in her at all beyond continuing to use her as his own personal interplanetary cab driver.

He gave her one long, considering look before saying, "My parents were focused on their work—my father's a fusion engineer. And my younger sister, maybe studying my example and deciding she didn't want to be anything like me, got married before she was twenty-five and now has two children. I haven't even seen the youngest one, aside from some pictures Naomi sent me."

"Wouldn't that be reason enough to go back?"

"For a short visit, sure. To stay? Not really. My sister and I were never that close. We don't have much beyond genetics in common."

It sounded cold, put that way, but Cassidy thought she understood. After all, you really couldn't choose your family…you were just supposed to love them, even if they were nothing like you. God knows if she could've picked out her father, he would've been nothing like Owen Evans.

"So, after the Consortium accused you of Theo's murder…." she began delicately, wanting to know what had gone wrong. Yes, Derek and his father had disagreed about his working on the GARP project, but that didn't sound like enough to have caused a serious rift.

This time Derek did push himself up out of his seat, as if he didn't want to remain sitting down while he recounted this part of the story. Instead, he leaned against the metal lintel of the oval opening that led into the corridor beyond. "It wasn't the murder," he said, voice expressionless. "It's that my father couldn't bear the shame of me being exposed as a homosexual."

Cassidy blinked at him. "Wait—what? You mean there are people who still care about that sort of thing?" Marriage between members of the same sex had been legal for so many centuries that she couldn't understand how anyone would still have an issue with it.

The look he sent her seemed to be equal measures amusement at her disbelief and anger that the person who still harbored that kind of bigotry was his own father. "Oh, yes. Some care. They don't broadcast it, because displaying that sort of genderism can have serious repercussions, both personally and professionally. My father probably would have stuck by me if all I'd been accused of was murder."

"So it's okay to kill a person, but not to sleep with someone of the same sex?"

"That about sums it up." Derek shifted his weight from one leg to the other and crossed his arms. "He found it easy enough to believe. After all, I hadn't really dated in high school, had one girlfriend my sophomore year in college, a few casual liaisons once I was done with my doctorate. Beyond that, there was no one in my life, which to my father seemed evidence enough that I wasn't into women, not that I was simply too busy to get involved."

"That's…ridiculous," Cassidy managed, after a pause in which she wasn't sure exactly what she should say. Her own father's faults had been numerous, but bigotry wasn't among them. No, he'd always taken everyone as they came, more or less, which was why, she supposed, that he'd never said a harsh word about her mother abandoning them both. Even when Cassidy had attempted to bring it up as a teenager, he'd brushed her questions aside, only saying that her mother had found herself in a place where she didn't want to be a parent anymore, and that was the end of it.

Derek tilted his head back against the cockpit wall, then shrugged. In the close-fitting jacket he wore, Cassidy could see just how broad those shoulders were, how they strained against the smooth fabric. She jerked her gaze back up to his face…not that that was any less distracting. Damn.

"My mother said he was being ridiculous, that the whole story was a complete fabrication, but my father wouldn't listen." Derek's dark eyes were far away, and Cassidy hoped he hadn't noticed the way she'd been staring only a few seconds earlier. "You see, he felt he'd been publicly shamed. The only thing he could do was distance himself from me. And so, even though my mother tried to intervene by hiring a lawyer and attempting to get rid of the public defender I'd been assigned, it came to nothing in the end. They trumped up something about the lawyer she'd hired not being properly licensed for a criminal case, had him dismissed. In the end, all she got for her efforts was an ongoing rift with my father. They weren't speaking when I was sent off to Titan, but of course I have no way of knowing what's going on with them now. I've been a little out of touch."

This last was spoken with the first true bitterness she'd heard in Derek's voice. God knows he had plenty of reasons to be bitter, but it seemed the one thing that had gotten to him most was not the time he'd lost on Titan,

but the pain the false charges and subsequent imprisonment had caused his parents.

"I'm so sorry," Cassidy said, knowing even as the
words left her lips that they were woefully inadequate.
But what else was she supposed to do? She didn't know
him well enough to get up and give him a hug, or whether
he'd even accept such a gesture at face value.

He gave a lift of the shoulders that didn't fool her
at all. "I can't change what happened. But if I go back
to Gaia, attempt to track down the people who framed
me—"

"Then you can prove to your father that everything
they said was a lie."

"Exactly."

Put that way, it sounded so simple. However, they
didn't have much to go on, not even the name of the
man who'd shot Theo. Then she realized what she'd just
been thinking. That pesky "they" again. It seemed part
of her mind had made itself up already, even though
she'd made no conscious decision to do so.

"Do you have a plan?" she asked, wondering if she
sounded as resigned to Derek as she did to herself.

For a few seconds, he said nothing, only watched her
carefully. Cassidy tried not to blink, although a flush she
couldn't quite control rose to her cheeks. Then he said,
"Does that mean you'll take me there?"

"If that's really what you want."

Another hesitation. "It's not what I want, precisely,
but more what I know I must do."

"Well, then," she said, turning away from him so she could access the nav-computer. As she laid in the coordinates for Gaia, all she could feel was an overwhelming sense of inevitability. "That's where we're going. We should be there in approximately seventeen hours."

NINE

EVEN THOUGH SHE'D SAID SHE WOULD DO IT, DEREK couldn't quite believe that she'd given in that easily. He stood there for a moment, the sharp edge of the lintel biting into his shoulder, watching as she started tapping away on the keyboard next to her. "You're serious," he said at last.

"As a black hole," she replied, not looking up at him.

Her hair had fallen forward, obscuring most of her face, so he couldn't get a good read on her expression. "Just like that."

She still didn't glance up. "Just like what?"

"No more arguments? No telling me it's suicide to go back to Gaia?"

At that question she did turn around, expression clearly annoyed. "Why? Are you trying to change my mind?"

"No," he said at once. That was the last thing he wanted. But she'd been so adamantly opposed to the scheme up until now, he couldn't quite figure out what had caused this sudden shift in her attitude. Was it the sob story he'd told her about his parents? Not that it was really a sob story, just the simple truth, but it seemed the havoc the Consortium's lies had caused in his family had affected her more than some notion of getting the truth out there for the greater good.

Whatever it was, he knew he wouldn't offer any further arguments. Seventeen hours. That would give him some time to plan. His benefactor hadn't been very forthcoming about offering further help, but Derek suspected he'd reach out once again. Just a little information, such as the name of the man who'd headed the strike team back in Hunan Province...the man who'd shot Theo between the eyes with as little concern as someone putting down a diseased animal. That would be a good place to start. If they could track him down, manage to wring a confession out of him....

"If you can, you should sleep," Cassidy offered. "Better to do it early in the flight, rather than when we get closer to Gaia. As far as I can tell, this ship has been scrubbed pretty well—registry looks legit, all licenses up to date—so we shouldn't encounter any difficulties. But you never know."

No, you never did. Your life could be humming along more or less smoothly, and then you could hit the mother of all solar storms.

Her mention of the ship's registry jogged his memory, and he realized he'd left the packet containing their new documentation sitting on the bed in Cassidy's cabin. "One minute," he said, then straightened up and headed aft, where he scooped up the envelope and undid the magnetic closure. Several pieces of plastic fell into his hands—Consortium I.D.s, one with Cassidy's photo, the other with an image he knew had come from his identification card back at the university in Tucson. He didn't bother to speculate where their benefactor had gotten the photos, since all digital images had to be stored in some database or another, and clearly their sponsor didn't have a problem with hacking in and getting whatever he wanted.

Derek's new name was Philip Chung, and Cassidy's Bethany Whitcomb. A smile touched his lips as he thought what his father's reaction might be to his son passing himself off as being of Chinese extraction, but it faded quickly enough. These days, anything Derek might do was probably beyond the pale.

Ident cards clutched in his hand, he went back up to the cabin and handed the "Bethany Whitcomb" one to Cassidy. She took it from him, gave it a quick once-over, then slipped it into her pocket. "They thought of everything, didn't they?"

"Looks like it. But this means we should be able to move about a little more easily, although we'll still have to avoid anything with a biometric scanner. I know one drop of my DNA would send up red flags all over the system, and after that stunt at Europa, I have a feeling yours will, too."

Resignation settled on her delicate features like a cloud. "Well, that's a cheery thought, if not entirely unexpected." She leaned forward and inspected a reading on the console, then nodded, as if satisfied, before settling back into her seat. "Anyway, I meant what I said about getting some sleep. God only knows what kind of crap we're going to be wading into once we get to Gaia."

Yes, he would try to sleep…after attempting to make contact with their benefactor first. "What about you? Does this thing have an autopilot?"

"It does, but I'm feeling antsy. I want to stay up here and keep an eye on things. I'll probably nap a bit, but at least this way if something does go wrong, I'll be right here to take care of it."

She said this casually, as if it was of no great importance, but Derek couldn't help frowning as he said, "You mean you're just going to sleep here in the cockpit?"

"Sure. I did it all the time on the *Avalon*." A quick flash of a grin, one that lit up her hazel eyes, and he couldn't quite prevent the sudden heat he felt in his gut as he looked down at her. "And actually, this chair is a lot more comfortable. It's not a problem."

Still, he hesitated, although he thought that diffidence stemmed more from a desire to stay in her company than because he truly doubted her ability to sleep in the captain's chair, whether that was on board the Avalon or on this newer, much more modern ship.

"Go," she went on, making a flapping motion with her hands. "Get some sleep. I'm fine."

Since he knew arguing the matter further would only irritate her, he replied, "Okay," then headed on back to his cabin. Once there, he pushed the button to shut the door, and sat down on the bed. He fished the handheld out of his pocket, activating the text-to-speech function. "This is Derek Tagawa," he said, hoping it wasn't the middle of the night wherever their benefactor was located.

If it was, they were either a night owl or extremely quick on the trigger. Pale blue words appeared on the screen. *What is it, Dr. Tagawa?*

He paused, then told himself, Nothing ventured.... "I wanted to ask if you could locate someone for me."

Do you think I haven't done enough for you already, Dr. Tagawa?

Oh, hell. "That's not it at all. But the only way for me to clear my name is to find the man who shot Theo Karras."

The screen remained blank for a few seconds, and Derek began to wonder if their sponsor had signed off in disgust, both at his demands and the obvious fact that he was headed back to Gaia. Then, *This would have been in March 2463, correct?*

He let out a breath. "Yes."

I'll look into and get back to you.

"Thank you," Derek said, but there was no reply, and he didn't dare ask for anything else.

But their benefactor was apparently on the case, which meant he thought he might finally be able to relax enough to get that sleep Cassidy had urged on him. He went to the small but rather elegant little bathroom, scrubbed his teeth and face, then returned to his cabin.

Now if he could just make himself stop thinking about her alone in the cockpit, curled up in that chair....

Every second took them closer to Gaia, and every nerve ending in Cassidy's body was screaming at her to turn the ship around, to head into the null space between gravity wells so she could engage the subspace engines and get them the hell out of here. Someplace safe, someplace that didn't have an extradition agreement with Gaia, like Eridani....

She knew she'd never do that, though. Once she gave her word, she didn't take it back, and that included ferrying Derek Tagawa to Gaia, even if doing so meant the two of them most likely ending up dead.

Shifting in her chair, she attempted to find the position most conducive to falling asleep. Yes, she'd gotten a good chunk of it back on Triton, but, as she'd told Derek, they had no idea what they'd be facing on Gaia. Better to do it as rested as possible.

So she adjusted her position again, took a final glance at the displays on the console, then shut her eyes. Everything was fine...for now. The ship wouldn't falter, would take them straight on to Gaia without her help if necessary. Not that she planned to sleep that long. Just a few hours. Just enough for her to get her edge back.

Taking a breath, she let her thoughts drift, let herself sink down into a blackness as deep as that which surrounded the ship. Relax…breathe….

She seemed to float in the dark for a long time, feeling it like a soothing warmth against her skin, welcoming and soft as the blanket she'd loved to death as a child. Gradually, however, the air touching her grew colder and colder, until it was like ice, like the absolute zero of outer space. Her eyes fluttered open, but she couldn't see anything. Only black, pressing like a weight against her eyeballs.

And then something seemed to hold her by the wrist, and she swung around, trying to see what it was that had grabbed her, and she saw that it was a corpse wearing the dark gray uniform of the GDF, face pale and bloated, eyes staring sightlessly at her. She tried to yank her arm away, but even though it was dead, it continued to hold on, was pulling her closer, drawing her toward the gaping maw of its mouth, its tongue black and swollen, somehow reaching out to her….

She screamed, and screamed again, even though she knew sound didn't carry in a vacuum. And then a pair of strong hands were on her biceps, shaking her, Derek's voice saying urgently, "Cassidy, wake up! Wake up!"

Her eyes snapped open, and she realized she was in the cockpit, one leg tucked under her, gone dead and asleep from the pressure of her weight. With a grimace, she slid it out, feeling the sharp prick of pins and needles as blood began to rush back into the limb.

"What was it?" Derek asked, worried dark eyes scanning her face.

"What do you think it was?" she snapped, angry at herself for losing control like that. "Just a nightmare."

His eyebrows lifted. "It must have been a hell of a nightmare. You were screaming like you were being murdered."

Maybe she had. It certainly felt that way. A shiver went over her, and she knotted her fingers together, willing the dregs of the nightmare away. "It's no big deal. I guess I must be more stressed than I thought."

No reply, only an expectant look as he stood there, rocking back slightly on his heels. For the first time she realized he was dressed for sleep, wearing baggy pajama bottoms and a tight-fitting T-shirt. His biceps bulged against the sleeves, and she swallowed and made herself look away. Why the hell did he have to be so…distracting?

"Okay," she said, relenting when it became obvious that he had no problem with standing there and staring at her until she told him what the dream had been about. "I was in space, and something grabbed me."

"Something?"

"A corpse wearing a GDF uniform," she snapped. "Satisfied?"

Actually, he didn't look satisfied at all. His jaw tightened, and his brows drew together as he regarded her carefully. "He would have killed you, given the chance."

Intellectually, she knew that, knew she'd only done what she must in order to stay alive. Sure, killing some-one was way outside her comfort zone, but she'd kept telling herself that those pilots had sure as hell intended to kill her and Derek, and stealing their ship was the only way to survive. And maybe her conscious mind had accepted that "ends justify the means" argument, while the whole time her subconscious had been saving up a huge ration of guilt, just waiting to launch it at her at the first opportune moment.

"I guess it was," she replied, giving what she knew was a very half-hearted shrug. All she wanted was for him to stop staring at her with those worried eyes, as if he feared this was just the beginning, that she was going to fall apart when he needed her most. "I don't like that I had to kill anyone, even though I was only doing what had to be done. I guess it just…caught up with me."

He reached out to her then, to lay what he no doubt thought was a comforting hand on her shoulder. But something about feeling the warmth of his flesh through the thin fabric of her shirt seemed to touch off a spark within her, something that seemed to shimmer and dance along every nerve ending. Although she hadn't intended to, she sucked in a breath, the gasp sounding hideously loud in the close confines of the cockpit.

For some reason she'd thought he'd pull his hand away then. He didn't, though. His fingers tightened on her shoulder for the briefest of seconds, then slid down to her arm. It was a caress. Cassidy knew there could be no other word for it. She also knew she should pull away, shouldn't let him continue to touch her. The situation was complicated enough already—did she really intend to make it worse?

Raising her eyes to his, she pulled in another breath. He was watching her with that same careful gaze she'd come to recognize, but beneath it was a steady, hot glow, one of desire. There was no mistaking it this time, no pushing it away and trying to call it something else. She could tell he was waiting for her to react. He wouldn't force this. The final decision would have to come from her.

Before she realized precisely what she was doing, she was pushing herself up out of the captain's seat, standing so she was only a scant few inches away from him. He smelled good, she realized, of soap and warm skin, and as she inhaled that enticing aroma, she knew she was lost. She could blame it on stress, on weariness, on being so damn tired of feeling alone, but she knew it was more than that, more than she wanted to acknowledge.

And then she was tilting her face up toward his, and he was bending down to her, and oh, God, that was his mouth on hers, soft and strong at the same time, and his tongue, tasting of peppermint. She let out some kind of incoherent sound, half sigh, half groan, and she was pressing against him, feeling the hardness of his muscles, feeling the hardness of something else through the thin fabric of his pajama pants. Heat flickered in her core, and she knew she wanted him in her, wanted it more than anything she could remember wanting. It seemed this desire had flared up out of nowhere, like a nuclear explosion, and she could only wrap her arms around him and pull him more closely against her, needing to feel as much of him as possible.

In that moment, he lifted his mouth from hers and asked, his voice hoarse, "Is this—is this something you want? Because I didn't expect this to happen—"

"I want it," she murmured, and brushed her hand against the bulge in his pants. "Believe me. I know it's crazy, but I don't care."

"Neither do I," he said, bending to kiss her again.

Ah, the delicious sensation of his mouth pressed against hers! No one had ever kissed her like this before, so full of need, of desire, with an intensity that seemed to push all other concerns to the side.

She didn't want to pull away from him, but there were other places on board this ship far better suited to the kind of activity she had in mind. So she ended the kiss, but gently, then took his hand and guided him to the largest cabin, the one he'd said should be hers. She'd been so focused on getting the ship away from Triton that she hadn't even come back here to explore yet, but what she saw now pleased here—a decent-sized state-room with a bed big enough for two, the walls a soft gray-blue, a small table up against a wall. The bag containing the items she'd brought away from Triton was sitting on that table, which meant the bed was blessedly unobstructed.

If she paused now, she knew she might lose her nerve, so she didn't stop, drew Derek toward the bed, sank down on it and pulled him down with her, feeling the weight of his body on top of hers, the hardness of his arousal against her thigh. He was kissing her again, but at the same time she felt his hands moving over her, finding the fasteners for her shirt, pulling it loose from the waistband of her trousers. Then it was his fingers against the bare flesh of her stomach, a touch that ratcheted up the heat within her, causing her to wrap her legs around him, pull him closer. It was as if she needed to have every inch of her body touching every inch of his, and so she didn't protest when he undid her bra, pushed it up and over her breasts, caught hold of both it and her shirt and pulled them away. At the same time, she grasped his T-shirt and yanked it over his head.

God, she wanted to groan aloud at the sight of him, at the hard muscles of his chest, his flat stomach, all that wonderful smooth golden-brown skin. How had he managed to stay in that kind of shape during his stint at the MaxSec? She'd have to ask him later…if she could hold on to the thought that long. Right now her body was screaming for him, for all of him. It had been way too long since she'd been with anyone, let alone someone like Derek.

Actually, she'd never been with someone like him. He was as far outside her experience as daily life on Eridani. But you know what they say about new experiences….

His hands were on her pants, undoing them as well, pulling them away. Somehow her underwear seemed to go with them. Not that she minded. One less obstruction between her and the thing she wanted more than anything right now. Her own fingers were pulling at his pajama bottoms, and then he was free, and she could see how much he wanted her, how big he was, and she didn't stop to think, didn't wait, only ran her hand down his shaft, feeling the smooth skin, the hot, heavy weight of his need.

He moaned, and she continued to stroke him, even as he shifted so his mouth could close on her nipple, his tongue moving in slow, teasing circles. She hadn't been expecting that, and gasped, but didn't release her hold on him, not even when one of his hands moved downward, found the wet heat at her core.

This from a man who claimed he'd never had much time for women? Cassidy wasn't sure she believed that, since he seemed to know exactly where to touch her, how to touch her. Slow and purposeful, fingers curling into her so she leaned her head back against the pillows and felt the pressure building within, the hot waves of arousal pulsing closer and closer together, until at last they coalesced into an explosion of pleasure, one that rippled all through her, aftershocks leaving her limbs trembling.

She must have let go of Derek while in the throes of ecstasy, because she felt him move against her, felt him heavy and thick against her inner thigh. So, so close....

In ages past, she might have had to worry about getting pregnant, or catching a disease. But she'd had all her shots, and she knew Derek, coming from MaxSec, where he'd been kept in solitary, would also be clean. It was so easy, then, for him to slide into her, for there not to be a single second of hesitation or doubt. Her hand moved up to glide along his neck, then run through his thick hair, even as her other hand slid down, feeling the muscles in his firm ass flex as he thrust into her.

And then all she could think about was how good he felt, how he fit into her so well, how they seemed to know exactly how to move together, to rock into one another as if they'd done this a hundred times before. His breathing sped up, but she could almost feel him trying to hold back his orgasm, to make sure he didn't reach climax before she did. She wanted to tell him that it was all right, that he'd already made her come, and he probably needed the release even more than she did. The words seemed to get caught in her throat, however, and all she could do was keep rocking him into her, feeling that pulsing warmth at her center once again, and she knew he wouldn't have to wait very long, wouldn't have to restrain himself for much longer.

The orgasm struck her with the force of a terrestrial hurricane, and she screamed as she came, letting it all go, not caring how much noise she made. Derek seemed to take that as his signal, because he sped up, driving into her, his own breathing quickening, coming in harsh rasps, and then she could feel it hit him as well, feel him drive into her one last time as his own orgasm shuddered through him. He moaned, fine jaw clenched, and then he collapsed onto her as if he didn't have the strength to hold himself up any longer.

Not that she minded. She liked the feel of his weight, liked feeling his slightly sweat-slick body pressed against hers. He felt real, and close, and she knew then that she never wanted him to leave.

After a long, heavy silence, he pushed himself off her and rolled over onto his side. One hand reached out to brush a stray lock of hair away from her face.

This was the moment when all the men she'd known would climb out of bed, using the excuse that they needed to get cleaned up, and hey, it had been fun, and they'd be in touch. Not that they ever called, and Cassidy found she didn't much care.

Now, though, she found herself holding her breath, wondering what Derek was going to do, what he was going to say. True, they were on a spaceship; there was a limit to how much distance he could put between the two of them. Even so, she braced herself for the inevitable rejection.

It didn't come. He watched her, dark eyes thoughtful. Then he said, "You're beautiful, Cassidy."

Under normal circumstances, she would have laughed, or made a sarcastic comment about his eyesight. But there was something so achingly raw in the way he looked at her, the way he seemed to take in every aspect of her face and body, that she knew she couldn't make the standard response. It would wound him. He'd opened himself up to her and told her about the rift with his father, had been honest and real, and she knew she had to accept the gift he'd given her, not throw it back in his face.

"Thank you," she said quietly, although she couldn't help adding, "No one's ever said that to me before."

His eyebrows lifted. "And here I thought bad eyesight had been all but eradicated."

There was nothing to do but laugh then, so she chuckled, even as she shook her head. "Let's just say that most of the men I've known haven't been real big on giving compliments."

"I don't like to think of it as giving you a compliment, only stating the obvious truth."

What could she say to that? Cassidy couldn't think of a good reply, so she settled for leaning over and giving him a quick kiss. That seemed safe enough. Just a light touch of her mouth to his, enough to show that she appreciated his remark, even if she wasn't quite ready to go another round.

It seemed that he had other ideas, however, since he reached out and drew her close, deepening the kiss, even as she felt him hardening against her and knew he was ready even if she wasn't.

Okay, scratch that. Her body was responding, heat moving through her all over again, and she pressed against him, let out a gasp as his fingers began to stroke her once again, all heat and fire and aching need. Then she was on top of him, riding him, and though usually she would shut her eyes in ecstasy, she wanted to keep them open, wanted to look at him, drink in every plane and angle of his face, the sculpted curves of his arms and shoulders and chest, the utter perfection of him. He was gazing at her as well, and their eyes locked, energy seeming to pulse between them, crackling with sparks, until she twined her fingers with his and held on while the orgasm racked through her, felt him spasm in her as well.

She collapsed next to him, panting, spent and happy and tingling in every pore. Now was the time when she should get up, go to the bathroom and clean herself off, put her clothes back on. True, they were far, far away from Gaia, and the proximity alerts would give them ample warning, but she should still be in the cockpit, monitoring everything, making sure nothing would go wrong.

All those were things she should be doing, but weariness came over her like a yawning dark wave, and she felt into it, let it suck her under. And then she was gone before she even realized what was happening.

TEN

HE WATCHED HER SLEEP, HER DARK HAIR MUSSED against the pillow. Some time earlier he'd pulled the covers up around her, and she'd stirred slightly but hadn't woken. Now was the best time for her to rest, while they were still out in the kingdom of the gas giants. Traffic would begin to pick up once they were inside the orbit of Jupiter, but he wasn't sure how long that would be. Some hours, even in this ship, so much faster than Cassidy's lost Avalon.

Although he knew he should be trying to sleep as well, he couldn't help taking this stolen moment, to gaze on her when she was finally relaxed and unguarded, the barriers she kept up at all times relinquished in slumber. She'd chuckled when he'd called her beautiful, but she was, even if she didn't want to acknowledge that truth about herself. Delicate as porcelain but stronger than titanium. A while earlier he'd thought he'd never met a woman like her before, and nothing in that estimation had changed. A mixture of toughness and trust, keen-edged intelligence and sudden, shocking vulnerability.

Years ago he'd realized he probably would never settle down, not the way his sister had. He was all right with that, as he loved his work, felt privileged to be making a difference in the world. Now, though, as he stared down at Cassidy Evans, his mind began to explore, ever so delicately, the possibility that there might be something more than the work, something more than the sterile days that had formerly comprised his life.

And that was crazy, wasn't it? Because they were heading toward Gaia, and if he really cared about having a future with Cassidy, he should be waking her up and telling her to redirect their course, to get them the hell out of this system and very far away from anyone who had a vested interest in making sure Derek Tagawa was caught and silenced…permanently.

Somehow he knew he wouldn't do that. It was a risk, and a terrible one, but he didn't want to live his life in hiding, as someone else. He'd worked too hard to be where he was. Cassidy knew the risk she was taking and had still agreed to come along, had understood that some things were more important than mere survival. Although he didn't agree with his father on a lot of things, personal honor was one ideal they both shared. Letting a lie live on, and allowing the people who'd killed Theo to get away with it, was not something Derek would allow himself to accept.

So he lay down next to Cassidy, moving slowly and quietly, and let himself fall into sleep, knowing that he wasn't alone in this, that somehow, impossibly, he'd found the one person he could trust to have his back.

The beeping of a handheld woke her. Cassidy opened her eyes and stared at the ceiling of the cabin, taking a second to orient herself. Besides her, Derek stirred, but his eyelids remained shut.

She glanced around the cabin, didn't see the device making the noise, then remembered hers had been shoved in the pocket of her trousers. Slipping out of bed, she located the discarded pants half-flung across a chair, but when she pulled out her handheld, it was blank and silent.

The beeping continued from a spot on the floor, buried underneath Derek's T-shirt and underwear. The only thing left were his pajama bottoms, and, sure enough, when she lifted those and reached inside the pocket, she could feel the handheld vibrating against her palm.

So why had he felt the need to carry the thing everywhere he went, even in his pajama pants?

Because he didn't want to miss a call.

The phone was locked, and she didn't have the code, so all she could do was cross over to the bed and nudge it with one knee. "It's for you," she said, extending the phone as Derek opened one bleary eye and blinked at her.

That bleariness seemed to disappear when he realized what she was holding. He sat up and reached to take the phone from her.

"Were you expecting a call?" she asked, wondering what exactly he'd been hiding from her.

"Not this soon," he replied, and plucked the handheld from her fingers, then entered the code to unlock it.

"Anyone I know?"

He must have caught the edge to her tone, because he said at once, "It's from our sponsor, benefactor… whatever you want to call him. Or her."

That information did make Cassidy relax slightly, although she wished he'd told her that he'd had further contact with that elusive person. "Then I guess you'd better answer it."

A smile quirked around the edges of his mouth, one that faded as he read the message. "You're certain?"

Because of the way he held the device, Cassidy couldn't see the letters on the screen. All she could see was the tightening of Derek's jaw, the way his mouth thinned as he read whatever their sponsor had just sent to him.

"Thank you," he said then. "We'll follow up."

That must not have been the end of it, because his brow puckered as he read the next message. "We will. Thank you again for everything." And then he did tap the screen to end the exchange, right before he glanced over at her, eyes gleaming.

"We've got him."

"Him who?" she asked.

Derek placed the handheld on top of the covers and then pushed himself out of bed. "The man who killed Theo Karras."

It turned out that they'd slept for a good six hours, and so Cassidy checked the cockpit and the instruments to make sure everything was still operating normally, and then took a quick shower before relinquishing the stall to Derek. Although he might have liked to share that shower with her, the cramped facilities made such an activity pretty near impossible.

But before they did any of that, she'd asked for the details on his previous interactions with their sponsor, and so he'd showed her the logs of the two brief conversations they'd had. She'd read through them quickly, then nodded and said quietly, "Thank you."

Maybe she had expected him to conceal them from her, but really, he had nothing to hide. He hadn't mentioned them earlier because he had so little to tell her. Also, he thought with a grin, they'd both gotten a bit distracted.

She didn't look distracted now, sitting in the captain's seat, scanning the readouts on the console, hazel eyes also flicking occasionally to the huge window that showed utter black all around them, although far off to the left was a pale orange disc that she'd informed him was Jupiter.

"Everything all right?" he asked, settling himself into the copilot's chair.

"As far as I can tell. We got a transmission from Ganymede, checking our registry since we were passing in close enough that they cared who we were."

That didn't sound good. "And?"

"And they sent us on our merry way and told me to have a nice day." Finally she turned toward him, and he was gratified to see that her eyes were dancing with amusement. "So whoever put together those fake I.D.s for us seems to have known what they were doing. They don't mess around on Ganymede—their people are good. They would've smelled a badly faked registry a million kilometers off."

Some tension he hadn't even known he was carrying in his shoulders seemed to ease itself slightly. "So we're good to go."

"As far as I can tell." Her expression sobered. "Since it doesn't look like anyone intends to pursue us in the near future, maybe you can tell me what your plan is."

This was the part he'd been dreading. The closer they got to Gaia, the more concrete and solid this chance at retribution became. And after receiving the latest transmission from their benefactor, one he hadn't yet shared with Cassidy because it had come in while he was in the shower, he was worried, as it seemed part of the plan would rest heavily on her.

"The man involved, Conrad Waite, is actually an operative under contract to MonAg."

Some of the color left her cheeks at the mention of the megacorp that had its fingers in basically every facet of the Consortium government, but she said steadily, "That a fact?"

"Yes. He's been in their employ for some fifteen years. Apparently handles a lot of their dirty work, but our contact said we didn't need to concern ourselves with that. Records show he was in Hunan Province during the right timeframe, although he left immediately afterward and went to South Africa."

"Doing something equally dirty, I assume."

Her wry tone made Derek want to smile, but he kept his voice even as he replied, "I'd say that was a safe assumption. Anyway, for the past three months he's been working out of Chicago, although our sponsor didn't give me any details."

"Chicago, huh?" She appeared to consider that prospect. "I always wanted to try deep-dish pizza."

A tradition the former Windy City clung to, even though so much else of the world had changed. "We'll try to squeeze that in. The interesting thing is that this Waite seems to consider himself something of a ladies' man."

Cassidy picked up on that right away. "And that's where I come in."

"I know it's asking a lot, but I think you have the best chance of getting close to him. Obviously, I have to stay far away, since he'll recognize me on sight."

"It's not a problem." Again that little gleam of amusement came and went in her eyes. "If there's one thing I know, it's how to meet men in bars."

Derek lifted an eyebrow. "Oh, really?"

"Yeah, really." She tapped her fingers on the armrest of her chair and met his gaze in that forthright way he liked so much. "Do you have a problem with that, Dr. Tagawa?"

"Not at all," he said. "But this isn't some shuttle jockey looking to pass the time in Luna City. He's a cold-blooded killer."

Not even a blink. "I know that, Derek. But he won't know me from Eve, and if he has as high an opinion of himself as your contact seems to think he does, then he'll be like every other guy out there…thinking with his dick."

"So that's your opinion of me?" Derek tried to sound arch, but he could feel a smile teasing around the corners of his mouth despite his best efforts to suppress it.

Wearing a matching grin, Cassidy got to her feet and stood on her tiptoes so she could press her lips against his cheek. "I like the way you think with your dick. It's powerful and responsive…just like your brain."

He could feel himself stir to life at her words, and he took her hands, pulling her against him. "Let's see just how responsive it can be…."

The plan, as it stood, was pretty damn simple—their sponsor sent a list of bars Conrad Waite frequented, along with a current image of him and a second list of aliases he might be using. How their mysterious benefactor had been able to get a hold of any of that stuff, Cassidy wasn't sure. She just knew she was damn glad that this shadowy, powerful personage had decided to come down on Derek's side, for whatever reason.

The murderer didn't really look like one. No, that wasn't quite right. He was a hard-looking man in his early forties, but just attractive enough that he probably wouldn't have a difficult time trolling the bars and nightclubs for a quick lay. And really, if she hadn't known who he was or what he'd done, she might have found herself attracted as well. Conrad Waite was a little older than the other men she'd been with, but not so much that she would've considered him out of bounds.

They took a suite in one of the glassy high-rise hotels that overlooked Lake Michigan. Years of environmental rehabilitation had returned the lake to its original deep, deep blue, and Cassidy stood at the window, staring at the water. Yes, she'd known that of course Gaia had open bodies of water, but she'd spent her entire life in Luna City or shuttling around the Gaian system. The only expanse of water she'd seen that was a bigger than an aquarium in someone's office was the reflecting pool in front of Luna City's main administrative building.

She wondered now why she'd never come here before this, never visited the world that had birthed both her parents. No excuse, really, save that her father had warned her off from an early age, saying that Gaia wasn't for the likes of them, and that if she ever set foot on its surface, she'd find herself forever dissatisfied with space and the cramped confines of spaceships and domed bases. At the time she'd scoffed inwardly, although she hadn't contradicted him, but now she realized he'd been right.

It was beautiful here, and she wasn't sure what she should do about that.

Almost better than the open water and the high, drifting clouds overhead was the shopping. After they'd checked into the hotel, the whole time worrying that some red flag would be raised, that something would be off about their faked I.D.s or their credit voucher, worries that came to naught, Cassidy had taken one look at the meager wardrobe she'd brought from Triton and knew that nothing in it, not even the pretty red tunic and pants Derek had selected for her, would be good enough for the people who frequented the high-end bars on Lakeshore Drive.

So she dragged an increasingly glazed Derek from boutique to boutique, buying what she thought would work, spending what felt like an insane amount of money, although she knew she was barely putting a dent in their voucher. And when her companion rolled his eyes after she went into the fourth—or was it the fifth?—shoe store, she told him sweetly that he could meet her back at the hotel if he didn't have the stamina for this sort of activity.

Of course he'd declined. She could tell he didn't want them to get separated, even in as harmless a venue as a women's boutique. As a sop, she'd taken him to a few men's stores as well, since his own wardrobe was as sorry as hers, and lord knows when they'd have the opportunity for this kind of shopping again.

At last they returned to the suite, where Cassidy hung up her new clothing and carefully arranged her shoe purchases on the floor of the closet while Derek flipped through the thousands of channels on the vid, looking for what, she wasn't quite sure. Anyway, she'd never owned so many clothes in her life, and part of her wondered if she'd been just a bit extravagant.

Hey, you gotta dress big to play with the big boys, she told herself, just before going in to take a shower and start getting herself ready. Although she thought she was okay with all this, she couldn't help feeling a few nervous tremors in the pit of her stomach. As Derek had told her, this wasn't some bored shuttle pilot looking for some fun during a layover. Conrad Waite had killed a lot of people, according to their source, and wouldn't scruple to kill her and Derek if he discovered who they were or what they were up to.

The suite had two bathrooms, and so Derek was getting cleaned up in the other one when she emerged from the shower and got to work. Her own bathroom was equipped with a molecular hair-setter, and so she flipped through the hairstyles shown on the screen, settled for thick, loose waves, and placed the device on her head. Within a few minutes, it beeped, indicating it was done. She lifted it away and set it back on the rack next to the sink, then inspected herself in the mirror. Damn. No makeup on yet, and she already looked about a hundred times better than she usually did.

She'd purchased some cosmetics as well, with the help of an extremely motivated salesgirl who realized her commission that day was going to be pretty darn good. In the past Cassidy hadn't bothered much with makeup, save some lip color when she was going out, but after following the salesgirl's instructions and applying the new cosmetics as instructed, she thought she might have to review that policy. She didn't know who the woman looking back at her from the mirror was, but it definitely didn't look like Cassidy Evans. Her eyes seemed huge, almost a smoky green rather than hazel, and her mouth had a definite glossy pout.

After that she emerged from the bathroom, selected a slinky dress in a dark, dark brick-red color, and fastened a pair of pewter-toned high-heeled sandals on her feet. Before today she'd owned exactly one pair of heels, so she practiced walking back and forth a few times before deciding that she thought she could manage things as long as she didn't have to break into a run. Then a pair of dark silver hoop earrings and a wide cuff for her right arm to match, and she thought she was pretty much done.

Derek was still in the other bathroom, so that was why she found herself staring out at the waters of Lake

Michigan, watching as the light changed subtly, the sun slipping behind the tall buildings and casting long, rippling shadows on the surface of the lake. She realized she was missing her first Gaian sunset, but she didn't know where she could've gone to watch it, except possibly the hotel roof. There would be other sunsets.

At least, she hoped there would.

Derek's voice came from behind her. "Holy shit."

She turned away from the window, saw him standing a few feet away, staring at her. "What's the matter?"

Something about the expression in his eyes seemed almost glazed, as if he couldn't quite believe what he was looking at. "Uh—nothing's the matter. It's just—" He broke off and shook his head. "You look incredible."

"I do?" she asked, feeling absurdly pleased, and fighting the impulse to go inspect herself again in the mirror. Funny how, if asked, she would have protested that she didn't care all that much about appearance and fashion. It had never seemed to matter to her. But now, seeing the look on Derek's face…well, she was very glad that he thought she cleaned up well.

"You're stunning. That is, I always thought you were beautiful, but—"

"'Always'?" she teased. "For the whole three days you've known me?"

"Yes," he replied, clearly refusing to be baited. "The first moment I laid eyes on you, I knew I was in big trouble."

How in the world could she reply to a statement like that? She settled for going to him and wrapping her arms around him, although she restrained herself from reaching up to kiss him. That would only lead to makeup ruination, and she wasn't about to redo all that hard work. She'd just have to remind herself to kiss him an extra few times, once all this was over with.

He held her tightly but made no move to kiss her, either, which told her he knew the reason for her current reticence. After a moment, though, he released her and took a step back. Some of the warmth in his eyes disappeared, and he suddenly looked very businesslike.

"So you know what you need to do," he said.

Cassidy nodded. The list of bars wasn't all that long, and had been arranged in order from most to least frequented. So she would go to them one by one until she came across Conrad Waite. And if not tonight, well, there was always tomorrow. She didn't much relish the thought of having to go through all this preparation over and over again. But if she came up empty tonight, at least she'd be looking good for an intimate evening with Derek and some room service.

"A couple of drinks, food if he insists…and then the oh-so-casual suggestion that he come with me back to my room."

"Perfect. He should fall for it. Don't make it too easy, though…you don't want him to get suspicious."

"Not a problem." She'd done that tease before, the show of false reluctance, all the while knowing exactly where an evening was going to end up.

Earlier Derek had asked to borrow her handheld, and now he pulled it from his pocket and gave it back to her. "I've linked our devices. Keep an open channel on yours, and I'll be able to hear what you're saying and doing. If it comes to it, I can be there in a few minutes, but then our chance will be gone forever."

That sounded dramatic, but she knew it was only the truth. If Conrad Waite caught sight of Derek, he'd know this wasn't a casual pickup. Worse, he'd know exactly where Derek was, and even if he didn't try to take out the escaped convict then and there, he'd definitely be in contact with his superiors so they could send in the authorities.

"I'll be fine," she said calmly, although she wasn't feeling all that calm. "He has no reason to suspect anything. Even if his handlers have sent out my image, saying it was my ship that took you away from Titan, I doubt he'd recognize me. Right now I don't look much like my official I.D."

Derek actually chuckled at that comment. "Well, that's true enough. I suppose I should thank God for unflattering identification photos." He glanced down at the expensive chronometer on his wrist...another of that afternoon's purchases. "It's almost nineteen hundred. Are you ready?"

"Ready." Was she? Well, it was too late to back out now, so she'd have to pretend she was, even if nervous little chills had begun to tickle their way down her back.

He reached out and took her hand, gave it a reassuring squeeze. "You'll be great."

After that there wasn't much to do except pick up her silvery metal mesh evening bag, slide her handheld, some spare cash, and her tube of lip color inside, then give one last nod to Derek before exiting the suite. All during the elevator ride down to the lobby, she forced herself to take in soothing breaths, to stare off into the middle distance when more hotel guests got in to ride along with her. One was a businessman in a dark, high-collared suit, and Cassidy could feel his eyes on her the whole time. But since she didn't make eye contact, he said nothing to her, and left the elevator without incident.

As she exited the hotel, a mech manning the doors hailed her an autocab. "The Borealis," she said as she climbed in, letting the computerized car know her destination. In truth, it was only a block or two away, a distance she could have easily walked...except that the woman wearing this expensive dress and these expensive shoes, and staying in that expensive hotel, would never walk when a cab could whisk her to her destination in comfort and privacy.

The car's windows were filtered, so she couldn't see much. Probably just as well, since she would've been gawking like a tourist, and that was not the sort of impression she wanted to make. Of course there was no human being driving to observe her behavior, but Derek had told her that all of the autocabs had digital surveillance, and if anyone were to go over the footage at a later date, better that she not do anything to draw attention.

"Borealis," came a tinny voice from the car's speakers as it came to a stop in front of an impressive-looking structure with a smoked-glass façade and what looked like embers of light moving within its walls.

She didn't have time to stop and puzzle out how they managed that particular effect. Instead, she waved her credit voucher over the reader embedded in the wall of the cab, then got out. This was where it would have been helpful to have Derek along, since she could feel herself teeter on her heels for a split second before regaining her balance. If he'd been there to put a steadying hand on her elbow, she would have fared a bit better.

But of course he couldn't come anywhere near a place where Conrad Waite might be loitering, so she gathered up her dignity and entered the bar. Luckily, it had been dim and dusky outside, and so her eyes didn't take long to adjust to the equally dim lighting inside Borealis, which was actually both a restaurant and bar. When the mech maitre d' approached her and asked if she would like a table, she demurred, saying she was just going to the bar. The machine inclined its shining head and indicated the way for her, and she thanked it, wondering at the extravagance of an establishment that could afford mech personnel rather than their much cheaper human counterparts.

She pushed that thought aside as she entered the bar and did a quick survey of its occupants. The place was fairly full, but she saw an empty table for two on the far side of the space, up against one of those enormous sheets of glass…or whatever it was…with the glowing lights embedded within. It was impossible to see the faces of everyone in the bar from where she stood, but that table offered a good vantage point. If it turned out Waite wasn't here, she'd have one drink and leave. Maybe that wasn't the best plan in the world, since if she had more than a couple of drinks on an empty stomach, she wouldn't be as effective as she liked. On the other hand, she'd be sure to draw attention to herself if she walked into a place like this and didn't order something. Well, she'd just have to hope they didn't mix things too strong. It was her experience that the more expensive establishments tended to be the ones to skimp on the alcohol.

She crossed to the table, aware of the eyes of the men who were there alone tracking her progress. That was another calculated risk, that someone who wasn't her quarry would come over and attempt to engage her. Luckily, she had some experience freezing out unwanted attention, so she figured she could handle the situation if it arose.

In here they had a human bartender and human servers, so it looked as if the Borealis' pockets weren't infinitely deep. Anyway, experiments with mech bartenders had ended in disaster—they lacked the instinctual talent of a good mixologist, and couldn't taste their concoctions while they were being programmed, so that was an experiment that hadn't gone anywhere, especially since even the best A.I.s weren't exactly good conversationalists.

The waiter approached and asked what she would like. She told him a Starblazer, partly because it wasn't very strong, and partly because it was something she'd drunk before on numerous occasions. The drink was popular in Luna City because the vodka and other components were easy to synthesize, and she wondered after she'd placed her order whether she should have chosen something else.

Can't be helped now, she thought, allowing herself to scan the bar's occupants now that she had a more or less unimpeded view. A number of couples, a few women who seemed to be there alone, slightly more men who were similarly unattached. It was hard to look at them without appearing to look at them, especially since she didn't want to make any unintended eye contact.

But then....

Her entire body seemed to freeze, and she forced herself to let her gaze drift casually past. Dark hair cut a shade closer than was considered fashionable. Plain dark suit. Hard jaw and steely eyes that seemed out of place in the upscale bar.

He'd noticed her, she could tell. Something about those cold eyes seemed to sharpen, and she could almost feel his stare fasten on her.

Showtime, she thought, took a breath, and then shifted on her chair so the skirt of her dress hiked up ever so slightly, showing more thigh. As she did so, she allowed her gaze to track back toward him, and when their eyes finally met, she smiled. Just a little. But it was enough.

He got up from his seat at the bar, taking his drink with him, and came toward her, moving through the people in the bar like a shark cutting through a school of fish. Her heart began to beat more quickly, but she ignored it. Her heart could do as it liked, as long as it didn't give her away.

When he was a foot or so away from her table, he stopped, then asked, "Is that seat taken?"

Oh, very smooth. But she only smiled a bit more and replied, "It is now."

Accepting her invitation, he sat down, seeming to dwarf the fragile construct of extruded carbon-fiber and faux black leather, then put his drink on the table. "I don't think I've seen you here before."

What was that, the second-oldest line in the book? She shrugged, aware of the way her hair fell over the soft, silky fabric of her dress, slipped dangerously close to her cleavage. The dress did have sleeves, down to the elbow, but was low-cut enough that she could see the way his eyes flicked toward the shadow between her breasts, then back up to her face. Not overtly, no, he wasn't that crass. On the other hand, he hadn't made much of an attempt to hide his interest.

"No," she replied, answering his question. "I'm from Fort Dallas."

"Texas girl, huh?" He lifted his glass and drank some of the amber liquid it contained. "You don't sound like it."

Of course not, because I have only the barest idea where Texas even is. "My parents made sure of that."

"Wise, I suppose." Appearing to notice that she didn't have a drink of her own, he said, "Can I get you something?"

"Oh, I've already ordered. Here it is."

And yes, there was the waiter, bringing her the Starblazer she'd ordered. Good thing it didn't look much different from any other number of drinks made with clear liquor and equally clear mixers. With any luck, this would be her only cocktail for the evening, and she wouldn't have to tell him what she was drinking.

She accepted the drink, thanked the waiter, and allowed herself a sip before returning her attention to Conrad Waite. Up close like this, she could see the hard lines running from his nose to his mouth, fainter lines etched around those steel-gray eyes. Obviously, he didn't see the need for any cosmetic work to hang on to his lost youth. "So are you a native?" Cassidy inquired.

"Of Chicago? No. I'm here on business."

"Oh, really?" It was harder than she'd thought to make herself sound innocent and interested at the same time, and not at all suspicious, considering she couldn't help wondering what that "business" might be.

"I'm an exec with MonAg." He said it as if she should be impressed.

Actually, his admission startled her, and then she realized it was a good cover, since it meant no one would question how much he spent on fancy bars and fine dining. And it was partly true, since he did work for MonAg…although she doubted he'd ever seen the inside of an office, unless it was to deliver a report on his latest nefarious acts. Probably not, though. Whoever was pulling his strings would probably make damn sure that there was no way of connecting them.

"That's impressive," she replied.

A shrug as he took another sip from his drink. "It pays the bills. What about you?"

She'd cooked up a cover story, one that would explain her presence here but, she hoped, wouldn't cause him to ask too many questions. "Oh, I'm here for a cousin's wedding." Most of the men of her acquaintance, let alone hardboiled killers, didn't want to know anything about weddings, and would do whatever they could to avoid the topic, so she figured that was a safe lie.

It seemed Conrad Waite was like his brethren in that aversion, as he smiled weakly and said, "Oh," in flat tones.

"It's her third, so I can't get too excited about it, but it did give me a chance to come back to Chicago. I do like this town."

"What about it do you like?"

She hesitated, mind racing. Her experience of Chicago encompassed a grand total of about six hours. Then she sipped at her drink before replying, "The food…the shopping." A pause, one in which she lifted her eyes from the drink she held and forced herself to look directly at him. "The people you meet."

"Really?" His voice was softer now, had a silky edge she recognized from the other times in her life when men wanted to get down to the serious part of a seduction. "And do you meet so many people?"

"A few," she allowed, then gave a sideways glance at him through her eyelashes. "I'm actually fairly particular."

"I like that in a woman."

Should she giggle? No, it would sound forced. She settled for giving him a slow smile, one she hoped promised all sorts of future delights. "Well, I'll let you in on a little secret."

"What's that?"

"I think I like you."

He moved his chair a little closer to hers. "Do you? Why?"

She sipped her drink, pretending to consider his question. "You have amazing eyes, you know."

"I do?"

Since it seemed the time was ripe for a little physical contact, she reached out and laid her hand on his arm, gave it a playful squeeze. Or as much of a squeeze as she could manage, as his muscles felt like rock under her fingertips. "I can't be the first woman who's told you that."

"Well…." He lifted his shoulders again. "Maybe I've heard it once or twice."

Oh, please. She tried not to think about how those flinty eyes were probably the last thing a lot of people saw. "See, I was worried I wasn't being original."

"I think you're original," he told her, leaning closer still. "When you walked in, you made every straight man in the place turn around and look at you. There's something…intriguing…about you."

Cassidy gave what she hoped was a casual laugh. "Oh, well, maybe they don't get a lot of Texas girls in here." And probably even fewer freighter jockeys, she mentally added, sipping at her drink and praying that he wouldn't see any more in her than he wanted to see.

"Probably not." He drank as well, but his eyes never left her. "Makes me think I might want to visit Texas in the near future."

She smiled, but inwardly she was worrying that she'd bit off more than she could chew here. All right, she'd done some quick study on Texas, knew enough that people still raised cattle there, although the oil industry was as defunct as the internal-combustion engines it had once powered. Fort Dallas was the biggest town, and it tended to be hot and humid. That was about all she'd crammed into her brain, but if Waite really started asking questions, she was sunk.

"Oh, I think there are probably far more interesting places a man like you could visit," she demurred.

"Such as?"

Was it too early? Probably not, judging by the predatory way his gaze raked over her. He didn't look like a man who was willing to pass up an opportunity to get laid…and although his eyes were sharp and somehow unsettling, there was just the slightest looseness to his movements that led her to believe he'd had a drink or two before he sat down at her table.

Wrapping a strand of hair around one finger, she tilted her head to one side and said, "Well…my suite at the Cosmopolitan, for one. They have very good room service." Then, trying to seem as casual as possible, she lifted her drink and took another measured sip.

Something in his eyes flickered, but otherwise he barely reacted. "Do they?"

"Yes. And there's a great view, although of course at night you can't see much."

Deliberately, he reached out and ran a finger down the bare skin of her forearm. "I don't think I'd be looking at Lake Michigan."

Don't shudder, whatever you do. Somehow she managed to force a smile and said, "Probably not…." She let the words trail off, and then giggled a bit. "Oh, where are my manners? I'm Bethany Whitcomb."

He smiled as well, although to her the expression looked as humorless and predatory as the grin of a shark. "Randall Newsome."

"Well, I'm very pleased to make your acquaintance, Randall. So…now that we're formally introduced…."

The grin widened. "Bethany, I would love to share some room service with you."

ELEVEN

ALTHOUGH INTELLECTUALLY DEREK KNEW THAT pacing didn't do any good, he couldn't help himself from walking back and forth across the sculpted carpet floor of the suite, every syllable of Cassidy's conversation being sent from the handheld in his pocket to the small bud in his left ear. Who could have guessed she was such a skillful flirt? In their own acquaintance, she'd been entirely straightforward and matter-of-fact.

But that, he realized, was because she respected him. She only played games with the people she didn't care about.

Even so, it was excruciating to listen to their conversation but not know exactly what was going on, although he could guess. The killer was probably sitting far closer to her than he should, might have already reached out to touch her—a hand on top of hers, a caress along her arm, maybe even a brush against her thigh if he was feeling particularly bold. And she'd let him, because the whole point was to draw him out of the Borealis and get him up to their suite.

After that...well, once upon a time, Derek had considered himself a pacifist. Now he knew he'd do whatever it took to get the truth out of Waite. Not kill the man, he hoped, although some ice-cold part of him knew the best thing to do would be to get rid of him once he'd confessed to Theo's murder. But that would make Derek no better than Conrad Waite, and so he knew he would never go to such extremities.

Otherwise, he'd taken what precautions he could. The suite itself wasn't under surveillance, but of course the elevators and hallways were. However, the system wasn't so sophisticated that he couldn't disable the micro-cams embedded in the ceiling directly above the door. And although they'd had to use their false I.D.s to check in here—the Cosmopolitan wasn't exactly the sort of place that rented rooms by the hour and took cash— he could always contact their benefactor and explain that their current identities had been compromised and that they needed new ones. And then pray they'd actually be forthcoming.

The excruciating flirtation streaming into his earbud ceased, and he realized Waite was paying for their drinks and that he and Cassidy were about to leave the bar. Derek glanced at his chronometer. He'd timed the cab ride she'd taken to get to the Borealis, and between that and the elevator ride from the suite, the whole thing had taken roughly eight minutes. That time could change slightly, based on street traffic and how busy the elevators might be, but at least it gave him a ballpark idea of when he might expect them to return.

He'd been back and forth on this, wondering if he should just lurk behind the door and then smash Waite over the head with a lamp or something, but that didn't seem like a very good plan. It was Cassidy who'd convinced him that he needed to be patient, that he needed to wait until she had the contract killer relaxed, and then make his move.

"So, what, I'm supposed to wait until you're in bed together?" Derek had asked with some sarcasm, and she shot him an impatient look and said,

"Of course not. But maybe after a little champagne, some food…."

The champagne had actually given him the idea. It was easy enough to call down to the concierge desk and request some sleep medication. Derek had popped open a few capsules, extracted the powder within, and made up a little packet that he'd hidden behind one of the sofa cushions. All Cassidy would have to do was pour it into Waite's drink when he wasn't looking, and that would be enough to slow him down. Probably not knock him out altogether, especially if he was fighting it, but it would give Derek the edge he needed.

So he went back to his room, sat down on the bed, and waited. A ding in his earbud told him they'd most likely just entered the elevator, although, since they weren't talking at the moment, he wasn't sure which floor they were on or how much longer it would take before they reached the suite.

Those questions were answered a few minutes later as he heard voices in the living area of the suite, followed by laughter.

"No, let me get the vid on so we can look at the menu," Cassidy said, still sounding bubbly and giddy and quite unlike her usual self. "Do you like champagne?"

"Who doesn't?"

"No one I know." A brief silence as they apparently were perusing the menu. "Oh, and lobster patties!"

"Sounds good," Waite said, and something about the smug satisfaction in his voice—the voice of a man who knew he was about to get lucky—made Derek want to charge out of the room and punch him in the nose.

But of course he would never do that, although he was ready to move quickly if things got out of hand. The one good thing about Conrad Waite, however—if you could even call it that—was that he might be a killer, but he wasn't a rapist. His whole game was seduction, not force. And since Cassidy knew all about that game beforehand, she should be able to handle things.

In his earbud, he heard Cassidy placing the room service order, with the little addendum that she'd make it worth the hotel's while if they could get the food and champagne up here as quickly as possible. Derek had a feeling that wouldn't be a problem; people in the high-end suites tended to get privileged treatment.

"All this suite for you?" Waite asked once she was done, and Derek winced.

"I don't like to feel cramped," Cassidy replied with a laugh in her tone. "Actually, I'd booked a smaller suite, but it had plumbing issues, so they upgraded me."

Damn, that woman could think on her feet. Here she was, on a world she'd never visited before, assuming a stranger's persona, and nothing Waite fired at her seemed to faze her.

"So what are you using the second bedroom for?"

"My shoe collection," she said blithely, and Waite chuckled.

"I like the ones you're wearing."

"You do? They're killing my feet, actually. Do you mind if I take them off?"

"No, I don't mind if you…take them off."

There was so much weight to those last three words that Derek could actually feel his blood beginning to boil. So far Waite hadn't tried to make a move on Cassidy…maybe he was waiting for her to have some champagne, get a little more tipsy…but if the room service was delayed, how long would he be willing to wait? She'd have to go along or blow the whole thing, and the very thought of her having to kiss the man who'd killed Theo Karras made Derek feel physically ill.

She giggled a bit, something he knew she had to force, but it sounded natural enough. A pause, and then she let out a sigh. "Ah, that's better."

"I've been told I give a great foot rub."

Oh, for God's sake....

But Cassidy only let out an easy laugh and replied, "I may take you up on that later." A distant chime sounded in his earbud, and she went on, "Oh, that sounds like room service. That was fast."

Derek allowed himself a small sigh of relief as she went to open the door and let in the automated robo-cart the hotel used for room service deliveries. It wasn't nearly as sophisticated as a mech, but it got the job done for a fraction of the price.

After that it sounded as if she was entering the amount of the tip on the cart's screen and sending it on its way. In the background he heard a clink of glasses, and guessed that Waite was prepping things while she wrapped up the business of shooing the cart out of the room. Then there came the unmistakable sound of a champagne cork popping, followed by a small silence, most likely while Waite was filling their glasses.

Then he said, "What should we toast to?"

"Making new friends?"

"I can drink to that."

They clinked glasses, and there was another pause as they drank. Derek could feel his hands curling into fists. He wasn't even much of a drinker, and yet he wished he could be the one out there with her, sharing a bottle of champagne and watching the lights of the city.

"Lobster patty?" Cassidy asked, and Waite made some sound of agreement.

Again it was quiet. Then she said, tone casual, "Have you stayed in a lot of different hotels in Chicago?"

"A fair number."

"I was told the Cosmopolitan had the best views. Why don't you take a look, and then come back over here and give me your unbiased opinion?"

"Don't you want to come look at it with me?"

"I could, but I don't want you watching my reactions. I want to know what you think."

"Fair enough." A clink, as if he'd set his glass down on the cocktail table. "You can pour me some more champagne in the meantime."

Derek let out a breath. There was her chance, and of course Cassidy was far too smart to let it pass her by.

"Sure thing. And I'll try not to eat all the lobster patties while you're looking at the view."

"If you do, we can always order more."

"True." It went quiet then, and Derek assumed Waite had gone over to the wall of windows that faced out over Lake Michigan and the curve of the shoreline. They could be made opaque for privacy, but Cassidy had left them clear. Because the suite overlooked the lake, with no other buildings between them and the water, you'd basically need to hover outside to even see in, but it was somewhat reassuring to have the option to blacken the windows if needed.

A few more quiet, subtle noises that Derek couldn't identify, but which he guessed was Cassidy retrieving the packet of ground-up sleep aids from the sofa and quickly pouring the contents into Waite's glass. Then a subtle metallic sound, maybe her picking up one of the lobster patties from the tray.

"So you did leave me some." Another one of those metallic noises, a little louder.

"They're pretty rich, I'll admit."

"But perfect with champagne."

"Oh, yes. And see, I topped yours off."

"So you did. Thanks."

They clinked glasses again, and Derek waited, wondering how long it would take for the sleep aids to filter through Waite's system. Not quickly enough, he thought, but there was nothing he could do except stay there in the second bedroom, not daring to move, hoping that the other man hadn't eaten enough to slow down the absorption of the medication.

"So what did you think?"

"Of the view?"

"Yes."

"It's pretty spectacular...but mine over at the Lakeview is impressive as well."

"Oh?" A small laugh, followed by, "Well, maybe you can show it to me later."

"I definitely have a few things I'd like to show you."

I'll bet you do, Derek thought, but still didn't move, only waited. It got even harder in the next moment, as he heard them both set their glasses down. A little gasp from Cassidy, then silence.

Was that bastard *kissing* her?

Even if he was, there wasn't a damn thing Derek could do about it. Not if he wanted this whole insane plan of theirs to work.

After what felt like roughly a century or so, Cassidy said, sounding a bit shaky, "Wow. I guess you do like the champagne."

"Among other things."

Another silence. Definitely a second kiss. This one seemed to last even longer, but then there was an odd thud, as if one of them had stumbled into a piece of the furniture.

Cassidy's voice. "Randall? Are you okay?"

A mumble.

"Maybe you should sit down. Can I get you a glass of water?"

A thump that could only be Waite dropping down on the sofa. His voice came next, hoarse, forced. "What did you do?"

"What do you mean, what did I do? I didn't do anything." A pause, and she added, "You do look a little green. Are you sure you're not allergic to lobster or anything?"

Waite groaned. "Can't…."

"Can't what? Can't move?"

Another incoherent sound.

"Let me get you some water." Another silence, and then Derek heard her say in a murmur, "Looks like he's down for the count. I think it's safe to come out."

Words he'd been waiting for. Derek got up from the bed, gathered the careful strips of sheet he'd been preparing for the past hour, and went out to meet their guest.

Cassidy never thought she'd be so relieved to see anyone as she did Derek when he emerged from the bedroom, expression grim. Conrad Waite was slumped into a corner of the sofa, face slack, eyes half shut.

"Maybe I gave him too much," she said as Derek approached her.

"He'll be fine." A quick glance from those dark eyes, one that seemed to take in her now swollen mouth. "What about you?"

She tried not to shudder. "Well, his technique isn't bad, but he doesn't seem to be too good at judging when a woman's actually ready for a kiss."

A pained look passed over Derek's face, and she knew that was the last thing he wanted to hear. Well, they'd both known it was a risk, and one she'd been willing to take. A kiss wasn't a huge deal. Anything more than that…she wasn't sure she had the strength for that kind of a sacrifice.

But luckily it hadn't been necessary, and she'd rather just dismiss the whole episode from her mind.

"Anyway, I'll live," she went on, her tone brisk. "What now?"

"There's no good way to tie him to the couch. I'll bring over one of the chairs from the dining set."

She waited while Derek fetched the chair, and then the two of them hauled Conrad Waite's limp form off the sofa and propped him up in the dining chair. At least it had arms, and so Derek went to work binding Waite's wrists to it while she crouched down and used strip after strip of the torn sheet to fasten his ankles to the legs of the chair.

"Well, it's not corrections-department issue, but I suppose it will all hold," she remarked, and Derek frowned.

"It will. I'd prefer something a bit more regulation, but that's not exactly the sort of thing you can go shopping for on Lakeshore Drive."

"No, probably not…unless they have any of *those* sorts of boutiques around here."

At first he stared at her blankly, and then a flush seemed to rise to his cheeks as he figured out exactly what kind of store she was referring to. Not the type of place he'd normally frequent, she guessed. Well, that really wasn't her thing, either, but….

"Anyway," she went on, trying not to grin at his discomfiture, "do you know how long he's going to be knocked out? Because I don't think you're going to get much information out of him in his current condition."

"True." Derek ran a finger along his jaw line and seemed to consider the comatose man in the chair. "One thing's certain, though—we'll need to be ready to leave quickly once we're done with him. So maybe you should pack your things while I stay out here and keep an eye on him."

"What about your stuff?" she asked, although she thought she already knew the answer to that one.

"Packed while you were out." His mouth tightened, and he didn't quite look at her as he added, "I needed something to do to keep me busy."

She could tell it bothered him. Even though he knew it had been necessary, he hated the thought of her being around Conrad Waite. Well, she hadn't liked it much, either. True, he wasn't the sort of kisser who thought sticking his tongue down her throat was an erotic maneuver, but it had taken pretty much every ounce of restraint she had to not knee him in the groin or shove him away when he kissed her. The man was a cold-blooded killer, and she wasn't naïve enough to believe he wouldn't kill her, too, if he found out what she was up to.

"Okay," she replied, tone casual. "I'll go get everything together."

After giving a final glance at the still comatose hit man, she went into the bedroom she'd claimed as her own and began pulling her new purchases out of the closet and stowing them in a hard-sided suitcase, also a new acquisition. As she did so, she tried not to sigh. While she understood that they couldn't stay here, not after they were done with questioning Waite, she kind of wished that they might be able to stop someplace just long enough so she could get a decent night's sleep.

From what she could tell when she'd sat down on it to strap on her sandals, that bed was very comfortable.

But it wasn't going to get any use tonight, so she methodically folded her clothes, then fetched the cosmetics and other toiletries from the bathroom, and put them away as well. The dress she was wearing definitely wasn't practical for a quick getaway, and she pulled it off and folded it, then drew on a pair of close-fitting black pants, a thin pale green top, and the jacket that matched the pants. Some low-heeled black boots finished off the ensemble, which she thought looked chic and efficient, but definitely not flashy. And she knew she could run in those boots if she had to.

Approximately ten minutes after she'd left, she returned to the living room to see Derek leaning up against one arm of the couch, watching Waite, whose head was lolling from side to side.

"How's sleeping beauty?" she asked.

"Starting to come around, I think." Derek's gaze swept over her, and he gave her a quick nod of what she thought was approval for her change of wardrobe.

At those words, Waite jerked in his chair, head lifting slowly as his eyes opened. They narrowed almost immediately as he saw who was watching him, although Cassidy was fairly certain he hadn't noticed her yet, as she was still standing behind Derek.

"Ta…gawa," Waite muttered.

"Oh, so you do recognize me. Maybe I should be flattered."

"Don't…forget…murdering scum like you."

Derek's jaw hardened, but his voice sounded even enough as he replied, "You're getting it backward, Mr. Waite. I'm not the murderer…you are."

As Conrad Waite made an incoherent sound somewhere between a groan and a grunt of disgust, Cassidy came around him and went to stand next to Derek. At once Waite's nostrils flared.

"You…bitch," he managed.

Derek started forward, but she laid a hand on his wrist. No sense in him getting all riled up right now. He had to show he was in control of the situation. "It's fine," she said. "I've been called worse."

"Bet you have," Waite snarled, and again Derek shifted next to her.

Although it was nothing more than the truth, that didn't mean she had to like it. "Sorry about my little deception, but I guess you weren't being entirely truthful with me, either, were you…Randall?"

Some kind of recognition gleamed in his eyes then, and he said, "You're her. The pilot of the *Avalon*. The one who helped pretty boy here escape."

She raised an eyebrow. "Wow, I had no idea I was famous."

Waite ignored the barb, steel-colored eyes fixed on her face. "Why're you helping him? He's a criminal." A pause, and he added, almost in a snarl, "I get it— you think you're in love with him or something, right?" A cool sidelong glance at Derek. "How many other women have fallen for that?"

She ignored the jab, seeing it as the gambit Waite meant it to be, just another way to mess with her head. Even so, she knew that "love" was a word she hadn't allowed herself to think, to even whisper to herself. She was not in love with Derek Tagawa. She barely knew him. Anyway, Cassidy Evans did not fall in love. That was for other people, not her. All right, so she cared what happened to Derek, didn't want to see him get hurt or caught. It was a far cry from that to love. She wouldn't let her mind entertain the notion for even a second.

"Who said anything about love?" she returned, tone purposely light, brittle. "But he is a spectacular lay, which is more than I could probably say about you…if things had gotten that far."

At that comment, Waite let out another one of those snarling sounds, and beside her Derek held back a chuckle, with only partial success.

"Another thing Derek and I have in common," Cassidy went on, "is that we're both very interested in the truth. And that's really why we have you here." She flicked a glance toward Derek. "Isn't that right?"

"It is," he replied calmly, pulling his handheld out of a jacket pocket, then setting it down on the coffee table. A green light glowed from one corner of the screen, indicating that it was recording.

Waite's eyes went guarded, but a sneer still pulled at his lip. "I have nothing to say."

"You might think that," Derek said, something in his voice sending a shiver of unease down Cassidy's spine, "but I'm fairly certain I can convince you otherwise."

No reply. The hit man's eyes were scanning Derek's face, looking for something. What, Cassidy wasn't sure. Maybe that he really had the guts to do whatever it took to get the truth out of Waite? She had to admit to herself that she wasn't sure if Derek really had it in him. After all, the man was a scientist, not some Consortium interrogator. And she wasn't stupid enough to think that Waite was the sort of man who would crack easily.

The silence was broken by Waite's hoarse laughter. "You can try...amateur."

Cassidy risked a quick sideways glance at her companion. His face was composed, still and quiet. If he'd had his eyes shut, she would've said he was meditating. His gaze never flickered.

"Are you sure about that, Waite? All you have to do is tell me what really happened in the GARP HQ in Hunan Province at approximately 2 p.m. local time on March 25, 2463."

Waite's gaze was steady as well. "I don't know what you're talking about. The spring of that year, I was working on a project in Capetown."

A bit of truth mixed in with the lie there, as apparently Waite had headed to South Africa after he dispatched Theo Karras and framed Derek for the murder. Cassidy could tell Derek noted it as well, because his mouth tightened for just a fraction of a second before he asked,

"You sure about that?"

"Of course I'm sure."

"Funny, you look a little young to be having significant memory lapses." Derek pushed himself off the couch and approached Waite, looming over him. In actuality, the two of them were similar in height, but at the moment Derek had the clear advantage. It was obvious that Waite felt it, too; Cassidy could see his hands straining against the sheets, knuckles turning white from the effort.

"I know they don't look like much," Derek said, "but they're enough to hold you in place, Mr. Waite. So you might as well save yourself the effort. And in case you've forgotten the question...where were you on the afternoon of March 25, 2463?"

"I told you. I was in Cape Town. That's in South Africa, in case you for—"

Crack! It happened so quickly that at first Cassidy wasn't sure of what she'd actually seen. Then she realized Derek had reached out, taken the little finger of Waite's left hand between his thumb and forefinger, then bent it backward until it snapped.

Their captive had gone white under his tan, and beads of perspiration stood out along his hairline, but he didn't cry out. His jaw clenched, and he said in a hoarse whisper, "You'll have to do better than that."

"Not a problem," Derek replied calmly. "You've got nine fingers to go. And toes after that, if you're still not willing to talk. After that it might get a little dicey. Guess we'll just have to see. But you can spare yourself a world of pain if you just talk now."

"I have nothing to say." The words were gritted out, his eyes glittering and defiant.

"Okay." A pause as Derek seemed to consider the situation. "Would you like all the fingers of one hand broken in order, or would you prefer if I alternate?"

"Fuck you."

Through all this, Cassidy could only look on in amazement mixed with some horror. Not that she thought Conrad Waite was deserving of any special consideration, not if he really had murdered Theo Karras and too many others to count. No, it was more that she couldn't believe Derek Tagawa, a man of science and learning, was capable of such violence.

He spent two years in MaxSec, she thought then. *That can do a lot to change a man. Who knows...maybe he's thinking of all the days he lost in there while he's working up the nerve to break one of Waite's fingers. Anyway, he's not causing any damage that can't be fixed by a couple of hours in a bonesetter. I'm pretty sure Waite's employers can afford that for him.*

"Alternating, it is," Derek said, and reached over and snapped the little finger of Waite's right hand.

This time a sort of gargled sound of agony emerged from the man's throat, but he clamped his lips together and otherwise remained silent.

"You really want to do this the hard way, don't you?"

Waite remained silent, and Derek glanced over at Cassidy, something in his expression softening for a moment.

"Maybe you should wait in the other room."

She shook her head. "No, I'm okay. It's better if I'm here in case he somehow busts out of those sheets."

"Oh, you definitely don't want to be here when I get out of these sheets," Waite snarled.

Ignoring him, Derek gave her the faintest of shrugs. "I'm not worried about it. If you're sure you're all right—"

"I'm fine," she said firmly, although she wasn't sure if she was fine. Maybe it was the lingering traces of the champagne she'd drunk and the cocktail before that, but something about the whole situation felt completely surreal, as if this was another Cassidy Evans standing here and calmly discussing whether she should be hanging around to watch her current companion torture a man into revealing his secrets. Surely that was the sort of thing that only happened in the more surreal thriller vids?

"You'll both get caught, you know," Waite put in then, his voice tight with pain but still completely in control. His gaze flickered to Cassidy. "But you—I can put in a good word for you, make sure you don't get charged with anything, if you just help me stop this mad—"

Snap! There went the ring finger of his left hand, and that time he did let out an audible howl, perspiration now streaming down the sides of his face.

"I'm pretty sure Ms. Evans isn't interested in any of your propositions," Derek said.

"Not at all," she remarked, although inwardly she wasn't sure how much more she could take of this, despite her earlier protestation that she was just fine with standing there and watching Derek break Waite's fingers one by one.

"Bitch."

Another of those lightning-fast moves, and there went the ring finger of Waite's right hand.

"Cocksucker—"

"I'll hazard a guess that now you're noticing the pain is cumulative, Mr. Waite. That's only four fingers, and you have six to go. So tell me, where were you on the afternoon of March 25, 2463?"

"I was in Cape Town, South Africa, you crazy motherfucking bastard!"

This time Derek grasped both of Waite's middle fingers at the same time and snapped them like twigs. Cassidy had to fight to keep herself from raising her hands to her ears to blot out the resulting howl.

"You sure about that, Mr. Waite?"

"All right, all right!"

"All right, what, Mr. Waite?"

Sweat dripping from his face had made large dark blotches on the expensive shirt Conrad Waite was wearing. "All right, I was in Hunan Province. I was informed we had a situation and that I needed to take care of it. So I did."

Derek didn't blink. "Can you please elaborate on what 'taking care of it' means?"

"Eliminate Theo Karras and make sure you were blamed for it." Waite shot a look of such venom at Derek that Cassidy was surprised when he didn't react at all. "Too bad I didn't kill you and frame Karras instead. That little twink probably would've enjoyed getting pegged in MaxSec."

At that remark, a look of such icy rage passed over Derek's face that Cassidy couldn't help taking a step backward. Waite obviously saw it, too, because he abruptly shut his mouth.

A long silence. Finally, Derek said, "He was worth a hundred of you." Then he picked up his handheld, swiped his thumb across the screen, and put it back in his pocket. "All right, we have enough. Time to go."

Thank God. Cassidy could feel the champagne and the lobster patties resting uneasily in her stomach, and she had the feeling she was probably going to vomit if she had to watch any more of this nightmare. "I'll get my things," she said, and hurried into the bedroom to grab her case.

Once there, she paused and ran a hand over her forehead, feeling her own brand of clammy sweat there. Could she ever look at Derek in the same way again?

Figure that out later, she told herself. *For now, we need to get going.*

When she returned to the main living area, she saw that Derek had his suitcase out as well. Waite was glaring at him. "You're just going to leave me here like this?"

"Relax," Derek replied, flicking a glance in Cassidy's direction. "It could be worse. At least you're trapped in a suite in a five-star hotel."

And with that parting shot, he inclined his head toward the door, indicating that she should go first. She didn't argue, but hurried out of the room, head down so the security cameras in the hallway wouldn't get a good shot of her face. A moment later, Derek followed, shutting the door on Waite's howls, which sounded curiously muffled. She realized he must have stopped long enough to gag the hit man, as otherwise the sounds he was making would surely have disturbed the other guests and caught the attention of hotel security.

"Let's go," Derek said briefly, and she knew she had no choice but to follow.

Now he had his evidence. She wondered what he was going to do with it.

TWELVE

NOT EVEN WHEN THEY WERE IN AN AUTOCAB AND being whisked across town to the maglev station would Derek allow himself to relax. He could feel Cassidy next to him, tense and silent, and he knew that he'd probably just ruined everything with her because of that display. But he'd have to push that aside for now. Either she'd come to understand why he'd done what he'd done, or she wouldn't. And if she couldn't understand that, well....

No, he wasn't going to go there right now. Every muscle in his body ached, and he felt vaguely nauseated. Strange. He'd been dreaming of this day for the past two years, and now that he had the hard evidence he'd wanted so badly, all he could do was think about the woman sitting next to him, and what she must be thinking of him in that moment.

Better to stick to neutral subjects. "We're taking the maglev because the security on the trains isn't nearly as high. The strats require biometric check-in before boarding."

"The what?" Cassidy asked, obviously confused. Those were the first two words she'd spoken since they'd left the suite.

Sometimes it was hard to remember that this was her first time on Gaia, that she'd spent her whole life on worlds with no atmosphere, in domed cities with artificial air and manufactured gravity, that the only real means of transport she'd ever known were spaceships of one kind or another, other than the underground rail lines on the Moon. "Sorry. The stratospheric liners."

She appeared to consider that reply, then asked, "Why can't we just go back to the spaceport and get our ship? It would be a lot faster than taking a train."

So much she didn't know about life here planet-side. But he couldn't hold that against her. Despite the gaps in her knowledge, she was one of the most capable people he'd ever met. "You've never flown in and out of Gaia. Consortium regulations prohibit using interplanetary craft for intraplanetary use. Everything's set up to make sure people use government-regulated transportation to get around. We could get in that ship and fly to the Moon or back out to Europa, or lay in a subspace course for Eridani if we wanted, but we can't use it to fly from city to city here on Gaia. It's either strats or maglevs, I'm afraid."

Another silence as she appeared to digest that information. "So where are we going, if we don't have to take a strat to get there?"

"Tucson."

A nod as she seemed to process his reply. Later he'd need to get Waite's confession in as wide distribution as possible, but before anything else, Derek wanted to get back home, show his parents that he was innocent.

All right, after torturing another human being, he supposed he wasn't exactly deserving of that label. Innocent of the crime for which he'd been convicted, then. That part was true enough.

He also knew that the identities they'd been provided would be compromised just as soon as the cleaning staff opened the door to the room tomorrow and discovered the little care package he'd left behind. Sooner possibly, if Waite managed to free himself. That was a calculated risk, though. Derek figured they had some time, and he planned to get in contact with their benefactor as soon as they reached the maglev station. True, there was surveillance everywhere you looked there as well, but his chances of being overheard were far lower there than here in this autocab, where everything he and Cassidy said and did was being monitored. Eventually someone might track down the recordings from this particular cab and learn that the two of them had headed to Arizona, but he planned to be long gone by then.

He wouldn't allow himself to think about just where they might go after they were done with their business in Tucson.

The autocab stopped in front of the station some five minutes later, and Derek swiped their credit voucher over the reader before getting out. Cassidy followed, still silent. Neither did she ask for any assistance climbing out of the cab, but maybe it was because she didn't need the help. He'd rather think it was that than because she simply didn't want him touching her. Not that he could really blame her for feeling that way.

At this time of night, the maglev station wasn't deserted, but neither was it as busy as it would have been during a more civilized time of day. People moved about, but with purpose, not paying any attention to him or Cassidy, or their surroundings. The place had been built during the Industrial Revival period of the late twenty-second century, and it was massive, gray, and thoroughly unappealing. Derek could see Cassidy giving it a once-over and looking unimpressed.

"I want to make a quick call," he told her, and she nodded. There was a quiet spot behind a blocky pillar a few feet to their left, one that was conveniently out of range of the closest surveillance cam. He sheltered in the lee of the pillar and drew out his handheld, then pulled up his last conversation with their sponsor, hit "reply," and said, "Are you available?"

A second passed, and then another. Cassidy stood a few feet away, watching him still in silence, but he couldn't tell what might be passing through her mind at that moment. Her face was blank and quiet, as if she'd decided the best thing to do right then was reveal nothing of what she might be thinking.

What is it now, Dr. Tagawa?

Funny how he could detect a clear note of impatience in those pale blue letters. "Sorry to disturb you," he said quietly, "but I'm afraid we're going to need new identities again. We used these ones to check in to the Cosmopolitan, and we've left some evidence behind that's going to stir up some trouble."

Evidence?

"Evidence named Conrad Waite," he said tersely.

Is the evidence still breathing?

"Yes."

No need for new identities. I'll have someone take care of it.

"You…will?"

Yes. It will be handled, and within the hour. Go ahead with your plans. I assume they involve you leaving Chicago.

"Yes, we're—"

No need to tell me. I'm tracking your I.D.s and will know where you're going.

He supposed he should have thought of that. Then again, he wasn't really used to living the life of a criminal on the run.

"Got it," he said after a pause. "I'll be in touch if we need anything else."

I have no doubt of that, Dr. Tagawa.

Despite everything, he felt himself smile slightly as he ended the convo and put the handheld back in his pocket. Cassidy had turned away from him and was scanning the enormous heads-up displays above the ticket kiosks.

"I don't see Tucson listed on there," she murmured as he approached her.

"It's not a direct destination. We'll have to take the maglev to Denver and then take a connecting train."

She accepted this explanation without comment, probably because her knowledge of Normerican geography was shaky enough that she couldn't get a clear picture in her head of where they were going. Funny, because he'd heard the schools in Luna City were actually fairly good.

No more time to worry about it now, since he saw from the ticketing display that the next train to Denver was leaving in less than fifteen minutes. He hurried over to the kiosk, Cassidy right behind him, and bought two tickets. They would be leaving from platform 93, which of course was on the opposite side of the station from the ticketing area.

"Come on—we don't have much time," he told her, and she picked up her suitcase and followed him, grimly hastening her pace to match his more long-legged stride. He wished there were some way for him to offer to carry her luggage, but he had a feeling she wouldn't appreciate such a gesture. Probably just as well; he was feeling exhaustion set in with every step, and knew he didn't have a lot of energy left in reserve.

They climbed into the maglev with approximately four minutes to spare, swiping the extruded plastic of their tickets through the reader at the door as they entered the train. Although Derek had never traveled this exact route, he knew that the maglevs were manned by human stewards who would make periodic sweeps of the cars to make sure all was in order. However, intervention generally wasn't necessary, as you couldn't even get on the train without a valid ticket.

The car they entered was not even a quarter full, and he pushed on toward the back, into the least populated section he could find. No point in taking the risk of having their conversation overhead.

At least Cassidy did allow him to swing her suitcase up into the overhead compartment, and he slid his in next to it, then closed the luggage bay. She'd already taken the window seat, which he thought only fair, although he doubt she'd be able to see much. This entire trip would take place in darkness, since they'd be pulling into Denver at around four hundred hours.

Enough time to catch some sleep, but he didn't know if he'd be able to manage that. The encounter with Waite had drained him and at the same time had left him keyed up, edgy. And although their sponsor had said he—or she—would take care of the man they'd left tied up in the suite at the Cosmopolitan, Derek couldn't help worrying over the problem in his mind, conjuring scenarios where Waite freed himself and escaped, or knocked over something in the suite and made enough noise that someone came to investigate, or—

"Hey," Cassidy said, and he looked up. To his relief, the look she gave him now was one of concern, not loathing. "We got away. It's going to be fine."

"For now, maybe," he allowed. She tilted her head, and he added, "That is, our 'friend'—he cast a significant glance toward the handheld in his pocket—"said he'd take care of the mess we left behind. So apparently these identities aren't compromised, and we should be okay. But still—"

"But you can't help worrying. I get it." She reached out and laid one hand on top of his. Only for a few seconds before she lifted it away, but even that brief touch was more reassuring than he cared to admit. Surely she wouldn't have done that if she were thoroughly disgusted by what he had done to Waite back in their suite. "Still, it sounds as if this person, for whatever reason, is really looking out for us. He—or she—hasn't steered us wrong yet."

No, he hadn't. Which made Derek wonder what was in all this for that person in the shadows, someone who seemed to have a good deal of resources at his fingertips. He couldn't be connected to the leak back on Europa. So that must mean there were several factions within the underground working independently of one another. It wasn't that surprising, if you stopped to think about it; such a large, shadowy group wouldn't tend to be all that homogenous. And in a dynamic like that, he supposed it wouldn't be terribly difficult to insert a few agents who tricked everyone into thinking they were working for the cause when in fact they were doing just the opposite.

"That's true," he replied, when he realized Cassidy was looking at him expectantly, waiting for him to speak. "We would've been dead, or caught, a long time before this without his help. I just wish I knew why."

"Maybe it's best not to question his motivations right now. As you said, there've been plenty of chances for him to reveal our whereabouts to the authorities, but he hasn't. Instead, he's done everything he could to keep us safe. So maybe you should stop worrying about it for now, try to get some sleep."

Practical, sensible words. He knew she was right, but could he release enough of the tension to let himself go, get the rest he knew he needed?

"I think we're safe here," she murmured, casting a quick glance around the cabin.

Probably. There wasn't anyone sitting within three rows of them, and all the people they'd passed hadn't even bothered to look up from their handhelds or computers. If anyone had been lurking on this train, waiting to spring, most likely they would have done so by now.

"All right," he told her. "I'll try." And he adjusted his seat so it reclined backward, then turned on the heat and the gentle massage function. If that didn't put him to sleep, nothing would.

She gave him a relieved smile and did the same, clearly impressed with the amenities even these simple seats offered. Well, it was a bit different from the cockpit of a spaceship, even one as sleek and up-to-date as the one they'd left behind in Chicago.

As he drifted off to sleep, he wondered if they'd ever make it back to the Windy City's spaceport to retrieve it.

When his face went still, eyelashes black crescents against his cheeks, Cassidy knew Derek slept. She also knew she should be doing the same thing, but slumber eluded her, despite her comfortable seat. Dark landscapes flitted by outside the window, lights of passing cities and towns shimmering in the darkness, then gone. It all felt so big, although she knew that was only an illusion. Gaia was really not a very large planet at all, was dwarfed by Jupiter and Saturn and Neptune. But of course man had never settled on any of those gas giants and never could—the conditions would kill an unprotected human being in less than a second.

Here, though, with the central plains of Normerica dashing past the window at a little more than 150 kilometers per hour, Cassidy got a sense of scale quite unlike anything else she'd ever experienced. On the Moon, one could take the underground rail from Luna City to Tranquility Dome, a journey of around an hour, but that distance felt tiny compared to this one. And it would take another not quite three hours to get from Denver to Tucson. With all the distance they were covering now, it was still only a little more than half their journey.

And what would be at the end of it? It was clear that Derek intended to go to his parents with the proof of

Waite's involvement in Theo Karras' death. She guessed Derek would edit the recording heavily, would take out the torture that resulted in Waite's confession. At least, that was what she would do if she were in his position. She couldn't imagine allowing her own father to see the kind of violence she was capable of. But she also couldn't have imagined that Derek would be able to do any of what he'd done back in their suite at the Continental, so what did that say about her as a judge of character?

Not a hell of a lot, apparently.

She risked a glance over at him, but he slept still. If he was tormented inwardly by the lengths he'd gone to extract that information from Conrad Waite, Derek didn't show it. His face was calm, peaceful. Studying him like this, she could see how elegant his cheekbones and chin and nose were, how finely molded his lips, how thick his eyelashes. All little details she hadn't really taken in before now, partly because everything had been happening so fast that she didn't have much time to really stop and think, and partly because she didn't want him to catch her staring.

Well, she had plenty of time to stare now.

And what did that say about her? As they'd left the suite after his interrogation of Waite, she'd been shaken by what she'd just witnessed. Now, though, that unease seemed to have disappeared, or at least lessened to a great extent. Was it simply that she'd had time to think about what a piece of shit Conrad Waite really was? Lord knows he hadn't shown much guilt over the man he'd murdered...and she knew Theo Karras had to be just one of many. There were probably quite a few additional victims scattered around the globe even after Derek had been sent to MaxSec.

Maybe some people would call that situational ethics, but she realized Conrad Waite wasn't worth shedding any tears over. Derek had indicated that their sponsor's people would take care of him, but was that Waite's own brand of "taking care" of something, or would they simply remove him from the Cosmopolitan and then dump him someplace where his handlers could pick him up?

More questions she didn't have the answers to. She doubted she ever would.

And that's fine, she told herself. *You don't have to know everything. The most important thing to know is that someone's helping us, someone who seems to have our best interests at heart.*

Otherwise, as she'd told Derek a short while earlier, they would've been dead a long time ago.

She shifted in her seat, turning back toward the window. Now she was regretting her lack of knowledge about the world that had birthed her ancestors. Maybe if she'd spent a little more time studying Gaia, instead of learning astrogation and new techniques for squeezing a little more speed out of the Avalon while at the same time reducing fuel consumption, she wouldn't feel so lost now. She'd know the names of those cities and towns flashing by, know how many people lived there, whether any of them had ever gone into space, or whether they'd spent their whole lives bounded by Gaian scenery, a blue Gaian sky.

Well, she was lucky in that, she supposed. She'd seen the glitter of far-off sunlight on Saturn's rings, drifted in blackness pierced by the delicate shimmer of a million stars. She'd watched Gaia rise beyond Luna City's domes, and seen the ice volcanoes on Io shoot hundreds of meters into its tenuous atmosphere. All of those things made her who she was now, and she knew she would have never given any of them up in exchange for a safe existence here on Gaia's surface.

Or not so safe, she thought then. *It wasn't that safe for Theo Karras…nor Derek.*

She wished they were someplace private. If they were, she would lean over and kiss him awake, show him that she understood why he'd stood there and calmly broken Conrad Waite's fingers. Not because he enjoyed it, but because he knew it was the only way to get to the truth. He wasn't a Consortium intelligence operative— he didn't have access to truth serums and mind-control drugs and all the other less damaging but otherwise just as invasive techniques others might have used in a similar situation. No, he only had his hands and his mind, both of which he'd used to brutal effect to get the information he needed.

But because they were on this train, and only fifteen feet away or so were other passengers either nodding in their own seats or trying to occupy themselves with watching a vid or catching up on work or whatever else it took to fill up the time, Cassidy settled for touching her forefinger to her lips, placing it gently on the back of Derek's hand, and then removing it just as quickly so she wouldn't wake him up. He stirred, but only a little, and she knew she needed to take her cue from him. There were still about two hours left before they reached Denver, and she might as well rest up now.

She had no idea what to expect when they reached Tucson.

THIRTEEN

TEMPERATURES IN CHICAGO HAD BEEN MILD, AS IT WAS now late September on Gaia, and the northern hemisphere of the planet was tilting toward winter. Here in Tucson, though, it was warm and dry, fiercely bright, and Cassidy wished she'd thought to purchase some protective lenses in one of those boutiques on Lakeshore Drive. Sunglasses…that's what they called them here on Gaia.

They'd switched trains in Denver without incident, and arrived in this bright desert city a little before eight hundred hours. They'd checked their luggage into an automated storage locker at the station, although she wasn't sure why.

Autocabs were queued up at the station, so that wasn't an issue, although she saw Derek cast a somewhat longing look at the aircar rental station.

"Why don't we get one of those, if you prefer it?"

she asked in an undertone. It was much busier here than in Chicago, not because Tucson was a larger city, but because they'd arrived right in the middle of the morning rush as people were heading in to work.

"Can't," he said shortly. "All aircar rentals require a biometric scan at check-in. We'll take an autocab part of the way and walk the rest. That way it won't have an accurate record of our destination."

Maybe at some point she'd get used to the way everything was watched and recorded here on Gaia. Sure, there was surveillance on Luna City, but not to the extent she'd seen here. Then again, on the Moon, there were only so many places you could go. A fugitive might flee to a different domed population center, but there were only seventeen in all. Sooner or later, you'd be tracked down. Whereas here....

Here you'd have a whole planet to lose yourself in. No wonder the authorities wanted to remove every opportunity for a person to slip the net. She had to hope Derek knew what he was doing, that they'd get out of Tucson before anyone figured out they'd been here.

An autocab stopped in response to Derek's hail, and they climbed into the back seat. He gave the cab a destination, but Cassidy didn't pay too much attention to what it was, since they were heading someplace entirely different.

But at least it was daylight, so she could stare out the window at the streets passing by outside, so different from the row after row of towering high-rises they'd left behind in Chicago. Yes, there were tall buildings here, especially clustered off to their left in what she assumed must be some sort of downtown district, but what caught her eye more than anything were the mountain ranges that surrounded the town. She'd seen mountains before, on the Moon and on Mars, but these felt bigger somehow, were deeply hued and majestic, and seemed to have some sort of vegetation growing on them.

The median at the center of the street had spiky vegetation growing in it as well, something that looked as if it should have been growing on an alien world, not Gaia itself. "What are those?" she asked as they passed by another one.

An expression of amusement passed over Derek's face, although before then he'd looked somber and far away. "Saguaro cactus. The lower ones are called prickly pear. They grow a fruit that's edible."

"Really?" It looked so very inedible, what with those spines all over the place.

"Really. I used to know a bar that made a mean margarita with them."

Maybe at some point she'd get used to not knowing much of anything about Gaia. Trying not to feel like an idiot, she echoed, "Margarita?"

"A drink made with tequila and a sweet and sour mix. It's a local tradition. Maybe if we have time we can stop in one of the local bars and have one."

That sounded like fun, and also refreshingly normal. Which meant she doubted they'd have time for a margarita, prickly pear or otherwise. Still, it was something pleasant to think about.

The cab took them past the downtown area, out into what were clearly residential districts. Having spent her whole life in domed cities where space was at a premium, she could only stare at how spread out everything was here, how every house sat on its own plot of land, with its neighbors a respectable distance away, not stacked on top of each other like the condo compounds in Luna City or the modular residences on Ganymede. And in front of those houses were more cactus planted in what she assumed were meant to be aesthetically pleasing patterns, although she couldn't quite figure those out. There were potted shrubs in Luna City, carefully spaced and even more carefully watched, but that was the extent of her exposure to gardening.

"What do you think?" Derek asked.

"It's big. Alive, in a way that Chicago wasn't. If it weren't for the lake outside and the size of the building, I could've said the Cosmopolitan was tucked in a dome somewhere. Even when I went outside, it didn't feel as if I was outside."

"I can see that. I was never much for big cities. You get spoiled when you grow up with this kind of view." His glance strayed to the mountains far off in the distance, and Cassidy couldn't really blame him. She knew she wanted to keep staring, to drink in this place that felt so alien and yet was the home world of her race.

The autocab turned a corner and came to a stop in front of a house with a high wall of some sort of smooth, pale substance. Molded duracrete? She wasn't sure; she'd never made much study of Gaian construction techniques. Far more interesting was the vining shrub that covered half of the wall, and the bright, bright pink flowers studded along its length. She had no idea anything that vivid grew naturally.

They got out, and as they began to walk, she understood why Derek had had them leave their luggage behind. It would't have been much fun to drag the heavy cases along in the heat, and since they were now going through a residential area without much foot traffic, the two of them would have looked extremely conspicuous, walking along with a couple of large suitcases in tow.

It was also warm, almost uncomfortably so. In the past she'd complained about the *Avalon*'s balky temperature regulator, but running a couple of degrees too warm was far different from the heat she was experiencing now. It had to be almost thirty degrees out there. Sweat was already beginning to drip down her back.

Apparently, Derek noticed her discomfort, because he said, "Maybe you should take your jacket off."

She should have thought of that earlier. Too used to having the temperature around her adjusted to what she was wearing rather than vice versa, she supposed. Pausing, she undid the tabs holding the jacket closed, then shrugged out of it and draped it over one arm.

That was better, although she wished the shirt she'd been wearing under it didn't have long sleeves.

"It's not too far. Just another block."

It seemed that a "block" down here on Gaia was far longer than the units with the same name used in Luna City. She trudged along, squinting in the bright sunshine. "How do people live here?" she asked. "It's so hot and sunny."

"Believe it or not, a lot of people enjoy this kind of weather. But then, they dress for it, too." He sent her an encouraging smile. "Well, that, and our houses have good climate control. Speaking of which, here we are."

He nodded toward a large, sprawling structure with square outlines, surrounded by another one of those high walls. In the center of the front wall was a large gate made of black metal twisted into elegant shapes, and through that gate she could spy more cactus and other plants she couldn't identify.

"That's your parents' house?" she asked. It was so large, she couldn't imagine all that space being for just two people. But then, if this was where Derek and his sister had grown up, then at one time it might not have seemed so big.

"Yes," he said, and this time she noted an undercurrent of tension in his voice, whereas before this he had sounded fairly relaxed.

"So…what now?"

"We go in."

He moved past her and went to the gate, then lifted the latch and entered the yard on the other side. How odd that the gate was just open like that, with no visible security measures she could see. Was that how they normally did things in Tucson, or were the Tagawas more trusting than usual?

Judging by what Derek had told her so far about his father, she kind of doubted that was the reason.

The front door was protected by a keypad, but Derek typed in a code and the door opened inward. Cool air drifted out toward them, and Cassidy permitted herself a small sigh of relief. At least they wouldn't be sweltering once they were inside. At the same time, she wondered if this was the best way to approach things…to simply walk in, when Derek's parents still thought him locked up on the other side of the Solar System.

Then again, it wasn't as if calling ahead to warn them had been a viable option. Had they been informed of his jail break? She sort of doubted it, since that was the sort of screw-up the government preferred not to advertise.

The house was quiet, the background hum of the cooling unit the only sound she could hear. No distant noise of a vid being watched, no soft music while someone worked.

Maybe that was it. Derek had said his father was an engineer and his mother a surgeon. It was quite possible they'd already left for the day.

"Do you think they're out?" she asked softly. And if they were, what then? The thought of just sitting here and waiting for them to come home seemed a bit creepy.

"They're retired," he replied, sounding mystified. "It's a little early for them to be running errands, but...."

Since she had no idea what a typical day for a retired Gaian entailed, Cassidy could only shrug and wait. This was his house—or at least had been, once upon a time—so it was really up to him to decide what to do next.

"Mom?" he called out. "Dad?"

If the silence that greeted his call weren't so unnerving, Cassidy would have been tempted to smile. It was somehow incongruous to hear him addressing his parents like that, grown man that he was. Then again, her own father would have given her what-for if she'd attempted to call him by his first name, no matter that she was legally an adult, so she didn't know why Derek should be any different.

Frowning, he moved down the central corridor of the house, one that opened out on either side into a series of rooms, one clearly an office, the other a sitting area of some sort. It was difficult not to stare, because it was all so very different from what she was used to, from the floor of some dark red ceramic tile to the woven hangings on the walls and the furniture that looked as if it had been made of real wood. Real. That was how it felt to her, as if everything in the house had been made by human hands out of natural materials, rather than

extruded of plastic or composite in a factory somewhere. It was strange, but very beautiful in its way.

They continued to the kitchen, a mixture of up-to-
date appliances and natural tile, everything spotlessly
clean. It had a small sitting area off to one side, with a
table for two, and on that table sat two mugs. So Derek's
parents must have been here recently, and most likely
planned on coming back. She couldn't imagine they'd
leave those mugs out like that otherwise, not when the
rest of the place was so tidy.

The kitchen overlooked a casual room with a sofa
and a couple of chairs, and a vid-screen mounted on
one wall. Directly opposite this was a wall of glass—but
then Cassidy saw two figures approaching it, talking and
smiling, and the wall slid aside. Not a wall at all, then,
but an automated doorway of some sort.

It was a woman in front, carrying some sort of long-
stemmed flowers in one hand, flowers she must have
just gathered in the garden out back. She came inside,
took a few steps into the room...and then seemed to
notice Derek and Cassidy where they were standing in
the kitchen. Her eyes widened, and she let out a gasp,
the flowers falling from her hand.

"My God," she said, standing there and staring at her
son as if she'd seen a ghost. Well, Derek was probably
not too far removed from a ghost in his parents' eyes.
Cassidy doubted that they'd ever expected to see him
alive again.

"What is it?" the man behind her said, entering the house as well. He paused next to his wife and went stock still, not blinking.

Cassidy could see some resemblance there, in the high, proud cheekbones and the shape of his face. Otherwise, Derek's features were more like his mother's, only stronger. Both parents had dark hair and dark eyes, although the mother's hair was streaked with gray.

"What is this?" Derek's father said, voice calm, cold, as if encountering escaped-convict sons breaking into his house was something that happened to him every day. "What are you doing here?"

Beside her, Cassidy could feel Derek tense. She recalled that he didn't have the most cordial of relationships with his father. When he spoke, however, his tone betrayed nothing of that tension. "Hi, Dad...nice to see you, too."

Derek's mother came farther into the room, even as her husband touched a control unit on the wall, shutting the door. Her eyes seemed to shimmer with tears. "Oh, Derek...I don't believe it. How did you get here? Were you released? We weren't informed—"

"I wasn't released. I escaped."

Dead silence. Derek's mother paled, and she stopped where she was, staring at her son. "What? How—"

"If that is so, then you have brought even more disgrace on this family," his father cut in, tone sharp as a knife. "And I will ask you to leave before you bring the authorities down on all our heads."

Cassidy tried not to flinch at his words. They weren't even intended for her—Mr. Tagawa had barely allowed a single glance in her direction—but they still hurt.

Derek didn't move. "I will not leave. I have evidence exonerating me. I want you to see it."

"I'm not the person who needs to see it. If it is valid, then take it to the authorities."

"The same authorities who would shoot me on sight before they'd listen to a single thing I had to say?"

Mrs. Tagawa raised a hand. "Please. I don't know how this happened, Derek, but if you have something you want us to see, then I think we should see it." Her husband opened his mouth, clearly intending to gainsay her, but she went on, ignoring his protest, "It's the least we can do."

"And be charged with harboring a known fugitive?"

"Your *son*," she said sternly, and there was something in the glance she sent her husband that made him subside. Then her gaze shifted to Cassidy. "And this is…?"

"Cassidy Evans," Derek told her. "Captain of the *Avalon*. She saved my life."

Despite the tension in the room, Cassidy still felt a little wave of warmth go over her. He'd introduced her as the captain of a ship, not bothering to mention that the Avalon was a beat-up old freighter now reduced to cosmic dust orbiting Jupiter. His parents had status, and he hadn't wanted them to look down on her.

His mother came forward into the kitchen and took Cassidy's hands in hers, giving them a gentle squeeze before releasing them again. "Then thank you, Ms. Evans. There's nothing a mother can do to show her gratitude for saving her son, but…thank you."

"You're welcome," Cassidy replied, knowing how awkward her response sounded. But what else could she say? "It's nothing" didn't really fit the bill here.

Derek's father, however, remained where he was. "What is this evidence?"

"Maybe you should take a seat," Derek told him, clearly used to his father's abruptness.

He stood there for a few seconds more, back ramrod straight, and then went to one of the chairs and sat down. His wife sent both Cassidy and Derek a reassuring look before going back to the family room and situating herself at one end of the sofa.

Cassidy reached over and touched Derek's fingers briefly. She didn't want to say anything aloud, as she wasn't sure he would appreciate her giving away anything as to the nature of their relationship, but she also wanted him to know that she was here for him. The briefest of nods, and then he moved past her and into the other room, where he made his way over to the vidscreen. He pulled the handheld from his pocket and aimed it at the data port on one side. Of course. Better that they see this on a large screen, rather than trying to squint at the much smaller one on the handheld.

Moment of truth, she thought. Now she'd get to see whether he'd done some surreptitious editing on that file while she was asleep, or whether he was willing to let the recording stand as it was, was ready to have his parents see what he'd done to Conrad Waite.

Both sound and picture faded in. The angle was a little strange, as the handheld had been sitting on the coffee table in their suite and pointed in Waite's direction, but you could still see him sitting there, tied to the chair, perspiration dripping from his forehead.

"…was in Cape Town, South Africa, you crazy motherfucking bastard!"

So he'd cut some of it out, but not all. Crunch went Waite's middle fingers, and Cassidy could see Mrs. Tagawa wince. Derek's father, on the other hand, sat stiff and straight in his chair, expression unchanged.

Then the recording got to where Waite said, "Too bad I didn't kill you and frame Karras instead," and Derek's father finally blinked. Not much of a reaction, but it was something. Something promising? She didn't know the man well enough to hazard a guess.

Derek picked up the handheld and severed the connection between the vid-screen and the device. "So there you go."

An uneasy silence. At last Mrs. Tagawa said, voice still with shock, "You broke all his fingers?"

"Not all of them," Derek replied, tone indifferent. "I didn't touch his index fingers or his thumbs."

"This proves nothing," his father said. "A confession—and not much of one at that—given under duress?"

"'Not much of one'?" Derek repeated, sounding incredulous. "Which part of 'I should've killed you and framed Karras instead' did you not understand?"

A frown creased Mr. Tagawa's brow. "That is still not an outright confession."

"Are you really going to sit there and try to tell me you don't believe what he was saying, that he was just lying to get me to stop?"

"Derek," Mrs. Tagawa said, her voice gentle, but so firm that her son subsided, although Cassidy could tell from the way his hands were knotted into fists at his sides that he was fighting with himself to keep from launching at his father. "I believe you. I never thought you capable of murdering anyone." Her husband's mouth tightened, but he didn't interrupt. "And it does sound like this man was the one responsible. That said, what do you intend to do next?"

Derek's shoulders slumped a bit. "To tell you the truth, I'm not sure. I can't go to the authorities directly, since I'm a fugitive, but I was hoping that maybe you could make a copy of this, take it to the local public attorney's office. You're both prominent members of the community here…it's possible there's someone in that office who hasn't been corrupted, who would be willing to listen to what you have to say."

"Impossible," Mr. Tagawa said, voice flat. "No one would listen to us."

What the hell was the man's problem? He wasn't even looking at Derek as he stood there by the vid-screen, features tight with an uncomfortable mixture of anger and disappointment. Even though she knew she should stay out of it, Cassidy found she couldn't stay silent any longer. "So that's it? Even though your son is innocent, was made a scapegoat to cover up the monstrous things they're doing in Hunan Province, he's just supposed to throw up his hands and go meekly back into custody? What about justice? What about what's right?"

The look Tagawa shot her felt roughly akin to one he might have given a cockroach he spotted crawling across his spotless floor. "Young woman, this has nothing to do with you."

"It sure as hell does," she shot back. "It was my ship he hijacked to get off Titan, so I'm involved whether I wanted to be or not. At first, I wanted to kill him— but then I heard his story, and I knew he was innocent. Don't sit there and tell me that the Consortium government isn't capable of covering up the truth, because I will laugh in your goddamn face."

Slowly, Derek's father got to his feet. "I will not be spoken to in such a way in my own house, no matter what you might have done to help my son." He clearly intended to go on, but his wife cut him off, saying,

"That's enough. Ms. Evans has been through a good deal, that's clear if nothing else is, and she was helping our son when she certainly didn't have to." She got up and went over to stand by Derek, a gesture clearly calculated to show her husband where her loyalties lay. "If you refuse to help him, I can't make you. On the other hand, if you try to stop me from helping him…well, you might want to consider what the consequences of such an action could be."

The threat was clear enough, even if she didn't bother to spell it out. If it came to a choice between her husband and her son, she would come down on Derek's side. Maybe she was inwardly berating herself for not doing more when he was first charged, although Cassidy wasn't sure what any one person could have done to prevent Derek's conviction. When the Consortium wanted something, it generally got it, even if that meant trampling on someone's rights, or sending an innocent man to rot in MaxSec.

"I suppose we will all do what we feel is right," Mr. Tagawa said, clearly unmoved by her threat. "Even if our opinions do not line up."

Derek cleared his throat. It was obvious enough that the last thing he'd intended was to cause any additional friction between his parents, although he'd probably guessed that something like this might happen, as he appeared upset but not overly surprised. For all he knew, they'd been fighting over the subject since the day he was shipped off to MaxSec. Actually, Cassidy was somewhat startled that they were even still together. Marriages had broken apart over a lot less.

"Look," he said, "I only wanted to prove to you that the lies the Consortium told about me were just that… lies. I did not shoot Theo Karras. As I said before, Theo and I discovered that the dead from the Cloud were not being respectfully handled, and we got clamped down on before word could spread. As Waite himself put it, the Consortium had a situation, and it wanted it handled. The government doesn't care about me, or Theo, or anything besides making sure no one finds out how dirty the GARP operation actually is."

Mr. Tagawa crossed his arms and said nothing, but his wife, dark eyes troubled, ventured, "But even though you do have something of a confession from this Conrad Waite, he said nothing about GARP or what you discovered. So how will you get the word out about that if you don't have any evidence?"

From the troubled expression that crossed Derek's features, she could tell he'd already thought the same thing. "I'm not sure. Probably I'll need to go back to China, get real concrete proof, and then…distribute it."

He hadn't mentioned that plan to Cassidy, but it made sense…in a way. On the other hand, getting within a thousand kilometers of the people who had framed him probably wasn't the wisest idea in the world. She had a feeling they wouldn't bother with trying to frame him this time. No, they'd put a pulse bolt between his eyes and call it a day.

"Distribute it how?" his mother asked.

"I know someone who can help me. And that's all I'm going to say on the subject. The less you know, the better."

She looked as troubled as her son, but she didn't try to protest. "I suppose there's no point in asking you to be careful."

"Oh, I'll be careful," he told her. "Whether that will be enough…?" The words trailed away, and he lifted his shoulders. "I guess I'll let the universe sort that out." His gaze moved past her and seemed to settle on Cassidy. "But we've been here long enough, and I don't want to run the risk of anyone finding out about this visit. The best thing I can do is keep moving."

"Derek—"

He bent slightly and kissed his mother on the cheek. "I hope you'll hear from me again. I hope—" A shake of his head. "Well, I hope it will somehow all work out. But if you don't hear from me—"

"I'll assume you're on the run and can't risk it." The words were spoken firmly, as if she wouldn't allow herself to contemplate the possibility that she might not hear from him because he was dead. "Take care of yourself, Derek."

"I'll do my best." He moved away from her then, pausing just long enough to say, "Goodbye, Father."

Mr. Tagawa said nothing, only looked on with his jaw tight and his eyes unblinking.

No reaction from Derek, save possibly the slightest narrowing of his eyes. He came toward Cassidy, gaze fixed on her as if his father didn't even exist, and said, "Let's go. We've spent enough time here."

FOURTEEN

On the cab ride back to the maglev station, Cassidy had remained conspicuously silent. Derek watched her fine profile as it was silhouetted against the 'car window, the bright Tucson sunlight throwing the outlines of her nose and mouth and chin into sharp relief. It seemed clear enough that she didn't dare broach the subject of what had just happened in his parents' house, although whether that was because she didn't want her words recorded by the cab's surveillance equipment, or because she was worried what his reaction might be, he wasn't sure.

Probably just as well. At the moment, he didn't think he could discuss his father without using language that might shock her. Or maybe not. She'd seen some of the rougher edges of life, probably far more than he had. Even so, she shouldn't have to be on the receiving end of the rage Derek felt boiling within him…rage that really should have been directed at Hiro Tagawa.

It's your own damn fault for thinking anything would be different, he told himself, attempting to push the fury away, the desire to have the cab turn around so he could walk up to his father and give him the punch in the face he so rightly deserved. No, that would be foolish. In general, violence didn't solve anything—breaking the fingers of Consortium operatives notwithstanding—although contemplating knocking his father out did give Derek a certain sense of satisfaction.

They got out of the cab at the maglev station and went to retrieve their luggage. Only then did Cassidy say, "So…what next?"

"We keep moving," he told her. "Everywhere we go, there's surveillance. Eventually, the Consortium's facial-recognition software is going to catch up with us. Right now no one knows exactly where I am, so the search isn't being pinpointed to a precise location. But sooner or later, a data point someplace is going to cross-reference with the known fugitives list, and then we're going to have ourselves a problem."

"And what's the bad news?" she quipped, although he could tell from the worried flicker in her hazel eyes that what he'd just told her had frightened her a good deal.

"The bad news is that we can't take a maglev to China, so fairly soon we're going to have to figure out a way to get our biometrics altered."

It wasn't quite as dire as he'd made it sound; he had a feeling their benefactor might know one or two people involved in that illicit but necessary business. First things first, though—they needed to get out of Tucson. And since it made sense to take a stratospheric flight from the West Coast, he thought they should purchase a ticket to Barstow. In that sprawling city, which had become the new population center in the southern half of California after Los Angeles succumbed to the rising oceans caused by global warming several centuries ago, he had to hope they would find someone who could make it possible for them to safely leave Normerica.

If not…well, he wouldn't let himself think about that now. There was always the Zephyr, still parked at the spaceport in Chicago and quietly racking up hangar fees. Maybe the best thing to do would be to send Cassidy back there, get her safely off-planet. This wasn't her fight, and he'd dragged her into the path of danger too often as it was.

She was looking up at him expectantly, waiting for him to answer her question about the biometrics, or maybe she was simply waiting to hear what his true plans were. He had a feeling she wasn't going to like what he was about to say, but he went ahead and said it anyway.

"Look, Cassidy…I think it might be better if you went back to Chicago and retrieved the ship. You can get away from Gaia—out of the system entirely—and I'll do what I have to in China. It would be safer that way."

Her brows drew together, angry dark lines against her pale skin. "Just like that, huh? Now that you don't have a use for me anymore, it's 'so long, Cass, it's been great'? What if I don't want go back to Chicago with my tail between my legs?"

Damn it, he hadn't been expecting that reaction. "Cassidy, that's not what I meant—"

"Isn't it? If I can't fly you someplace or act as bait for a company hit man, then I'm superfluous, right? Just extra baggage?"

Approximately five or six careful, reasoned replies rose to his lips…and then he realized she was too angry to listen to any of them. So he did the only thing he thought might work. He set down his suitcase, plucked hers from her hand, and then pulled her against him, kissing her thoroughly right there in the maglev station. For just the briefest instant, he felt her resist, body rigid against his, but then she relaxed, her arms going around him and her mouth opening to his.

It was amazing what this woman could do to him, send such a rush of heat through his body that he could feel himself stiffening, pushing uncomfortably against the pants he wore, which were just slightly tighter than he would have preferred. Someone in the terminal let out a wolf-whistle, and he had no doubt that the shouts of "get a room!" were soon to follow, and so he released her gently, keeping his gaze intent on her face the whole time.

"I don't want to get rid of you," he said. "But I don't want anything to happen to you, either."

Her breasts were rising and falling as she struggled for air, and he could see the flush that infused her fair skin. "I appreciate that. But I'm a big girl, Derek. I can handle myself."

She'd already provided ample evidence of that, but he still found himself wavering. He'd never forgive himself if something happened to her. On the other hand, he couldn't forcibly put her on a maglev bound for Chicago. Even if he somehow managed to do that, she was just stubborn enough that she'd probably get off at the first stop and come right back after him.

"All right," he said at length. "But I have no idea what we're getting into. Hell, I'm not even sure how we're getting into China. So we'll take this one step at a time."

"Barstow first."

"Barstow first," he agreed. "And after that…we'll see."

"That works for me," she said, and bent to pick up her suitcase with one hand while looping her free arm through his.

Still worried I'll bolt? he thought, a smile pulling at his lips. *No worries there, Cassidy. From now on, I don't plan to let you out of my sight.*

The maglev had lost all novelty for Cassidy at this point, but she was just glad it was pointing westward and not back toward Chicago. Really, what the hell had Derek been thinking?

That he wants you to continue breathing, she thought. She couldn't really argue with that particular sentiment, as she would prefer to keep on breathing as well, but she'd also come too far to walk away at this point. Whatever happened, she'd stick by him.

Why she felt such loyalty to someone she'd only met a few days ago, she didn't quite know. Or maybe some part of her mind and heart had already guessed, but she wasn't willing to acknowledge that truth. Not openly, not yet. At the same time, though, she knew she couldn't bear the thought of not being around him, of never knowing whether he'd succeeded in his quest or not.

Even if it got her killed.

They didn't speak as the train sped west, the desert landscape blurring past the window. Maybe they had too much to say. She wished she could think of something that would comfort him after that gruesome scene with his father, but she had the feeling Derek wanted to pretend it had never happened. It must be awful to have a parent who disapproved of you so heartily, and she still couldn't quite figure out what Mr. Tagawa's problem was. After all, even if he hadn't stayed in Tucson and taught at the university, Derek was still a successful man, a scientist assigned to a very important project.

Well, except for the part where a key component of that project had turned out to be a complete lie.

Her stomach rumbled, telling her that it didn't much appreciate running around day and night, and not getting anything to fill it up. Derek must have heard as well, because he smiled slightly and said, "There are vending machines in the forward car, if you need something to eat."

"It's fine," she replied. "I'd rather wait until we get to Barstow and can have some real food." His expression didn't change, so she added, somewhat worried, "That is, assuming we can get real food in Barstow."

He chuckled. "Oh, we can get real food there. I know a place where we can get some chilaquiles that'll make you weep."

"Chila-what?" she replied, trying to get her mouth to pronounce the unfamiliar syllables. Anyway, did she really want food that would make her cry?

"It's a dish we eat here in the Southwest. It's good."

Since he didn't seem inclined to elaborate—maybe he wanted her to be surprised by these chilaquiles, whatever they were—she asked instead, "So you've been to Barstow before?"

"Several times over the years, for conferences at the university, that sort of thing." He shifted in his seat, clearly uncomfortable in the cramped space. This train car didn't feel quite as luxurious as the one they'd taken from Chicago. Maybe, since this was a shorter route, the designers had thought they could get away with skimping. "I made friends with some of the professors, and they took me around to their favorite places to eat around town. It's the best way to get to a know a city— sample its restaurants."

"Mmm," Cassidy replied, feeling once again as if she were on an alien world, rather than one from which she was only a single generation removed. Not that Luna City didn't have its eating establishments, but the food at most of them was fairly bland, only a few steps up from the ready-made rations she took along to eat when she was traveling the route between the Moon and Titan. There were a couple of restaurants that specialized in hydroponically grown produce, along with meats brought in specially from Gaia, but those places were way above her pay grade. The lobster patties she'd shared with Conrad Waite were probably one of the best things she'd ever tasted, despite the company she'd shared them with.

So the thought that a city could have such variety in its restaurants that they contributed to its personality was an alien one to her…but she didn't mind giving it all a try. If nothing else, it sounded like a good way to re-energize before they left Normerica for China… which, she thought she'd read somewhere, once had quite a regional cuisine of its own. Maybe its refugees had preserved something of it, but she'd never had any dishes that claimed to be Chinese.

The landscape outside the window steadily grew greener, and she found her gaze pulled to those unexpectedly verdant hillsides. For some reason, she'd thought all this area would be as dry and dusty as Tucson.

"Not what you were expecting?" Derek asked, apparently noticing her distraction.

"No," she replied, still staring out the window. "I thought this was supposed to be a desert."

"It was, about three hundred years ago. But the rising oceans cooled the air, and the monsoon rainstorms became more widespread, and so it eventually greened up. It's still nothing like the really green places—the upper Midwest, the United Kingdom—but it's very different from what it used to be."

"It's beautiful." She didn't have a name for the scrubby green shrubs that looked halfway between honest-to-goodness trees and mere bushes, nor the bright yellow flowers that danced on the breeze, but somehow that didn't matter. For the first time she understood what her father had been talking about when he told her it was dangerous to go to Gaia, that you'd see things there that would make the world of living shipboard and domed cities feel cramped and small, colorless and sterile.

"Yes, it is," he agreed, although she felt his gaze on her rather than the scene outside the window.

Color rose to her cheeks, and she made herself keep staring outside rather than look at him. It would be nice to have Derek's warm olive skin, which never showed much of a flush. Oh, well.

"How much longer until we get to Barstow?" she asked then. She knew it was probably a transparent attempt at redirecting the conversation but couldn't come up with anything better to deflect his attention.

"Less than an hour. Luckily, I know the town a little, so I can get us to a hotel without too much trouble. I just have to make sure it's not one I've stayed in before. The last thing we need is anyone recognizing me."

That was for sure. She knew how lucky they'd been so far, but there was no point in taking unnecessary risks. "Do you think that'll be a problem? Running into someone who knows you, I mean."

He grinned. She loved the way his dark eyes lit up when he smiled, the small cleft that appeared in his chin. "In a town of a little more than two million people? I doubt it."

Two million. The number made it sound vast, although she knew Chicago was much, much larger than that. But she'd only seen one small section of that megalopolis, and so hadn't gotten much sense of its true scale.

She nodded, and they lapsed into silence again. Derek seemed to be staring off nowhere in particular, and his smile had disappeared. Something about his mouth seemed somber and quiet, and she wondered if he was thinking about his father, or simply attempting to figure out their next move. Either way, he didn't look too happy.

Without thinking, she reached over and laid her hand on top of his, not squeezing it, not doing anything except letting him feel the warmth of her skin against his. That did seem to help, as his expression relaxed slightly, and the corners of his mouth turned up just a little.

That was better. One way or another, she'd prove to him she was a valuable asset to have along on his quest.

Although it had been almost five years since his last trip to Barstow, Derek didn't think it had changed all that much. A little bigger, a little noisier, with the frenetic, disorganized energy of a place that had grown far larger than it ever should be and still hadn't quite figured out what to do about it.

The travel advisor on his handheld gave him a list of possible places to stay, and he chose one not too far from the stratport, a hotel he'd never heard of but which had a good rating. Not that that necessarily meant much; it was common knowledge that those ratings tended to be based more on how much graft passed hands to inflate the recommendations rather than on an establishment's actual merit.

But when they got out of the cab and went into the hotel lobby, he was reassured by what he saw—gleaming travertine floors, walls painted a glossy slate blue, front desk of rough-polished aluminum. High end, but not over the top. The desk was manned by real people, and within fifteen minutes he and Cassidy had a room and were headed up in the elevator.

Since it was otherwise unoccupied, he felt it safe to say, "Sorry there weren't any suites available."

She lifted an eyebrow. "Well, that place in Chicago was impressive, I'll admit…but did you really think we needed to have separate bedrooms?"

Damn. He still wasn't used to her forthrightness. Most of the women he'd known would never have come out and said such a thing so baldly. "I didn't want to presume—"

A laugh as she shook her head and gave him a mock-annoyed look. "You're not presuming. But maybe I am?"

"No," he said at once, wanting to shoot that idea down before it even had a chance to get started. "I—that is, I wouldn't mind a repeat of that night on board the ship."

"Good," she said with a wicked grin. Then she put her hand on her stomach. "Although I think you'll need to feed me first."

"That I can do."

They got out of the elevator and went to their room, which was located about halfway down the corridor. It looked back over the city, showing the sprawl of downtown, the shimmering high-rises, the mountains on almost every side, closer to the north and east, much farther away to the south and west, those ranges hiding the view of drowned Los Angeles. Otherwise, it was much like pretty much every other hotel room he's stayed in when in Normerica—large bed; small table with two chairs; a convenience station with a coffeemaker, infrared heating unit, compact refrigerator; a shower nicely outfitted with faux-stone tile and a separate dressing area.

Just as he was stowing his suitcase in the closet, the door chimed. Cassidy shot him a puzzled look, and he lifted his shoulders before going to answer it. Waiting outside was a small room service mech.

"For you," it said, a tray extending from its side. On the tray rested a thin plastic envelope.

Mystified, he said, "Thanks," and removed the envelope before shutting the door again. The envelope had a small bio-sensitive square holding it closed, and he placed his thumb on it. Immediately the envelope opened, and several pieces of plastic and actual paper slid out.

"What is it?" Cassidy asked.

"Looks like our fake credentials. Probably our sponsor was waiting to see which hotel we checked into so he would know where to send everything."

"Impressive," she remarked, casting a quick glance over the contents of the envelope.

It was an audacious plan, actually, but one that made sense. Faking government credentials was nearly impossible, but pretending to be staff from the biggest vid-news network gave him and Cassidy a reason for traveling to China without putting them under too much scrutiny. And lord knows scrutiny was the one thing they needed to avoid at all costs.

He supposed he should be glad that their benefactor was covering all possible angles, but there was still something a little disconcerting about all that smooth, behind-the-scenes efficiency. But he supposed he should let that go for now. First things first.

"Still hungry?" he inquired, knowing exactly what her answer would be.

"Starving."

So he said "Margarita's" into the handheld, and it gave him a quick map and an estimated trip time. They were actually so close that he thought they could walk. It would feel good after so many hours cramped up in the maglev.

"Margaritas?" Cassidy inquired. "Do they have those here, too?"

"No—that is, yes, they do, but 'Margarita's' is also the name of the restaurant where we're going."

"Does Margarita's have margaritas?"

"Of course," he said, offering his arm. "Not up to Tucson standards, but I think they'll do."

She looped her own arm through his, then said, "Lead the way."

It was a pleasant early autumn day, the temperatures barely touching 25 C, a fresh breeze moving over the high desert town—desert no longer, although people still referred to it that way. He found it fascinating to watch Cassidy's face as she looked at the shops and restaurants they passed, at the people hurrying to and from their places of work, at the hundreds of different makes and models of aircars that filled the streets. These were all commonplaces he took for granted, but aside from brief glimpses in Chicago and Tucson, this was her first real introduction to life down on Gaia. Maybe it felt more real now, since they were striding along the sidewalk instead of being removed from everything in the back seat of a cab.

In the early twenty-third century, some large towns had installed moving walkways, but then protests were made about them taking away the charm of a city—not to mention being detrimental to health and fitness—and so they'd all been torn out. The sidewalk they traversed now was not so different from those made centuries ago, although the invention of duracrete had made them virtually maintenance-free.

Around them he heard Anglic and Spaniola and the odd snippet of Nippon and Szechuan, as a good many of the Cloud's refugees had ended up here in addition to the area around Tucson. Normerica's official language was Anglic, but that didn't keep people from speaking the language of their forebears around others in their family or extended social group. He could speak Spaniola and Nippon, and had a smattering of Szechuan, although he was much better at reading than speaking it. Being able to read signs had come in handy when he was working in Hunan Province, although of course there was no one around to speak Szechuan to these days.

But that only made his thoughts turn to the devastation he'd seen there, and he didn't want to think about that right now, not on a day as lovely as this, not with a woman as beautiful as Cassidy Evans by his side. The breeze was picking up her hair and blowing strands of it around her face, causing her to constantly reach up to brush them aside, but she didn't seem annoyed. No, she appeared fascinated, as if she'd never had to manage the wind blowing her hair in her face before.

He supposed she hadn't, not if she'd spent her entire life shipboard or in Luna City. In that domed settlement, everything was carefully regulated and controlled. No fresh September breezes there, that was for sure.

After a walk of some ten minutes, they arrived at Margarita's. It was set back a little from the street, with a large open courtyard area where one could dine *al fresco* if the weather permitted.

Cassidy gaped at the metal tables and chairs. "Do people eat outside here?"

"Sure, when the weather's pleasant. Would you like to? There's a table over there under the pergola where there's some shade."

Her brows drew together at the word "pergola," and he realized she'd probably never heard it before. But when she saw the spot he'd indicated, still out in the fresh air but protected by a wooden structure with bougainvillea vines covering it, she nodded. "That looks beautiful."

They went and took their seats, and a minute or so later a young woman who looked like she was probably working her way through the university came and brought them their menus, along with some water. Although many restaurants had taken to sending their bill of fare directly to patrons' handhelds, or used heads-up displays next to their tables, Derek had always liked the places that did it the old-fashioned way, with a menu printed on real paper and backed with cardboard or faux leather. It made the food seem more real, somehow.

Cassidy was frowning as she stared at the menu, obviously confused by the unfamiliar dishes.

"Do you want me to order?" he asked in an undertone. "Normally I wouldn't presume, but...."

A look of relief passed over her features. "That's probably a good idea. Otherwise, I'd end up ordering dessert for the main dish or something."

Smiling, he asked for a couple of house margaritas, and then chilaquiles for Cassidy and chicken enchiladas for himself. That way they could share a bit, if she wanted to taste something different. And, if she still had room after that, the best flan on this planet or any other.

The server took the menus away, promising that the margaritas and water would be out in a few minutes, then went back inside the restaurant.

"So...." Cassidy began after sipping at her water. "What now?"

Part of him wanted to leave the question of their next move aside for the moment, to simply sit here and feel the wind on his face, smell the faint aroma of spices and warm oil from inside the restaurant, but he knew that would only be wasting their time. He glanced around, saw that they were the only ones sitting outside, mainly because it was now almost two and so past the time most people would be taking a break for their midday meal.

"Put out an SOS," he replied, then dug in his pocket and got out his handheld. Although there was no one around him, he thought it was prudent to type out his question rather than use text to speech. After pulling up his last conversation with their benefactor, he tapped in the message, *In Barstow, need help with biometrics. Thank you,* then sent it.

"Do you think they're really going to keep bailing us out?" Cassidy asked, her tone wry.

"They have so far. Otherwise, we're going to be in trouble. I've visited Barstow before, but I was here for academic conferences, not looking up ident-scrubbers."

"Too bad," she remarked. "That probably would've been more useful."

Derek could tell from the gleam in her eye that she was joking, and so he merely lifted his shoulders. It was during that lull in the conversation the waitress returned with their drinks, and she set them down, said their food would be ready shortly, and disappeared again. It seemed obvious enough that she wasn't in the mood to loiter or ask too many questions, which was fine by him. He really didn't want anyone overhearing what he and Cassidy had to say to one another.

His handheld beeped, and he looked down to see a new message. *Working on it. Will get back to you soon.*

Thanks, he typed in return before sliding the handheld into his pocket. He looked up at Cassidy, who was watching him, gaze expectant.

"So?"

"Looks like he—or she, or they—hasn't given up on us yet. I assume we'll be contacted again when they have something. In the meantime, enjoy your margarita."

She hadn't touched it yet, was obviously waiting for him to be ready. Then she reached out and wrapped her fingers around the stem and lifted the glass in the air. "To tilting at windmills," she said.

The reference surprised him, but he raised his glass as well and clinked it against hers. "To dreaming the impossible dream."

A grin, and then she swallowed some of her margarita, eyes widening as she did so. "Damn…that is really good."

"You sound surprised."

"I suppose I am." She drank some more, then set down her glass. "Gaia is surprising me. I thought it was crowded and over-regulated, and no one ever got time to enjoy anything because everyone was working all the time, but…."

"Like most over-generalizations, that's partly true… but only partly." He allowed himself another swallow of his margarita, savoring the sweet-sour flavor and the warm, aromatic undercurrent of tequila. "People do tend to work long hours, and there are cameras everywhere, watching much of what they do. On the other hand, there is still open land and trees and flowers and…."

"And margaritas," she finished for him, sipping at her drink again.

"Not everywhere, but in this part of the world, definitely."

For a moment she was silent, appearing to savor her margarita, and he wondered if he should warn her to slow down, that tequila could sneak up on you, especially on an empty stomach. But she was a grown woman and could make her own decisions. Besides, she'd be counteracting the tequila with some chilaquiles in the very near future.

"I think I get it now," Cassidy said, but she didn't get any farther than that, as the server came back with their food.

"Anything else?" she asked brightly, although it seemed clear that she hoped there wouldn't, in fact, be anything else.

"I'm fine," Derek told her, and Cassidy chimed in,

"No, I'm good."

After they were alone again, Derek prompted, "What do you get?"

"Why you're fighting so hard for this. Why you didn't just pack it in and let me take you away to someplace that doesn't have an extradition treaty with Gaia."

"Because of the margaritas?" he quipped, although he could tell from her expression that she didn't appreciate the joke.

"Because of the margaritas and restaurants like this and all that green land we rode through. And those purple mountains around Tucson. The way the city lights reflected on the water at Lake Michigan. All of that."

He looked at her, and his heart broke a little. Because that was exactly it. For all its flaws, this was his world, and abandoning it would have left a scar on his soul. And that was also why he wanted so badly for the truth to be known, because he understood that most people had no idea what their government was actually doing, save the usual propaganda about keeping Gaia safe while increasing its wealth and power in ever-expanding colonies throughout the galaxy. Maybe he would end up changing nothing, but at least he would have made the attempt.

For Cassidy to look at him and understand that, to realize what was so important to him—well, he'd never been with anyone before who had that kind of insight. Perhaps it was only her perspective as an outsider that allowed her to see things in an entirely different light… but he didn't think so. Not entirely, anyway. And that made the situation a lot more difficult, because he understood now, more than ever, how special she was, and how much he wanted to survive all this. Not merely because of a need for vindication, but because he wanted a future with her in a way that he'd never wanted one with any other woman.

"Yes, because of all that," he replied quietly. "And a lot more."

Their gazes locked, and he could see the hope and need and worry in her because it so clearly echoed what they were both feeling. Then she broke the contact and gave a half-hearted laugh. "I suppose we'd better eat this before it gets cold."

"Yes," Derek said. "I suppose we should."

FIFTEEN

THEY DID EAT, AND THE FOOD WAS AMAZING TO CASSIDY, layered with so many different flavors and textures that she wasn't sure she'd ever be able to identify what they all were. Derek ordered a second round of margaritas, and somehow they'd both known to let the conversation flow to more casual subjects—the food, the places he'd traveled, the way he'd spent the holidays at his maternal grandmother's house, acquiring her love for the cuisine of the area, as it sounded like his mother's family had lived in the Tucson area for generations.

"That's how I learned to speak Spaniola," he said, as they lingered over some divine, rich dessert he called flan. "My mother only used Anglic, but my *abuelita*— my grandmother—she wanted me to have something from that side of the family."

What was it like to have that kind of history, to know that your people had lived somewhere for hundreds and hundreds of years? Cassidy couldn't begin to imagine it. True, her father had boasted sometimes about their Welsh heritage, about how the people of that land had been great warriors and poets, but he'd certainly never bothered to take his daughter there so she could see for herself. Then again, that would have been violating his "don't set foot on Gaia" policy. Had he been running from something, or was it simply that he didn't want to go back to a place which reminded him of where he'd met his long-lost wife?

Cassidy had forced her thoughts away from such things, as there wasn't much she could do about it at this stage of the game. Better to concentrate on Derek's face and the sound of his voice, then take a rather wobbly walk with him back to their room, where she was fairly certain of what was going to happen next.

And that turned out to be the case, because once they were inside, he went and immediately opaqued the windows, then turned back to her and pulled her against him, his mouth tasting of the creamy sweetness of flan and the tang of margaritas. She wasn't sure who reached out to undo the fastenings of the other's clothing first, and it didn't really matter—the garments fell to the floor with a sort of dreamlike flutter, and then she and Derek were on the bed, hands reaching out to touch the other, to break the tension that had been building for the past day or so.

She wanted to taste all of him, and so she took him into her mouth, caressing him with her tongue, teasing him to the brink, until he let out a laugh that was half groan and pushed her up against the pillows, fingers stroking her, moving into her, and that wasn't the only thing that was moving, since he began to kiss his way down her stomach until his tongue reached where his fingers had been only a few seconds earlier.

Nothing to do then but let him make love to her with his mouth, wrenching a climax from her even as she reached up to grab one of the pillows and muffle her cries with it—after all, she didn't know how thin the walls in this hotel might be. As the orgasm continued to ripple through her, he moved, pushing against her, sliding into her, hips rocking in a rhythm that seemed to come naturally to them, even though this was only their second time together.

She could feel him tensing, could feel him reach his own climax, the heat of his orgasm within her. Just that sensation at her core was enough to make her come again, and she let it run through her, bring every nerve ending to sudden, flaring life as she wrapped her legs around him and pulled him even farther in, wanting to hold him there, to keep him inside her for as long as possible.

Eventually they did break apart, but only so they could reach out and hold the other close, until they fell asleep like that, sated with food and drink and sex.

The beeping of Derek's handheld woke them eventually, and Cassidy pushed herself up on her elbows, blinking and trying to reorient herself. A vid-screen was installed on the wall across from the bed, and in the lower corner, green numerals were blinking "19:48." So they'd been asleep for some hours.

Derek managed to push away the covers and stumble over to retrieve his pants and the handheld concealed in one of the pockets. "It's them," he said briefly after looking at the screen. He flicked a button, then said, "I'm here."

From where she sat in bed, Cassidy couldn't see the message. Maybe she should have gotten up and gone to take a look, but she figured Derek would tell her soon enough. Besides, it felt so nice in here. She hadn't even gotten a chance to enjoy the bed at the hotel in Chicago.

"Got it," Derek said. "And they're expecting us?" A pause, and he added, "We can be there in half an hour."

We can? she thought blearily, but nonetheless she forced herself out of bed and tottered off to the bathroom, where she set about freshening herself up as best she could without taking a shower. A minute or so later, Derek came to stand in the doorway of the bathroom, watching as she set down her lip color and then ran a brush through her hair.

"Looks like you figured out that we have a command performance," he said.

"It sounded that way," she replied, attempting to mimic his casual tone. Never mind that they'd both been panting and moaning in each other's arms only a few hours earlier. "So what's the plan?"

"Our sponsor has a contact for us, someone who can take care of our little biometrics problem. Once that's settled, we'll see about booking passage to China."

"About that," Cassidy said, then hurried on when she saw a flicker of dismay cross his features, "are there even that many flights there? I was always under the impression that the only people going in and out were scientists, engineers, government contractors...you know, people like you."

"It's true," he agreed. "But there are people going back and forth in an official capacity, and Barstow stratport is the natural departure point for the west coast of Normerica, so there's usually at least one leaving every day. I checked, and it goes out tomorrow morning around nine hundred. We need to be on it."

"And no one is really going to question our particular 'official capacity'?" she inquired, giving her hair one last flick of a brush. Nowhere near as glossy as she'd appeared in Chicago, but she supposed that wasn't too much of a problem. Ident-scrubbers couldn't be all that picky.

"I doubt it. All the news agencies send people over from time to time, even if the only thing most of them do is hang out in Shanghai and drink, then send back fake reports about how well GARP is handling everything."

"Typical," she said, and he couldn't help grinning.

"Well, I suppose they have to do something to justify their salaries. Anyway, the scrubbers are expecting us, so we should get going."

"I'm ready," Cassidy told him, and hoped that wasn't a lie.

Derek didn't know why he'd expected the identity-scrubbers to be located in some back-alley warehouse or dingy apartment in one of Barstow's less reputable neighborhoods. Too many cop vids when he was a child, he supposed, before one of his parents came along and told him he should be watching something more educational. Even when he hadn't been allowed to watch his fill, those sorts of shows could color your imagination for years to come.

In reality, the address they'd been given was in a glossy high-rise building, one that contained a number of data-related businesses. Because he had no idea whether the scrubbers had subverted the security in the entire building, Derek had cautioned Cassidy on the way over that they shouldn't discuss anything of their reasons for being there while in the public areas of the high-rise. They should be safe once they were inside the suite the scrubbers were using, but until then, it was smarter to keep their mouths shut.

She'd understood at once, and stood quietly at his side as they went up to the tenth floor, then followed the signs to a door near the end of the corridor. The glowing hologram on the door said that the organization in question was called PLM Enterprises, but that didn't give much indication as to the true nature of its business.

His finger didn't even make contact with the touch pad by the entrance before the door opened and an unsmiling young woman in a severe-looking suit stared out at them. "We've been waiting for you," she said, and something in her tone seemed to indicate that they weren't very happy about it, either.

Nonplussed, Derek followed her into the office, Cassidy only a pace behind them. The door shut on its own, and they all walked down an austere hallway unrelieved by a single picture or wall sculpture. At the end of that corridor was a set of double doors. The young woman opened the one on the right and said, "Go on in."

There didn't seem to be anything to do except follow her instructions. Derek entered the chamber, which was large and far warmer and darker than the rest of the office suite. Here, the walls had been painted a dark red, and everywhere were banks of computers, vid-screens, heads-up displays…and a slightly more ominous-looking screened-off section in one corner, which was where he guessed the retinal and thumbprint alterations were done.

A chubby Hispanic man in his late forties, not much taller than Cassidy, came out from behind the screen. The loose-fitting clothing he wore somehow made him look even chubbier. Unlike his assistant, he smiled when he saw Derek and Cassidy, then said, "Right on time. This won't take long."

"It won't?" Cassidy asked, sounding dubious. Her gaze shifted to the screened-off area and then moved back to the stranger.

"No. And it won't hurt, either." Incongruously, he winked. "If I may have the I.D.s you're currently using?"

Derek removed the wallet he'd purchased back in Chicago from his jacket pocket, then extracted the I.D. Cassidy did more or less the same thing, retrieving hers from the bag she carried. The strange man, who didn't seem inclined to introduce himself—probably just as well—gave them a quick once-over, murmured "nice work," and slipped them into the breast pocket of the pale blue lab coat he wore.

"Who'd like to go first?"

Neither of them said anything. Cassidy shifted her weight from one foot to the other, looking even more uncomfortable, so Derek said, "I will." He glanced over at her and added, "Nothing to it."

"So you say," she replied. But he could see the way she fidgeted with the strap of the bag she carried and guessed that she was less than thrilled by the prospect of having someone poking at her eyeballs.

It wasn't something he looked particularly forward to, but if that was what it took to get them on a stratliner and bound for China without inviting any unwanted attention, so be it. "Let's do this," he told the stranger.

Another one of those cherubic smiles, and the man led Derek behind the screened-off area, where there was the sort of reclining chair you'd see in a dentist's office, along with a variety of other equipment he didn't recognize. The stony-faced young woman who'd let them in was standing there as well, although Derek couldn't quite figure out where she'd come from. A door on the far side of the cavernous room, he supposed. Now she was wearing a pale blue lab coat as well, covering the suit.

"Fingers first," said the man, and before Derek could even react, the woman had taken his left hand, smeared some icy-cold liquid across his fingertips, then set about applying what appeared to be a complete set of false prints to his fingers. This took her only a minute or so, and then she shifted to his other side and did the same thing to his right hand.

Once she was done, the unnamed man, who Derek assumed was in charge, picked up one hand, then the next, peering at the doctored fingertips the way Derek had seen his colleagues staring at field samples they'd collected. "Looks good," the man murmured. "Let's test it."

The young woman retrieved a portable biometric scanner and held it out toward Derek. "Place your thumb on this."

He did as requested, and immediately the words "Philip Chung, 34, Santa Fe" flickered into existence above the scanner. All the information already connected to the false I.D., which seemed to have been joined flawlessly to the fake fingerprints he'd been given.

"So far, so good," said the man. "Next step. I'll have to put these drops in your eyes…."

Derek did his best not to blink as the stranger let a precise drop of clear fluid fall into one eye, then the other. This was the part he really hadn't been looking forward to; he'd never required surgery to correct his vision, so he'd never had much experience with people poking around his eyes. But he held himself still as the young woman approached on his left side, holding a tray on which rested a clear plastic receptacle. In that receptacle were two filmy objects that he guessed were his new retinas. He swallowed and forced himself to stare up at the ceiling.

Some tough guy you are, he thought, keeping his gaze fixed on the flat, pale yellow surface. *You can float in vacuum, break a man's fingers one by one, and crack an arm with a judo kick when necessary, but you can't look at a few pieces of artificially grown tissue?*

He decided he couldn't.

There was a smile playing around the chubby man's lips, one that seemed to indicate he'd noticed Derek's squeamishness and was amused by it. But he didn't say anything, only gestured for the young woman to move closer. Then, so quickly Derek barely noted the movement, he used a delicate instrument to retrieve one of the retinas before depositing it in Derek's left eye. A twinge, and the man went on to duplicate the process, attaching the retina so quickly that it was over before Derek had time to react.

"Now blink," the man instructed. "First the left eye, then the right."

Derek did as he was told. Everything felt fine, which seemed odd to him. He would've thought he'd notice something different.

"How's your vision? Any blurriness?"

"No," Derek replied, giving a quick glance around the screened-off area. There didn't seem to be any material change in how he saw the world.

"Excellent." The man beamed. "Test the eye, Alice," he said, and once again the assistant stepped up, this time with a retinal scanner. It flashed the same information the thumbprint reader had. The man nodded in satisfaction before telling Derek, "You can get up now and send Ms. Whitcomb in."

It was somewhat disconcerting to hear the scrubber using Cassidy's assumed name, but maybe he was saying, in a subtle way, that they needed to get used to those names, to only use them, to leave Derek and Cassidy behind, as one slip-up could be fatal. "Thanks," Derek replied, pushing himself up off the operating chair. For just a second he thought he noted a slight dizziness, but that could've been his imagination.

When he went out into the main room, he saw Cassidy sitting in one of the chairs there, flipping through what looked like newsfeeds on her handheld. The expression of relief that crossed her face when she saw him was somewhat warming, although it was possible the relief was just as attributable to the procedure appearing to be harmless as the fact that he'd escaped unscathed.

"Your turn," he told her.

She nodded, but as she went to step past him to the makeshift surgery, he reached out and took her hand. "It'll be fine. Over before you know it."

Her fingers squeezed his slightly, a gentle pressure. "I know. But thanks."

Then she was gone, disappearing behind the screen. Derek could hear the soft murmur of voices back there, then quiet. To occupy himself, he double-checked the stratliner departures from Barstow, but the schedule hadn't changed. Since it seemed they were good to go, he went ahead and booked two seats for him and Cassidy. Not in first class, though; the networks might pay a premium to have their top talent shuttled around, but they definitely wouldn't spring for that sort of thing for a lowly research team.

Just as he was wrapping up the reservations, Cassidy appeared, looking slightly bleary-eyed but otherwise fine. "So you survived," he remarked, standing up and slipping the handheld into his pocket.

"More or less." She blinked. "It feels strange."

"It does?" he asked, alarm bells going off in his head. "Maybe you should have him look at your eyes again. It's not supposed to feel any different at all."

In answer, she gave him a deprecating smile and replied, "No, I didn't mean it that way, only that I'm not used to having anyone do anything to my eyes, so it feels…odd. I have a feeling my eyes feel off to me because everything seems the same, and my brain is telling that it shouldn't be."

"You'll get past that," the scrubber said, peeling the self-skinning latex gloves he'd been wearing first from one hand, then the other, and tossing them in a nearby waste receptacle.

"So what do we owe you?" Derek asked as he began to pull the credit voucher from his wallet.

"Nothing."

Cassidy shot the man a mystified look. "What?"

"It's on the house. Free. Gratis. If it's true that what you're up to is going to give the Consortium the mother of all black eyes, then the least I can do is give you a few free retinas and fingerprints."

Some part of Derek wanted to protest, but after looking at the uncharacteristically grim set of the chubby man's mouth, he decided to let it go. "Well, thank you for that. We appreciate it."

"Very much," Cassidy chimed in.

"And I appreciate you appreciating it," the man said. "Now, Alice, if you could show our guests out?"

The unsmiling woman nodded, and led Cassidy and Derek back out to the entrance to the suite. "Have a better one," she said, before entering the code to open the door.

Derek almost wanted to grin at the young woman, just to see how she would react, but decided against it. Instead, he just said, "You, too," and went out into the corridor, Cassidy right behind him. She shot him a questioning look, but he only shook his head and cast a significant glance upward, indicating the hidden but still most likely present security equipment.

A nod, and the two of them went back to the lifts, headed outside, and called for an autocab. It pulled up only a few minutes later. Even though the back seat offered an illusion of privacy, Derek knew that impression was specious at best. They'd have to wait until they were back at the hotel before they could talk…*really* talk.

Now, though, he was startled but happy to feel Cassidy slide over to get closer to him, have her rest her head on his shoulder. "I'm tired," she murmured. "I think those margaritas are catching up with me."

Margaritas and enthusiastic sex, followed by a fun little chaser of minor surgery to doctor your identity. He couldn't blame her for being tired. Weariness began to catch up to him as well; he could feel it in the slump of his shoulders, now that it seemed a few milestones were behind them. Yes, tomorrow was going to be a challenge, and he had no idea what awaited them in China, but he decided it was better to wait and see what happened rather than rile up his brain with a baker's dozen of manufactured scenarios, none of which might actually come to pass.

"It's been a long day," he agreed. This sort of exchange seemed safe enough, the sort of thing any couple might share while taking a cab ride back to their hotel late at night. "We'll get a good night's sleep, and then we'll be ready for our flight tomorrow."

At his words she shifted a bit, moving so she could look up into his face. Despite the shadows he could see under her eyes, a hint a smile played around her mouth. "Okay...but I'm not sure I want to spend all that time sleeping."

A rush of warmth went through him, and he marveled that she could still be so willing after everything they'd faced lately. Not that he was going to say no. "I think we can arrange that," he said, dropping a kiss on top of her head and pulling her closer.

He wouldn't let himself wonder what he possibly could have done to deserve such a woman.

SIXTEEN

AFTER RETURNING TO THE SUITE, THEY DID MAKE LOVE once more, and almost immediately afterward Cassidy felt herself falling into a deep, deep sleep. Her last coherent thought before she drifted into darkness was that she hoped Derek had remembered to set the alarm on his handheld, because there was no way in hell she'd wake up on time otherwise.

Apparently he had, since it began a strident beeping at precisely six-fifteen, far earlier than she wanted to get up. She moaned and pulled one of the extra pillows over her head in a vain attempt to blot out the annoying sound. Almost at once she heard a muffled chuckle, and Derek plucked the pillow away from her.

"We have to be there an hour before the flight leaves to check in."

"Just another reason why I miss having my own ship," she grumbled. Having to follow someone else's schedules and rules was definitely no fun. But since the Zephyr-class ship was still sitting back in Chicago and the Avalon was gone forever, she didn't have much choice but to push herself out of bed. Now that she was a little more awake, she was able to focus more clearly on Derek, who stood a few feet away, wearing only a pair of loose-fitting pants and with his hair slightly damp, which seemed to indicate that he'd already showered. A flicker of warmth kindled within her, and she knew it wouldn't take much to fan that spark into a raging fire.

Unfortunately, she really couldn't afford the time to give in to that urge, not if she wanted a proper shower when she could still get one.

"It's not fair, you walking around like that," she remarked, digging in her luggage for a clean pair of panties. "Positively distracting."

"Sorry," he replied, although he didn't sound very contrite.

"Please tell me you've built some time for breakfast into this ungodly schedule of yours at least."

"I have, or I would've let you sleep until seven. But we need to keep things moving."

Despite his bare torso, he looked very brisk, very businesslike. So she knew it was better to shower quickly and allow enough time to pack and eat, especially since she had no idea what would be available once they got to Hunan Province. She sort of doubted there was anything like Margarita's in that once-thriving region.

Although her thoughts couldn't help wandering to what it might have been like to share the shower with Derek, she still enjoyed herself, marveling at the feeling of the seemingly endless flow of water over her bare body, the sweet scent of the shampoo and creamy lather of the soap the hotel had provided. And since the bathroom here also had a molecular hair-setter, she gave herself another headful of long, loose waves before wrapping a towel around herself and going out to get dressed.

"That'll never work," he remarked as she plucked a fresh shirt and pair of pants from her suitcase.

"What won't work?" she responded, glancing down at the clothes she held. They seemed simple and comfortable, the perfect thing to wear on a long flight.

"You looking like that. Everyone's going to think you're one of the news anchors instead of only a member of the research crew."

The off-hand comment oddly pleased her, but she managed to shrug and say, "I kind of doubt that. But thanks."

Derek smiled and finished buttoning his shirt. His own suitcase was sitting open on a rack at the foot of the bed, and as she watched, he folded the lounge pants he'd been wearing earlier and put them away. The bathroom had been conspicuously clear of his own toiletries, so Cassidy assumed he'd packed them once he was done.

A quick glance at the chronometer on his wrist, and then he asked, "How soon will you be ready?"

"Ten minutes, max. I want to throw on some makeup, and then I'll close everything up and be good to go."

She proceeded to do just that, not bothering with much more than some lip color and a quick flick of the eyelash darkener. Back on the *Avalon,* she wouldn't have done even that much, but she was going out in public now and figured she'd better look as if she'd made some sort of attempt at being presentable.

Judging by the way Derek was gazing at her as she finished packing, she had an idea that she might be a little bit more than merely presentable. That was fine, though. Being on the receiving end of such open admiration was a new sensation for her, but she wasn't going to lie and try to tell herself she didn't enjoy it.

"Ready," she told him, quite unnecessarily, as latching her suitcase shut was indication enough that she was done with her preparations.

"Good. There's a restaurant right here in the hotel, so I figured we could eat there, save some more time."

Since she didn't have any better alternative to offer, she nodded and went on out to the hall, letting him perform one last inspection of the room to make sure they hadn't left anything behind. Apparently satisfied, he closed the door behind him, and then they took the elevator downstairs.

"Are we going to eat first and then check out, or vice versa?" she inquired.

"We're already checked out. I took care of it while you were in the shower. We can still leave our bags at the concierge if you like, but—"

"No," she broke in. For some reason that didn't feel right to her. Not that she had anything enormously valuable in her suitcase, but it was the only thing she could really call hers right now. She didn't want to leave it with strangers. Maybe it would seem odd to the staff at the restaurant for her and Derek to have their luggage with them, but so be it. The hotel was close enough to the stratport that such behavior couldn't be all that unusual.

He nodded, and they traveled the rest of the way to the ground floor in silence. The restaurant wasn't too far from the bank of elevators, and the man at the hospitality desk there didn't seem put off at all by the suitcases they carried. Instead, he guided them to a table by the window, activated the electronic menu embedded in the tabletop, and left.

Luckily, the items on the breakfast menu weren't nearly as exotic as those on the bill of fare at Margarita's, so Cassidy was able to select eggs and toast and sausage, although these all promised to be fresh, not the processed soy substitutes you got in Luna City. The setup here was more like what she was used to as well, where you pressed the touchscreen to indicate your selections, and then they'd be brought out to you by a server. She also ordered coffee, thinking that she needed it, and also that it would probably be better than anything she'd had on the Moon.

Derek made his own selections, and then he said, "We have about forty-five minutes to get to the stratport."

"Is that enough?" she asked uneasily.

"It should be. We're less than five minutes away, and places like this are used to people in a hurry. Our food should be out in no time."

He was proven correct in that, as a waiter came by with their coffee less than a minute later. Cassidy always took hers black, mostly because she never completely trusted the additives you got in the spaceport cafes she tended to frequent, and so she blew on the surface of her coffee to cool it down, watching as Derek tipped some cream—which looked real—and one small half-spoon-ful of sugar into his.

"What's the procedure like?" she inquired.

"The procedure?" he echoed, cup of coffee paused halfway to his lips.

"At the stratport. Remember, I've never flown that way."

"Nothing too bad. They'll scan your fingerprints and your retinas, check your bags. You'll also be scanned for weapons. It feels a little intrusive, but it goes quickly enough. After that we'll go to a waiting area until the flight's called. From here the trip should take about five hours. They'll feed us some kind of lunch, prob-ably, but I can't vouch for the quality, so it's good we're filling up here." Up until then his expression had been serious enough, but then his dark eyes twinkled slightly. "Anything else?"

"No," she replied, wishing she had more experience with all these things so she wouldn't feel like such a rube all the time. "That seems pretty basic."

"It is. But they are very security conscious, so...."

He let the words trail off, but she knew what he meant. There was no way they could have possibly gotten on board a stratcaster without their little visit to the identity scrubbers the night before. Even thinking about it now, Cassidy felt a nervous flutter in her stomach. Yes, both her prints and her retina had been tested and apparently passed, but that was with the scrubber's equipment. Would the modifications he'd made really stand up to a real-world test?

Well, she supposed they were about to find out.

The food arrived then, and she made herself eat, forcing her thoughts away from what might lie ahead. It was harder than she'd thought it would be, partly because they had a view from the restaurant of one of the runways at the stratport, and she saw several of the sleek silver craft taking off and landing. In a little more than an hour, she and Derek would be on one of them.

He seemed to guess at the reason for her silence, or maybe he was worried that the hotel restaurant's surveillance might pick up their conversation if they spoke about anything too suspect. Whatever it was, he ate quietly, too, cleaning his plate, and Cassidy did the same. As he'd said, better to eat now when the food was good. And it was good, hot and fresh. Funny how little things like that could make such a difference.

When they were done, Derek ran the credit voucher over the reader embedded in the table, and they were set. After collecting their suitcases, they were gone, heading to the front of the hotel and the line of autocabs waiting there for patrons.

It was another mild, sunny day, and Cassidy took a deep gulp of the fresh air before the cab door closed behind her. She couldn't help wondering if she'd ever get to breathe air that fresh again.

Despite telling himself that it would all be fine, that the scrubber obviously had known what he was doing, Derek couldn't help holding his breath as he placed his right hand down on the scanner while simultaneously looking into the retinal imager. *If this goes south, I hope Cassidy knows to get out of here and pretend she doesn't know me....*

But nothing did go wrong. The light on the scanner went green. The official manning the scanning station glanced briefly at his I.D. and the data displayed by the device, then handed Derek back his identification before saying, in a very bored tone, "Have a nice flight, Mr. Chung."

He let out a breath but didn't look back, knowing that doing so would only reveal his worry that Cassidy might not be so lucky. However, less than a minute later she was through the station as well, clutching her suitcase. "Now what?" she murmured.

"Bag check," he said, and pointed.

This part of the process was considerably less worrisome, considering neither of them had anything more incriminating in their bags than a few changes of

clothing and some necessary toiletries. After their suitcases were scanned, they were tagged and sent off to be
loaded on the stratliner, and he and Cassidy were given
electronic vouchers to reclaim their luggage at the end
of the flight.

During this whole time, he could see her trying to
look around at the stratport without appearing to really
look around. In reality, it wasn't that different from the
spaceport at Luna City, except that here you saw blue
skies and darker blue mountains instead of the bone-
bleached surface of the Moon and the eternal black of
space. But it was the same sort of architecture, functional rather than elegant, although on one wall there
was a rather attractive mural depicting the area before
climate change had altered its appearance so drastically.
The same mountains, but a true desert landscape, high-
lighted with the spiky outlines of the Joshua trees that
had once covered the area, now almost extinct.

The waiting area was likewise nondescript, rows of
chairs with dark green cushions, people looking bored
or impatient, depending on their particular reasons for
taking this flight. Here it was slightly different than in
other stratport sections, simply because no one heading
to China was going there to vacation or visit family. For
the most part, there was no one left to visit.

In recent years, though, Shanghai had begun to
bounce back, and now had a population of almost ten
thousand. Nothing compared to its glory days, when it
had teemed with millions of people, but Derek supposed

you had to start somewhere. Shanghai was their first destination, a destination shared with the scientists and engineers and support staff currently waiting along with him and Cassidy.

The men and women waiting to embark shot a few curious glances in their direction, and he could feel himself stiffening. The pool of experts going to and from China was small enough that there was always the possibility someone might know who he was. It was a calculated risk, one he couldn't avoid. But he saw no flickers of recognition from any of the people who shared the waiting area, and he realized their curiosity was more because they couldn't quite figure out who he was or why he was there.

And, he realized, with a small pang of jealousy that was quite unlike him, it was also because some of the men were looking more closely at Cassidy than he would like. Not openly ogling, but still.

In fact, one of them detached himself from the group he was with and came over to where Derek and Cassidy stood, blatantly ignoring Derek while going straight to Cassidy.

"I don't think I've seen you before," the man said, flashing what he probably thought was a charming smile at her. "Are you with GARP?"

"No," she replied calmly, as if being approached by strange men in stratports was something that happened all the time. She even flicked a lock of hair back over her shoulder, and the man's smile widened at what he seemed to think was a sort of invitation. "My partner and I are with NBN."

The barest hint of a glance in Derek's direction before the stranger returned his full attention to Cassidy. "Really? I don't think I've seen you on the vid before."

"Oh, I'm not a vid-caster. My official designation is research assistant, but just between you and me, that's a fancy name for lackey."

That remark elicited a chuckle, and Derek could feel his hackles go up. Never mind that he knew deep down Cassidy was handling this just right, that being friendly…but not too friendly…was far better than coldly shooting the guy down. Even if they had the horrible luck to be seated by him on the strat, it would only be for a few hours, and then he'd be off to his own assignment, and they'd be going on to their own far more subversive mission.

"Isn't that right, Phil?" she added, sending a sweet smile in his direction. "Of course, Phil's a senior research assistant, so I guess that makes him a senior lackey."

"Something like that," Derek agreed, although it pained him to do so. The stranger's glance in his direction was dismissive, and Derek had to quell the desire to tell the jackass that he was pretty sure he possessed just as many advanced degrees as the stranger, or more. After all, Derek didn't know him, so he had no idea whether the man was an engineer or a scientist, or maybe even support staff.

"First time going to China?" the stranger persisted.

"The first," she told him. "I'm sure it'll be quite an adventure."

"You don't know the half of it." He paused, acting as if an idea had just occurred to him, although Derek had a feeling the man had been considering the notion pretty much the whole time he'd been talking to Cassidy. "Say, if you're going to be in Shanghai for a while, you should let me show you around. This is my third trip there, and I know all the good places to go."

"Well, as appealing as that sounds," Cassidy replied, something in her tone telling Derek that she considered such a hookup only slightly more appealing than being pushed out an airlock, "we're heading out up-country almost as soon as we land. So I don't think that will work, unfortunately."

For a second or two, the stranger looked disappointed. But then he perked up, saying, "What about when you come back? I'm actually stationed in Shanghai—I'm part of the staff at the air-quality station there. So I'm very flexible."

The way he said that seemed to indicate his "flexibility" extended far beyond his schedule, and Derek had to grind his teeth and remind himself that chopping a strange man in the neck in a stratport waiting area was not a particularly good idea for anyone who wanted to remain inconspicuous.

Cassidy shifted her weight, clearly uncomfortable now. "Well, our trip is sort of open-ended, so I can't really make any commitments. But—"

The universe saved her then, as the speakers hidden in the walls came to life, saying, "Flight 89A, stratliner to Shanghai, is now boarding. Make sure you have your electronic tickets prepared for scanning."

"Thank God," Cassidy murmured to Derek after the stranger startled, then excused himself to go meet up with the rest of his team. "I was starting to think the only way to get rid of him was to knee him in the nuts."

"You and me both," he replied grimly. "You handled it well, though."

She flashed a grin at him. "Honey, believe me, this isn't the first time I've had to fend off a stranger in a spaceport. Okay, first time in a stratport, but the techniques involved aren't all that different."

In that moment he felt a warm rush of emotion go over him, one he couldn't quite identify. Admiration, tinged with amusement, but it was far more than that. She was constantly surprising him, this woman who had more or less fallen into his life, and he knew he wanted to keep being surprised by her.

Was it fair, then, for him to be dragging her halfway across the world, and for what? Some sort of vindication?

No, it was more than that. If the only thing at stake was his personal reputation, he would've taken Conrad Waite's confession and disseminated it to as many people as possible. Even that wasn't so very important. Derek knew his mother had had her belief in her son's innocence substantiated, and that would have to be enough. His father was a lost cause, but oddly, Derek found he could live with the situation if he had to. They'd been estranged even before Theo's death; the accusation of murder and resulting prison sentence had served to deepen the rift, but they certainly hadn't caused it in the first place.

Perhaps he was being naïve, but Derek believed the truth about the supposed "cleansing" of the Asian continent should be exposed. After all, he had only seen one of these processing plants. Who knew how many of them were scattered about the region, performing their grisly tasks with no one to see or know? And if he didn't try to get the word out, who would?

He felt a brush of fingers on his sleeve, and looked down to see Cassidy gazing up at him, expression troubled. "Everything okay? We really should be getting on board."

"I'm fine," he told her. "Let's do this thing."

SEVENTEEN

FLYING ON A STRATLINER HAD SOUNDED AS IF IT MIGHT be vaguely glamorous, but in reality the main passenger cabin was cramped, with not enough leg room and a seat that felt as if it should have been replaced years ago. Derek had graciously allowed her the window spot, but after takeoff and the first few minutes of flying through Gaia's atmosphere, there really wasn't all that much to see. A dark blue expanse far, far below that he told her was the Pacific Ocean, and above them the equally dark blue reaches of the upper atmosphere. She couldn't quite see the stars, and she couldn't see land. It was as if they were flying in limbo, neither here nor there.

All in all, she was looking forward to landing…or would have been, if it weren't that they'd be heading out into the wastes of China's interior, searching for the all-important evidence of the Consortium's illegal practices there. What exactly Derek intended to do with it, she wasn't sure, but it seemed as if their benefactor was extremely connected, in all possible senses of the word. Maybe Derek planned to pass the evidence on to him… or her…and see that it got sent to the right places.

Would that be enough to exonerate him? In a perfect world, maybe. In this one, it seemed more likely that it would simply provide another reason for Consortium authorities to lock him up and forget the code to his cell.

There wasn't much she could do about it now, though. She'd agreed to come along with him, and once she'd given her word, she'd see it through to the end. Anyway, she was fooling herself if she thought this was all about not breaking a promise.

A quick glance at the man sitting next to her reminded her exactly why she was here. His expression was abstracted, mouth tight as if he were thinking of something not entirely pleasant. Musing about what lay ahead of them? Probably. He knew far better than she what exactly they had to look forward to when they headed out to Hunan Province. He knew, and was going anyway, because it was the right thing to do, and Derek Tagawa was not a person to flinch from doing the right thing.

Quite a change from the men she'd encountered so far in her life. She had to wonder if her father would laugh at her for falling for some crazy-eyed dreamer, when she'd always vowed that she'd live her life alone.

A life alone. That was the last thing she wanted now.

She reached over and wrapped her fingers around Derek's hand, wanting the reassurance of his touch. Luckily, the clueless stranger who'd attempted to pick her up in the waiting area at the stratport was seated at the very front of the main passenger compartment, while she and Derek sat in the rear, so there was no chance of the man seeing her holding hands with someone who was supposed to be only a work colleague.

Derek said nothing, but she could feel him twine his fingers with hers and give the faintest of squeezes. It wasn't as if they could say anything of any import, not with strangers sitting directly in front of them and to the side. But she could feel his strength in even that quiet touch. *I'm here,* it seemed to say, and she had to content herself with that.

All the same, she hoped they would land at an inopportune time—the middle of the night would be perfect—so they'd have to find a place to stay and wait to strike out on the next leg of their journey in the morning. Maybe it was cowardly of her, but she wanted to be with him wholly before they ventured into dangerous territory. It might be the last chance she ever got to lose herself in his arms again.

Since she couldn't say any of that aloud, she had to settle for allowing her hand to rest in Derek's, to feel the warmth of his flesh against hers as they flew westward at speeds that would have been unimaginable a few centuries earlier. In that moment, she wished the stratliner weren't quite so fast. It was bringing them closer and closer to China, and she worried that, once there, they might never leave again.

Shanghai didn't seem to have changed much in the three years since Derek was last there. Possibly a little more congested, a bit noisier, but that was to be expected, he supposed. Humanity would always try to fill a void when it could. The Cloud hadn't settled as heavily here because of the ocean breezes, and people had started coming back some five decades or so after the mass dying.

For all its frenetic energy, though, the place was still struggling. Only the areas along the waterfront looked basically unscathed, as they were the first places to be cleared out and repopulated. The further inland you went, the more you saw vast districts of empty buildings, still blocked off and patrolled by Consortium forces. It was a grim sight if you allowed yourself to look…but the city's current population worked very hard not to look, to concentrate on the sections of Shanghai that were up and running again.

By the time they had reclaimed their luggage, it was almost eighteen hundred hours, local time, and Derek wondered if they should stay the night here in town. After all, he and Cassidy only had an hour or so of daylight left, which wouldn't get them very far. Something told him that they needed to keep moving, however, so after grabbing some noodles and soy at a diner in the stratport, he rented them a heavy-duty aircar, murmuring a silent prayer of thanks under his breath that once again his altered biometrics passed muster.

When he'd told her that they should press on, Cassidy had exhaled a slight breath but hadn't offered any protest. Not that she'd needed to—he'd seen the weariness and the disappointment in her eyes. He didn't ask, but he thought he knew the reason for the disappointment. After the long flight, and with dark approaching, she'd probably hoped they would stay here in Shanghai for one night at least.

"There still aren't a lot of hotels operating here in the city," he said by way of explanation as he guided the 'car through the streets, which somehow managed to be choked with traffic even though the city's population was not all that large. "I've stayed at all of the ones that are safe to stay in, and the risk of being recognized is too great. It's better if we get out of Shanghai."

She didn't protest, only stared out the 'car window at the unfamiliar streets. "How long to get to Hunan Province?"

"It's a good ways—more than a thousand kilometers, and not all the roads have been cleared yet. A day and a half, if we're lucky."

"So…." A shake of the head, and she said, "What's your plan, Derek? Are we going to sleep in here?"

That actually had been his plan. Once they were out of Shanghai, they'd be in areas controlled directly by the Consortium's peace-keeping troops. His and Cassidy's press credentials should allow them safe passage, and he'd purposely rented a large vehicle with extra ground clearance and room to stow a good number of supplies. Speaking of which….

"It's safest that way," he replied. "About an hour outside of Shanghai is a supply depot, sort of the last outpost of civilization before you enter the true wasteland. We'll get some camping equipment there, whatever we need to get us into Hunan. No one's going to think it odd that we're stocking up before we head into the waste. But…."

"But what?"

"You'll need to do the shopping while I wait in the 'car. I know there's a good chance someone at the depot will recognize me, as I've been there several times in the past. I'll make up a list and send it to your handheld."

Her expression as he told her this was dubious, to say the least, but then she forced a smile and said, "Hey, I'm fine with any excuse to go shopping."

There wasn't much comparison between shopping for designer clothing on Lakeshore Drive in Chicago and picking up survival gear in a dirty outpost on the borders of the China waste, but he recognized her remark for what it was—her way of making light of their situation, of letting him know she was okay with handling this part of the mission. Funny how he'd been thinking of it that way for quite some time. Possibly that was his mind's way of making this crazy plan seem more official, less a wild goose chase that could very well end up with both of them dead.

But no, he didn't want to think that way. Not here, not now. They'd gotten this far, which meant they at least had luck on their side.

No, not luck. He'd never much believed in luck. He did, however, very much believe in the unknown benefactor who'd provided a helping hand almost every step along the way. They hadn't heard anything from him, or her, for the past while, but Derek supposed it was because he hadn't asked for anything. If their sponsor really was tracking their I.D.s, then that person already knew they'd landed in Shanghai and rented a 'car there. No doubt he or she was sitting back and waiting to see if any more assistance was required.

Derek hoped not, but that was probably being foolishly optimistic. There were still so many things that could go wrong.

Realizing that Cassidy was staring at him, obviously expecting a reply, he said, "Just don't go crazy with the hiking boots and the gourmet SRPs."

"There's such a thing as a gourmet SRP?" she inquired, tone dubious.

"You'd be surprised. I've had a few, when the brass came to visit the station. We didn't have the luxury of a cook, so the higher-end SRPs were about the best we could do. Twice the price of the regular meals, but there's a reason for that."

She appeared to consider his comment. A lopsided smile pulled at her mouth, and then she said, "Okay...I promise I'll only buy a few. Well, maybe half. A girl's got to keep her energy up, you know."

Since there was such a teasing note in her voice, he could only shrug and say, "I suppose that's fine. Even with all the running around we've been doing, we've barely put a dent in that credit voucher."

He'd halfway expected her to make another joke in reply, but instead she nodded, expression suddenly serious. "I'm glad," she told him. "I want there to be a lot left on it so we can blow it on first-class tickets someplace really crazy when all this is over."

"Such as?"

"I'm not particular. Paris. Rome. Helsinki. Eridani." Shifting in her seat, she gave him a direct look, the kind that made an unexpected and not unwelcome heat rouse itself in his groin. "Just someplace where we can lock ourselves up in an expensive hotel and not come out of the room for days."

"Days?" he repeated, lifting an eyebrow.

"Days," she said firmly. "That's what room service is for, right?"

"True." At least, he supposed room service had been utilized in such a capacity before, although the few times he'd availed himself of it, it was only for a hurried breakfast before running off to a meeting or conference.

He had to admire her confidence, even if it was really only bravado. Giving herself something to look forward to made the more immediate future a little less frightening, or at least that was what he surmised. And he had to admit to himself that he wanted to be a part of Cassidy's future, whether it was locked up in the grandest suite in the Hotel Crillon in Paris, or settling down somewhere far away from all this madness.

Where that particular thought had come from, he wasn't sure. A life of quiet domesticity wasn't something he'd ever aspired to, but now, on reflection, he thought it might not be half bad…especially if he had someone by his side who would make sure that it might be quiet, but it would never be dull.

Good. Now they just had to get through the next few days.

The depot wasn't as large as Cassidy had imagined it, being a somewhat haphazard collection of insta-construct barracks that someone had put up years ago and which had somehow survived, even though such buildings generally had a lifespan of a decade at most. In the waning light, the place looked even more rundown, and she could feel a cold sensation churning in her gut, telling her she didn't want to go in there.

Which was silly, because Derek had already told her he'd been there several times. That was the whole point of her carrying out this errand instead. No one knew who she was. She could pop in, get the items they needed, and be right back out again with no one noticing.

At least, that was the plan. He told her to make sure her network I.D. was visible at all times, tacked to the collar of her jacket. To be safe, she pulled her hair back into a clip so there was no chance of it falling over the identification.

Knowing there was no reason to delay any longer, Cassidy got out of the 'car and strode as confidently as she could toward the building's entrance. She had to walk through some sort of screening device as she did so—checking for weapons, she guessed. But since she didn't have anything on her more dangerous than a wallet, the lights on the machine stayed serenely green.

Inside, the depot did look a little bigger than it had from the parking lot, and its organization left a bit to be desired, as she saw hiking boots stacked next to blankets, and all-weather tents dumped in a pile next to collapsible carbon-fiber bicycles. Even so, she slowly managed to gather all the items she needed, with the exception of the vid-recorder Derek had requested. She still wasn't entirely clear about that, as he could shoot footage just fine with his handheld. But she supposed the vid-recorder would produce higher-quality images, and it was more in line with the sort of equipment a news crew would have with them. Since it was a fairly expensive device, it was probably kept locked up behind the counter somewhere.

After wandering for a bit, she finally found someone manning said counter, an Asian man of indeterminate age who watched her with wary dark eyes as she approached. He asked a question in Chinese—she was sure of that much, even though she couldn't be certain of the dialect—and she shook her head.

"Sorry, I only speak Anglic."

"You looking for something in particular?" The words were heavily accented, but clear enough.

"A vid-recorder."

His gaze slid to the I.D. clipped to her collar and then back to her face. "What you need a vid-recorder for if you working for NBN?"

"My partner dropped ours," she said glibly, giving him the first lie she could think of. "He always was a klutz. And now I'm paying for it out of my credit voucher, because if the higher-ups ever find out he broke a piece of equipment that valuable, it could be his job. And mine, if they're feeling cranky enough that day."

A long silence as the man stared at her, face blank. Cassidy forced herself to not react, to remain standing there wearing what she hoped was a half-annoyed, half-amused expression. If the man asked too many questions, she didn't know what she would say. Derek hadn't warned her that she might get an in-depth grilling over something as innocuous as a vid-recorder.

"Okay," the man said at length, and she smiled, not allowing herself the relieved sigh she really wanted to make. He moved a few paces to his left and then pushed past a screen of some sort of wooden beads, disappearing into what she guessed must be a storeroom of some kind. The beads kept clacking against one another after he was gone, and something about the noise seemed to set her teeth on edge.

As she waited, she allowed herself to glance around the depot, although she wouldn't let her gaze settle on one particular patron for longer than a second or so. The place wasn't all that crowded, but there were five or six other people browsing the wares. The customers, male and female, were a mix of Asian and Caucasian, and she heard both Chinese and Anglic being spoken. None of the people there seemed to be paying any attention to her or what she was doing, however, a fact for which she was grateful. This wasn't so hard after all.

The shopkeeper or clerk or owner—Cassidy couldn't be quite sure what his exact role was—returned carrying a latching plastic case, which he set down on the counter. "All I got is last year's model," he said. "That okay?"

"As long as it takes video images, that's all we need," she said, adding, as it looked as if he was going to open the case and inspect the contents, "I'm sure it's fine. Just let me know the total for all this stuff, and we're set."

"You don't want to test it?" His tone was too flat to be openly curious, but she could tell he thought it strange that she didn't want to inspect the equipment.

"I trust you," she replied, shooting him her most winning smile.

A lift of his shoulders, and he started going through the contents of the large net shopping bag she'd been carrying, scanning each item and then setting it aside. The number in the holographic display that hovered over the register kept growing and growing, and she swallowed.

Looks like we're putting a dent in that credit voucher after all....

Cassidy didn't pretend to be an expert on Gaian prices, but she had a sneaking feeling that she was being charged a good deal more than any of these particular items were worth. Maybe he felt justified passing along some sort of surcharge because of being poised out here on the edge of the waste, or maybe he thought she was some silly Normerican with an expense account, some-one he could take advantage of. Either way, she wasn't going to protest. They needed the supplies, and it wasn't as if there was anyplace else they could go.

At the end she handed over the credit voucher and let him swipe it. She didn't bother to look at the total remaining. They still had plenty to get them wherever they wanted to go, once they were done here in China and safely away.

"You can take the bag," the shopkeeper offered, and she essayed another smile and piled all her purchases into it, at the same time wishing—as she had when she first entered the store—that they weren't quite so low-tech around here. One of the self-propelling carts she'd used back in Chicago would've been handy for hauling all this stuff around.

But obviously the owners of the depot weren't too concerned with customer satisfaction, since they were clearly the only game in town, and so Cassidy shouldered the bag and began moving toward the exit. A quick glance around told her that no one seemed to be paying any attention to her.

Some of the tension in her neck eased slightly. For some reason, she'd had this thought in the back of her mind that the Consortium authorities had put her and Derek on some "most wanted" list, getting their faces out there so the general public would be able to recognize them on sight. Silly, she knew, because although of course the Consortium was actively looking for them, it also wanted this whole business kept as quiet as possible. Broadcasting hers and Derek's faces wasn't exactly the best way to go about that.

As she was exiting the building, she accidentally grazed the shoulder of a man who was just heading inside. *Damn shopping bag,* she thought, before saying automatically, "I'm so sorry. This thing is bulkier than I thought."

He was tall and dark-haired, probably around her age, or a year or so older. "No problem," he replied, not really looking at her.

She smiled, said, "Okay, as long as I didn't knock you off your feet," and began to walk toward the 'car where Derek was waiting.

The man didn't say anything, just gave a brief abstracted nod. It was only because she risked another look back at him that she noticed he'd stopped and was staring after her, head tilted to one side, as if he had noted something familiar about her but couldn't really figure out why.

Well, that wasn't good. It was probably something as silly as her reminding him of his secondary-school girl-friend or whatever, but any kind of attention felt unwelcome right then. She hurried to the 'car and went around to the back, which Derek had already unlocked for her. After setting the bundle of supplies in the cargo area, she moved quickly to get inside the vehicle.

"Let's move," she said in an undertone, and Derek pushed the starter button immediately.

"Something wrong?" he asked, even as he began backing out of the parking space. Well, it wasn't really an official parking space, just a spot in between two other vehicles where they could fit.

"I don't know." She glanced out the window of the car, but the man had disappeared—gone inside, most likely, or at least stepped out of the pool of bright illumination at the entrance to the depot. By then it was quite dark.

Derek didn't respond at first, was busy with guiding the 'car out of the lot and onto the highway. On the way out here, he'd let the aircar drive itself, but it looked as if he wanted to be in control for this leg of the journey. After they'd put a half-kilometer or so behind them, he said, "Care to elaborate?"

"Just a feeling. I bumped into this man as I was leaving the building, and—"

"Man? What did he look like?"

Good question. She'd gotten a brief impression that he was good-looking, and that was about it. "About my age…Caucasian…dark hair. Attractive."

A flicker of dark eyes toward her, and then Derek returned his attention to the road. "Anything else?"

"Not really." She frowned, trying to remember. It was hard when she hadn't really looked at him directly. "Maybe he had blue eyes. I'm not sure. Anyway, at first he didn't seem to even notice me, but as I was walking away, he gave me this weird look, like he was trying to figure out if he recognized me or something."

Derek's fingers tightened on the steering wheel, but he sounded casual enough as he spoke. "I don't know if it was that, exactly. To be frank, there aren't a lot of women who look like you out here in the hinterlands."

The off-hand compliment made her cheeks heat a little, and then she shook her head. "No, I don't think that was it. He wasn't giving me that kind of look, if you know what I mean."

"If you say so." He shrugged. "Did he see which vehicle you got in?"

"I don't think so."

"Then we're fine. We'll put some distance between us and the depot, and then we'll find a place to park and rest for the night. The GPS shows a wood of some sort about twenty kilometers from here. That's probably a good sheltered spot."

She nodded, mostly because she didn't have any arguments she could offer at the moment. Something about the encounter with the stranger still felt off to her, but she decided to keep her misgivings to herself. After all, she was so on edge right now, she was probably reading something into what had really been an "oops" moment, and nothing else.

At least, she had to hope that's all it was.

EIGHTEEN

THEY'D FOUND SHELTER IN A STAND OF TREES, TOO meager to be called a real forest, but it was enough to hide the aircar from anyone who might be passing on the highway. One of the items Cassidy had bought at the depot was a portable sanitation unit, and so, although it wasn't quite the same as having a fully equipped bathroom, neither was it nearly as bad as having to go behind a tree and use a leaf or something equally uncomfortable.

Dinner had been a couple of the SRPs, washed down with pouches of water. Afterward, they sat on the open tailgate of the 'car and gazed at the stars. Before the Cloud, this wouldn't have been possible; China's skies had been far too choked with pollution. But now the heavens above them were clear, the stars and planets and satellites blazingly bright.

"So that's the Milky Way," Cassidy murmured. Somehow, her head had ended up on his shoulder, but Derek didn't mind too much.

"You've never seen it before?" he asked, surprised. Surely it should've been clearly visible from anywhere she traveled within the Solar System.

"Of course I have." She lifted her head then, gaze fixed on the velvety-dark skies above them. "I guess that's not what I meant. It's just that I had no idea what it would look like from down here on Gaia."

"And?"

"It's the same…but it isn't. Not as bright, but at the same time it feels as if it's shimmering more."

"Atmospheric disturbance, I would guess."

At that reply, she shifted so she could give him a mock-severe look. "You scientists—always taking the romance out of everything."

"Everything?" he inquired, and she grinned.

"Well, not everything."

She reached for him, pulling his mouth down to hers, and that was enough for him. They'd already laid out their sleeping gear in the back of the vehicle, laying down the seats to give themselves enough room, and he pushed her onto that soft surface now, hands finding the fasteners of her clothing, fingers moving over her soft warm flesh once it was freed of its shirt and jacket. She did the same, pulling off his garments and tossing them over into a corner somewhere, and then by some unspoken agreement their bodies were locked together, no foreplay this time, only a joining brought on by mutual need, as if they didn't want to waste any time before coming together again, reaffirming their decision to be with one another.

Afterward, they slept, undisturbed the sound of the wind in the trees, or the night birds calling to one another from far away. A hundred more kilometers into the waste, there wouldn't be any birds, save the ones brought in to slowly start repopulating the area, but here all was safe, the air still clean enough, the trees and grass growing as if nothing had ever come along to change the very face of the landscape.

Bright dawn woke Derek first, slanting in through the 'car's windows. He stirred, blinking, and then felt Cassidy stretch and yawn against him.

"Did we really sleep the whole night through?"

"Looks that way," he replied, adding mentally, Good thing, too…we're going to need all the energy we can get today.

After levering herself up to a sitting position, she said, "Will we make it to the station today?"

"Maybe, if we get an early enough start." He glanced at the chronometer that was still strapped to his wrist. "We're doing well. It's not even six-thirty yet."

She made a face, looking more adorable than she probably intended, with her sleep-mussed hair, the blanket pulled up to cover her nakedness. "That's way too early in my part of the universe, but I'll do what I can. Have you seen my underwear around here?"

A brief search turned up the discarded garment shoved into a corner, and she pulled on her panties and her shirt, sans bra, then slid out of the back of the vehicle, no doubt intent on using the sanitation unit. He knew she'd want some privacy for the next little while, and so he stayed where he was, scrabbling around his own discarded clothing until he located his handheld. No messages from their benefactor, which he assumed only meant that he or she was waiting in the background, not bothering to intervene unless necessary.

He pulled up the map function and did some quick calculations. If they left in the next half hour or so, then they should make it to his former research station…and the processing plant…by late afternoon. His plan was to cut off the main road before then and come in from the south, rather than the northeast, and get as much video as he could in a short period of time—say, no more than twenty minutes or so. Yes, he wanted the evidence, but he also knew the longer he and Cassidy lingered, the greater the chance that they would be caught. It should be clean enough. This vehicle shouldn't be on anyone's watch list, and as long as he didn't let anyone get close enough to recognize him, they should be fine.

Should. There was the operative word, and he knew there had been a disconcerting number of "should"s in his mental processes.

Cassidy returned, looking freshly scrubbed, the ends of her hair damp where the water she'd splashed on her face had caught them. "Well, I'd still kill for a hot shower, but I'm starting to feel almost human," she said, reaching up into the back of the 'car for her suitcase.

"You got coffee, right?" That was all he needed to feel human, or at least functional.

"Still in the bag."

He rooted around, found the pre-filled container, then flicked the tab to heat it up. This kind of coffee was only about two steps up from rocket fuel, but it did the trick. The gourmet espresso would have to wait until they were back in civilization.

While he was pulling out some clean clothes of his own, Cassidy prepped her own coffee, took a sip, and then made a face.

"I know," he said.

She just offered him a rueful grin and forced down another swallow. "Whatever doesn't kill you, I suppose."

Although she'd meant the remark as a joke, Derek couldn't help experiencing a sudden wave of foreboding. So far, quite a lot of things had tried to kill them. He could only hope no more were waiting on the road ahead.

Seeming to sense his mood, Cassidy remained silent after that, getting dressed quickly and pulling her hair back in the same clip she'd worn the day before. The sun began to rise, burning off some of the morning mists that had settled around them, and Derek could feel the beginnings of what promised to be a damp, hot day. He wondered if Cassidy had any experience with humidity.

Of course not. Up until now, every place she's lived has been rigorously climate-controlled.

It crossed his mind to warn her, but he decided against it. She had enough to worry her, and maybe the day wouldn't turn out to be as hot as he feared. Besides, the heat would only be a problem when she went out-doors, as their rented vehicle had very good cooling control.

They climbed into the 'car, and he turned off the self-navigation system. He wanted to be in control in case they came across anything the vehicle's admit-tedly limited computerized brain couldn't handle. It was designed for a multitude of road and weather condi-tions, but armed pursuit was something quite outside its programming.

Cassidy remained silent for some time, watching the green landscape outside pass by. At length she remarked, "I'd thought it would be dry and dead."

"It was, once," he replied, keeping his eyes on the road, which had narrowed down to one lane in either direction. This was all the area required, as hardly any-one came this way anymore. "The Cloud devastated the vegetation in the area as well. But it's bounced back bet-ter than we'd hoped. It's helping to clean the air just as much as our equipment is."

"If that's the case, why is it all still empty? I'd think that if there's enough decent air here to support plants—"

"Well, the plants want CO2, not oxygen. Besides that, there are still some heavier elements around that can play havoc with human respiratory systems if they're exposed to them for too long. Even those of us stationed here couldn't be here indefinitely—we had to be rotated in and out every eighteen months."

A nod, and she fell silent again, watching the landscape pass by. The bright green of the semi-tropical vegetation had to look even more alien to her than the desert landscape outside Tucson or the scrub junipers and live oaks growing around Barstow. At length she asked, "Is that why you're not worried about running into Liam? The eighteen-month rotation?"

He shook his head even as he slowed the vehicle slightly to navigate around a two-meter sinkhole that had opened up in the road. Aircars could manage some ground perturbations, but it was always better to give them a wide berth when possible. No one was coming toward them in the other lane; in fact, he hadn't yet seen a single vehicle. That didn't strike him as particularly unusual, as sometimes days would pass before any visitors came to the GARP facility where he'd been stationed. The Consortium actively discouraged traffic in this part of the world. The stray thought reminded him that they'd be coming up on a checkpoint in an hour or so. The personnel there were switched out often enough that he doubted they'd run into anyone who might recognize him, but he still wasn't looking forward to running that particular gauntlet.

Eyes still fixed on the road, Derek replied, "My mother told me that Liam had requested a transfer while I was awaiting trial. Too many bad memories at the facility, I suppose. Anyway, last she'd heard, he'd gone to the monitoring station in the Antarctic."

"Well, that's one way of getting away from it all."

"You might say that." Under normal circumstances, Cassidy's wry tone might have made him smile, but now, doing so only would seem to mock Liam's pain at his husband's death. Derek could only hope that Liam had managed to move on during the intervening years. "Even if he's not in Antarctica anymore, it's safe to assume that he won't be anywhere near the GARP station, or the processing plant. In fact, I have a feeling that they reassigned everyone and brought in new staff, just to be certain there wasn't anyone around with any connections to me or the work I was doing."

"Typical scorched earth, I guess," she commented, before lifting her pouch of water from where it sat in the center console and taking a sip.

"Exactly."

They fell into another silence after that, and sometime later she reclined her seat slightly and shut her eyes, dozing as they ate up mile after mile. He supposed that was for the best, although he knew, were their situations reversed, that he wouldn't have been able to do the same. It could have been the cheap caffeine still coursing through his veins, but he was keyed up, tense. He'd come from the edge of the Solar System to this place, and now their destination was less than half a day away.

But there was still that checkpoint to get through....

Cassidy awoke as she felt the 'car come to a halt. Had she really slept so long that they'd made it all the way to the GARP facility?

Blinking, she focused on the landscape outside the vehicle's windows, then realized they still seemed to be out in the middle of nowhere. The only signs of civilization were a cluster of prefab huts, far too small to house a group of scientists and engineers—let alone all the equipment required for their various projects and tests—and, on either side the road, another pair of even smaller huts. A shimmer across the road showed where the electronic fence had been set up, and approaching the vehicle was a hard-faced woman wearing the drab gray-green of Consortium ground forces.

Cassidy shot Derek a frightened glance, and he gave her the barest shake of his head, murmuring, "Checkpoint. It'll be fine."

Somehow she doubted that, but there wasn't time to reply, only to get her seat up to a more dignified position and to tug at her clothing so it was more or less lying where it needed to be. Luckily, she'd pulled her hair back that morning, and it seemed to have stayed in place. She could only hope nothing about her appearance would raise any alarm bells.

Derek pressed the button to roll down the window, had his I.D. and credentials showing he was with the network ready. As the guard stopped outside and looked at him expectantly, he said, "Good afternoon, officer."

"Afternoon," she replied briefly. "Your business in the Zone?"

"Documentary for NBN," he said. "Here's my I.D."

He passed the card to her and she took it, then scanned it through the reader hanging from her hip. From where Cassidy was sitting, she couldn't see the light on the reader glow green, but since the guard nodded and handed Derek his I.D. after a brief pause, she had to assume everything was all right.

"Credentials?"

Derek handed those over as well. They were actual paper documents, barcoded with the particulars of their fake "documentary" assignment. No reason why they shouldn't pass muster as well, but Cassidy found herself trying not to bite her lip in worry as the guard scanned those, too.

"And you?" the hard-faced woman asked, peering past Derek to where Cassidy sat. "I.D.?"

She gave it to Derek, who relayed it to the guard. A repeat of the scanning process, during which Cassidy made sure she remained quiet, expression bland, as if she did this sort of thing all the time in various locations around the globe.

Then the guard said, "All right, looks like you're good to go, Mr. Chung, Ms. Whitcomb. Have a good one."

Derek nodded at the woman, who stepped out of the way and gave some sort of signal, as the crackling energy fence across the road abruptly lifted, granting them access to the region beyond the checkpoint. After releasing the brake, the vehicle moved forward smoothly, slowly, as if Derek didn't want to attract attention by appearing too eager to get out of there. Then the 'car began to pick up speed, but gradually, and within a few minutes, the checkpoint had dwindled to a few specks on the landscape behind them.

Maybe she hadn't exactly been holding her breath, but Cassidy found herself breathing a little more easily once they were completely out of eyeshot. "Any more of those we need to worry about?"

"Not on this road. From here it's more or less a straight shot."

She nodded, then glanced outside. Here, the vegetation didn't look much different from the small treed area where they'd slept, although it did seem a little thinner, a little weedier, not quite as lush. And she was certainly no expert on the many moods of Gaia's sun and sky, but something about the quality of light seemed to have shifted, grown slightly yellow and dim.

"Are we in the Zone now?" she asked.

"Yes. At least, this was one of the worst-hit areas. But of course the entire continent…and more…suffered."

Suddenly the air tasted acrid in her mouth, harsh against her throat. "Do we need any kind of breathing equipment?"

He glanced over at her then, reaching out to lay a reassuring hand on her knee. "We're fine. Every vehicle in China is equipped with heavy-duty atmospheric scrubbing filters. Even without that, we'd be fine unprotected for a while. If you're going to be out in it for more than an hour or so, then yes, it's recommended that you wear a light filtration mask. But we're okay."

His tone sounded calm, casual, and she told herself to relax a bit. After all, he'd lived and worked here for some time, and hadn't suffered any ill effects.

Well, except for getting framed for murder and being sent to Titan to rot.

Even so, she found it hard to let go of the tension, which seemed to be ratcheting up along her neck and shoulders with every mile that passed. If Derek suffered the same nerves, he showed no sign of it, expression cool, serene almost, as he guided them down the deserted highway.

For him, this was the culmination of a quest. For her...she wasn't sure what it was for her. She only knew she had to let him do this, had to allow him to place an end cap on the cover-up that had so irrevocably changed his life. It took more strength than she had imagined to allow him to go on driving, to keep herself from putting her hand on her wrist and saying, Stop. Just turn around so we still have a chance to get out of here and be safe.

Denying him this, though, would be grossly unfair. She'd said she'd see this thing through with him, and she would. If only it didn't hurt so much, the thought of losing him, of losing what they might have together, if the universe would only give them the chance. Before Derek, she'd never thought of a future with an "us" in it. She hadn't planned on falling in love.

And that was the craziest thing of all. Could you love someone you'd only known for a few days? If anyone had asked her that question even a week ago, she'd have said that of course you couldn't. You could be attracted. Infatuated, even. But in love, to the point where you were willing to risk your own life to help the person you cared about achieve the thing they wanted the most?

No way.

Well, that's what she would've said then. Now she knew differently. Oh, the second he'd taken off his helmet, back when he'd been hijacking the Avalon, she'd been struck by Derek's good looks, even though at the time she'd thought he must be a mass murderer or serial rapist or something equally horrible. It wasn't the first time she'd been attracted to someone at first sight, although she'd never felt that certain pull quite so forcefully before Derek. And after she'd gotten to know him, had understood everything he'd gone through, why he needed so desperately to prove the Consortium's culpability in both Theo Karras' death and the truth of what was going on at that processing plant…somewhere along the way, admiration had turned to affection, then love. She couldn't imagine having to live without him.

He turned toward her, dark eyes warming as his gaze met hers. But then he frowned slightly. "Are you okay?"

"Fine," she said, although she knew her voice sounded too tight, too strained. "Just thinking."

"About?"

"You."

Seeming a little taken aback by that, he replied, "Is that a good or a bad thing?"

"Good…mostly." She swallowed, forcing a smile. "Something about you reminds me of a piece I read once."

"What's that?"

She shifted in her seat. "Oh, you'll probably think it's silly."

"I doubt I'll think it's silly."

No, he wouldn't. He took her seriously, asked for her opinion, treated her like an equal, even though his background and education had given him far more standing in Gaian society than her own spotty upbringing as the daughter of a freighter captain. Not quite looking at him, she said, "I never really went to school. My father taught me some math, the astrogation I needed to pilot a starship, but when I was younger, I used computers to learn how to read, to write. So I read a lot. I was always poking around in the free libraries, because the newer stuff you had to pay for was pretty much out of our budget."

"*Don Quixote*," Derek said.

She blinked at him. "What?"

"You made a reference to *Don Quixote* a while back…now I understand why."

"Right. So anyway, there was this poem I read once. I don't even remember the whole thing, but there was this line that stuck out for me. 'I could not love thee, dear, had I not loved honor more.' Anyway, it reminds me of you. Why you're doing all this." Belatedly, she realized the line she'd quoted had the word "love" in it, and so far Derek had never said that word to her. Acted as if he cared, sure. But loved her?

For one long, agonizing moment, he said nothing. Then, voice so quiet she could barely hear him over the hum of the engine, "It's not entirely accurate. I'm fairly sure I love you more."

Heart swelling, not knowing what to say, she reached out to him, and he lifted his right hand from the steering wheel so he could clasp her fingers in his.

"So maybe it's unfair," he said, still in those soft, intense tones. "Maybe I should stop now and turn around. It's not too late."

Part of her wanted to say yes, to tell him that was the right thing to do, that it was more important for the two of them to be together than for the truth to be revealed. However, far more of her knew that it wasn't, that they couldn't live with themselves if they didn't do whatever they could to reveal the truth of what was going on in Hunan Province.

"No," she told him, clinging to his hand and wishing they weren't separated by the console so she could be closer to him. "I know you have to do this. I want you to do this. And I want to help you."

He lifted her hand to his mouth, kissed the backs of her fingers so gently that she could feel tears begin to prick at her eyes. That was no good, though. She knew she had to keep it together, for both their sakes.

"Thank you," he said, and that was all, but she thought she understood.

Then he released her hand, placing his back on the steering wheel, and she knotted her fingers in her lap. After a long pause she asked, "How much farther?"

"An hour or two."

She nodded. What else could she do? She loved him, and he loved her…and in a few more hours, she'd find out if that love had any kind of future at all.

NINETEEN

DEREK GRIPPED THE STEERING WHEEL SO TIGHTLY he could see his knuckles stand out, white against the golden-brown of his skin. It was the only thing he could think of to do to prevent himself from turning the 'car around, taking them back to safety. He'd known what he felt for her—or at least, thought he did—but he hadn't been sure of exactly how much she cared in return. Now that he knew she loved him, how he could he continue with this mad dash toward…what? Vindication? Absolution?

But somehow he kept driving, because Cassidy had said she believed in him, would do this thing with him. She seemed to understand that if he left this unfinished, it would hang over him for the rest of his life. On the other hand, if anything happened to her….

He would never forgive himself. Even a lifetime of solitary confinement on Titan wouldn't be enough to atone for that unpardonable sin.

You'll just have to make sure nothing does happen to her. Easier said than done, of course, but telling himself that seemed to make it a little better. After all, they'd survived against all odds this far. That luck just needed to hold a little bit longer, and then he'd be able to give the Consortium the black eye it so richly deserved, and he and Cassidy could move on to explore the rest of their lives together.

On the side of the road was a rough signpost, now scarred by the weather, telling him the GARP facility was now ten kilometers away. No mention of the processing plant, of course. GARP was the public face of the Consortium's rehabilitation of the Asian continent. The processing plant—and any others like it—was a dirty secret it hoped no one would find out about.

But he knew that road, knew if he passed the turnoff for the facility that had been his home for almost a year, then drove a few more kilometers, he'd come to the processing plant. Would it be choked with traffic the way it had been that fateful day two and a half years ago? Maybe. It was hard to say, as he didn't know how often the convoys went there with their grim loads of human remains. But he had a feeling it had to be a daily occurrence. Otherwise, it would take centuries to process those corpses, rather than merely decades.

Part of the reason he'd rented this particular vehicle, however, was that it had beefed-up ground-effects equipment, and could navigate terrain far tougher than a man-made road. They'd go past the GARP facility, then turn off into the rough so they could come up at the processing plant from underneath, avoiding altogether the road the convoys used.

Up ahead he could see the right-hand turn that would lead him into the GARP compound. They drove past, not speeding, since he didn't want to draw any attention to the 'car, or at least no more than any vehicle going by might attract, since there was so little traffic here otherwise.

Cassidy's gaze flickered toward the facility as they passed the turnoff, but she didn't say anything, apparently sensing that he wasn't in the mood to talk about his time there. She only stared out the window, jaw tense, then resolutely shifted in her seat so she could keep an eye on where they were heading.

Derek knew that the trucks heading to the processing plant took a different road, the one that cut east-west approximately two kilometers from here. Since loitering around outside in bad air was something to be avoided, those convoys weren't the sort of thing a casual observer would ever notice. Whoever was watching the monitoring equipment in the facilities building would note the traffic, but that was easy enough to explain away. All Consortium brass had to do was say those vehicles were hauling contaminated soil and plant matter. It wasn't as if they'd allow anyone from the GARP facility to get close enough to discover otherwise.

"Check your harness," he told Cassidy. "It's going to get bumpy from here on out."

She nodded grimly, fingers touching the buckle of the seatbelt stretched across her lap, then moving up to tug on the piece of the harness that descended from the roof of the vehicle and crossed over her chest. "Everything feels okay to me."

"Good. Here we go."

Derek cut off the main road, feeling the jolt as the 'car left the tarmac and began traveling across the hummocky ground. A second later, the compensators kicked in and the ride leveled out somewhat, but it was still nothing like driving across duracrete.

Risking a quick glance at Cassidy, he saw that she still had her right hand clasped around the webbing, just a few inches above her shoulder. "You okay over there?"

"I'm fine. This is—different."

One could say that. He'd done some off-road driving back home in Tucson, and again here in China, so he knew what to expect. But for someone like Cassidy, who might have had the opportunity to go topside in a lunar rover but most likely had never traveled in anything smaller than a shuttle? It had to be a jarring experience.

"We'll come up from underneath," he said reiterating the plan, as much for his own benefit as hers. "The convoys come in from the east, so we'll angle in from the southwest. They move quickly, as they want to get their loads under cover as soon as possible, so that means they'll be distracted."

"But the place must be under surveillance, mustn't it?"

"Of course it is." He paused, recalling what he'd seen of the plant, the details he'd gone over and over again in his mind, searching for any kind of weakness. "But part of the reason approaching from the southwest will work is that there's a large pipeline coming out of the plant on that side, one that empties into a complex of storage tanks. We can use the tanks as cover, and move underneath the pipeline to get close enough to the plant that we can get inside."

Her expression told him she wasn't overly thrilled with this plan, but she only nodded. "Guards?"

"I didn't see any. Doesn't mean they don't have them, but I have a feeling they're relying on video surveillance and the remoteness of the plant to protect them." He shook his head, recalling all the strictures he'd been told about not going outside for too long, all the warnings that the GARP personnel needed to stay close to their facility. Those admonishments had sounded like common sense at the time, as no one wanted to risk lung scarring just to wander around a not very scenic part of the globe. He'd known that there were very real consequences to breathing that air for too long…it was only that the Consortium had used those consequences as its own personal electric fence.

Cassidy's gaze was fixed ahead, as if she were attempting to see the processing plant. It was still several kilometers off, and the haze in the area cut visibility down to far less than that. "Okay, so, assuming we get

close enough to actually get inside without being seen…
what then?"

"I get some damning video of what exactly this
plant is processing, and I send it to our 'friend' ASAP.
After that, we go. I'm not planning to hang around long
enough for anyone to catch up with us."

At his reply, she shifted in her seat, turning her gaze
back toward him. "It seems you're placing a lot of trust
in our mysterious benefactor."

Her tone was mild enough, but Derek could hear the
question underlying it. "What other choice to we have?
He's helped us out so far, and I can't see any reason for
that except that his goal is the same as ours—to expose
the Consortium's dirty practices, and so to hopefully
get people riled up enough about it that they'll actually
do something for once. But that part will be out of our
hands. I just want this knowledge to be public."

A brief pause as she appeared to think his words
over. "And what if—what if our sponsor has been playing us all along? What if this is an elaborate setup, just
so we can get caught?"

That same concern had occurred to him, although
he'd pushed it away, telling himself there was a fine line
between being cautious and being paranoid. "What's the
point? If that had really been his plan, he could have had
us at any number of points along the way. There's no reason for him to have waited until we were this close to
our goal."

"I suppose that makes sense," she said, although something in her tone seemed to indicate she wasn't entirely convinced.

Still, she didn't offer any further protests or questions, and they drove the last kilometer to the plant in silence, each occupied with his or her own thoughts. As they approached, the structure seemed to loom up in the haze, ugly, somehow managing to be squat and towering at the same time. Or was he only superimposing his own impressions on it because he knew what was happening inside?

That didn't matter now. What mattered was slowing down, scanning the landscape for other vehicles or guards or anyone or anything else that might raise the alarm. He saw nothing, however, and at length the vats and the pipeline he'd mentioned to Cassidy came into view, a huge combination of structures in a flat yellow-gray color that seemed to simultaneously blend with the landscape and offend it.

He parked the 'car behind one of the vats, scanning the area for surveillance equipment. Nothing appeared to present itself, and so he nodded at Cassidy, indicating that it seemed to be safe to get out of the vehicle.

"The air?"

"It's okay. In and out, this should be less than a half hour. That's not enough time to do any damage."

In response, she nodded and opened her door, then slid out. He did the same, pocketing the key and then pointing toward the pipeline. Another nod, and she fell in behind him, following him as they used the massive pipe to shelter their progress.

The taste of the air was one he remembered, somehow thick and acrid at the same time, giving him a faintly irritated throat. That irritation would go away soon after he was back breathing filtered air and had drunk some water to get rid of the gunk, but in the meantime, it was an annoying distraction. Behind him, he could hear Cassidy cough quietly. It had to be even more unpleasant for her, since she had never experienced it before.

But he wouldn't let himself be distracted by that, nor the rustle of the grasses around them, nor the weighty feel of the warm, humid air. Because now they were approaching the building itself, and he could see that where the pipeline attached to the building, there was some sort of door directly below it, mostly likely to allow personnel access to the pipe in case it needed servicing.

He held up a hand, indicating that Cassidy should stop, and she paused a few feet away from him. Still he'd seen no sign of any cameras, anything to show this area was under surveillance, but he thought it better to be as circumspect as possible anyway, just in case.

Still without speaking, he pointed at the door, which appeared to open with an old-fashioned wheel-type locking handle. No keypad or biometric scanner in sight, which relieved him immeasurably. He certainly didn't have the skills to circumvent that kind of security, although he supposed he could've attempted to have their sponsor hack into the system and insert his biometrics if necessary.

But it didn't appear such measures would be required, and so he approached the door, Cassidy still behind him, and gripped the wheel, then attempted to turn it. The thing wouldn't budge, so he hauled on it again, still to no avail.

"The other direction?" Cassidy whispered.

He supposed he should have thought of that, but generally, there was a right and a wrong way to do these things. Nothing ventured, however, and so he tried turning it to the right. This time it did begin to move, although slowly and with an alarming squeak. Probably no one had opened it for a year or even more.

It swung open, revealing a dark opening barely six feet high. An unpleasant, oily smell rolled out, and Derek felt his nose wrinkle. But foul odors certainly weren't going to stop him, not when he'd come this far.

He turned back toward Cassidy, who was watching in silence, an expectant look on her face.

This was going to be the hardest part. She'd come with him this far, and he knew she'd want to go inside with him. But he also knew he would be far less conspicuous on his own. Better that she should stay here, someplace sheltered and shielded from prying eyes. If something did go wrong, she had a clear route back to the 'car, and could get away before anyone realized that Derek Tagawa had not come here alone.

Nothing for it, though. "All right, I'm going to go in now—"

"Don't you mean *we're* going to go in now?"

He didn't reply, only watched her, saw comprehension dawn in her expression, followed swiftly by anger.

Her hazel eyes flashed, and color burned high along her cheekbones. "What, you expect me to just sit out here while you go in there and risk getting caught?"

"Yes," he said calmly. "One person can escape detection more easily than two. Also, I'll feel better knowing that you can get away clean if things go south." Her mouth tightened, and he took a breath and continued, "This is the best way. You have to trust me on this."

For a long moment she said nothing, only stood there staring at him, jaw tense, eyes snapping with anger. Then, "If you get yourself killed, I will never forgive you."

Relief flooded through him. "I'm not planning on it." He reached out and pulled her against him, gave her a kiss—just one, and quickly, because he knew if he let his lips linger on hers, he wouldn't want to stop, might lose his resolve, even at this late stage of the game.

She returned the kiss, her fingers threading through his hair and holding him in place for a second or two longer than he'd intended. Then she let him go, even giving him a slight push toward the door. "Hurry."

"I will." He pulled his handheld out of his pocket. "Send me a ping if you see anything out of the ordinary."

"Sure," she replied, her tone wry. "The only problem is, everything here looks out of the ordinary to me."

He grinned and shook his head, then forced himself to turn away from her and go inside the building, breathing lightly so as little of the foul smell as possible could penetrate his nasal cavity. Behind him, Cassidy shut the door, and he flicked the light on his handheld, letting it guide him along the access corridor. Beneath the sturdy boots he wore, the ground seemed to gleam with a sticky dark substance, one he didn't dare inspect too closely.

As he moved along, he thought of the insanity of trying to infiltrate a facility with no knowledge of its layout, its security…its, well, anything. But it wasn't as if they had much of a choice.

Even as those thoughts crossed his mind, though, he felt his handheld buzz. He'd turned off the audible alerts, just to be safe. Pausing, he turned it back toward him so he could see the screen.

Thought you might find this useful.

The message disappeared, and in its place appeared a schematic of a building—the one in which he stood. Off to one side was a small glowing yellow dot. Acting on instinct, he began to move—and the dot moved with him.

"Thank you," he murmured, but there was no response.

Well, he wasn't going to worry about that. Now he was no longer flying blind, could see that the passageway he was in continued for approximately another fifty meters before dead-ending in what appeared to be a staircase. He headed in that direction, watching as the yellow dot moved along with him, until he came to the stairs. They were dingy gray metal, obviously placed here for emergency access and then rarely used. All the better.

He began to climb, trying not to think about Cassidy waiting outside for him, nor of how many people might be currently working in the facility, each one of them a separate opportunity for him to be discovered. Curiously, though, his spirits rose with each step he ascended. Perhaps it was simply the knowledge that their benefactor hadn't abandoned them, was still watching out for them.

After going up approximately twice the height of a standard story in a high-rise, he came to a landing with a door. A sign next to the door proclaimed it to be "Level 1A," but he had no idea if this was his intended destination. He looked down at the schematic on the handheld, noticed that the glowing dot indicating his location had turned red. All right, so not this one.

He climbed again, coming to another landing, this one labeled "Level 2A." Now the dot had turned green.

His heartbeat sped up a little, and he made himself take a long, deep breath, knowing that he had to keep his wits about him more than ever. At least he was dressed simply, in a plain dark gray jacket and gray pants, an outfit that shouldn't attract too much attention even in a place like this, unless all the workers wore bright yellow coveralls or something similarly distinctive.

But he couldn't worry about that now. What was far more worrisome was the keypad located next to the door.

The handheld buzzed again, and he looked down to see that the schematic had disappeared temporarily, and the screen instead showed a sequence of numbers.

846329101176

Derek tapped in the digits, and the door swung open. No time to even murmur a thank-you; instead, he slipped inside and took a quick glance around.

He stood on what appeared to be a metal gangway that ran around the circumference of a circular space and overlooked a mass of machinery. In the background, he could hear a steady chug-chug-chug sound. The air here smelled even worse than it had in the tunnel, but at least he seemed to be alone for the moment.

His handheld beeped again, and he could see his dot morph into a green arrow pointing to his right. Clearly, that was where he was intended to go. Walking quickly, he made his way approximately ten meters away from the entrance to the stairwell, then stopped. He could see why this was where his benefactor wanted him to go.

The machinery clogging the space ended abruptly, and below him was a conveyor belt carrying what seemed to be an unending stream of bodies in various stages of decomposition. That was a quirk of the Cloud, it seemed; some were now only skeletons, while others looked as if they had been dead for only a few years, or at most a few decades, not centuries.

Bile rose in his throat, but he forced himself to grab the vid-corder he had slung over one shoulder, pick it up, and aim its lens toward the unspeakable sight below. A minute of the conveyor belt itself, and then panning toward the hulking piece of equipment the belt fed into, taking with it its grisly cargo. It was from this machine the chug-chug-chug sound emanated, and it would take a person with far less imagination than he had to guess at what was going on inside that machine.

"Got it," he whispered.

His handheld buzzed. Link to your device. I'll take care of the upload from there.

He did as instructed, bringing his handheld up against the side of the vid-corder, letting the beam carry the data from one device to another. A second went by, then another.

Got it, came the message. Good work. Now get your ass out of there.

Derek couldn't argue with that. He slid the vid-corder by its strap back over his shoulder, then hurried back toward the stairwell.

Only the way was no longer clear. Six guards in black uniforms stood there, flanking two men Derek had hoped he would never see again. One was Conrad Waite, eyes cold and hungry, and the other was General Marquez, ranking officer in charge of the Zone, and the person who had been responsible for making sure Derek got a one-way trip to Titan.

"Hello, Dr. Tagawa," said General Marquez. "It's been a while."

TWENTY

I<small>T SHOULD HAVE WORKED. THEY'D BEEN SO CAREFUL.</small> There hadn't been any signs of surveillance, video or otherwise, in this neglected little corner of the facility. The minutes had ticked by, and Cassidy had waited, telling herself it was going to be fine, that the place was huge, and who knew how long it would take Derek to reach a spot where he could get some truly incriminating footage?

But then the two trucks pulled up, and the men in the black uniforms had gotten out, and she realized things had gone horribly, terribly wrong.

She hadn't put up any resistance. What would have been the point, except giving them a chance to beat her up a little?

Now she sat in a small gray room, hands shackled in front of her. Those were the only restraints they'd used. She could get up and walk around, but what was the point? There was nothing in here except the chair in which she sat. No table, no other chairs. Not your standard interrogation room, then.

Right. As if you have any idea what one of those would even look like.

In the wall to her right was a door, and above an illuminated ceiling. The light was just a little too bright, and made her want to squint. She guessed that was on purpose.

And her mind kept churning away with, *Where's Derek? What did they do to him? Is he hurt? Does he know I've been captured?* Somewhere at the bottom of all that was, *Did he get the recording?*, but that seemed trivial compared to the hopelessness of her current situation.

Also, she was thirsty, the odd acrid aftertaste of the air she'd breathed while outside still somehow caught in her throat, but she kind of doubted anyone was going to come in and offer her a drink. She supposed it could be worse. At least she didn't need to go to the bathroom. Not yet, anyway.

The door opened, and a man wearing the gray-green uniform of the GDF's ground command stepped in. Judging by the silver stars tacked to his high collar, she thought he must be a general of some kind, but beyond that she couldn't guess at his rank.

A general? she thought. *They sent a general to question a nobody like me?*

"Ms. Evans," he said, stopping a few paces away from her. "My apologies for the wait."

Cassidy felt her eyebrows begin to lift, then forced herself to stop. No point in giving away anything more than she had to. As to why a multi-star general would come in here and start apologizing to her....

"It's no problem," she replied coolly, belatedly realizing that he'd addressed her by her real name. So much for the fake I.D.s and credentials their benefactor had secured for her and Derek.

The general didn't react, only said, "You do understand that you were trespassing in a highly secure area."

"Was I? Darn that navigation unit—I'm going to file a complaint with the rental 'car agency."

Still no reaction. Not a furrowing of the brows to indicate irritation, or a quirk of his thin lips to show some amusement at her flip remark. She didn't even know precisely why she'd responded that way, only that it was her natural tendency to retreat to sarcasm when she was nervous or uncomfortable.

"Ms. Evans, we both know why you were there. And I also know that you would never have come to Hunan Province at all if you hadn't been coerced by the escaped convict Derek Tagawa."

Coercion? Was that a new definition of mind-blowing sex that she'd never heard of? But the general's reply had told her which direction he intended to take this, and she tensed.

"You don't know that," she said. "I could've just been interested in touring some of Gaia's more scenic contamination zones."

This time she saw a distinct tensing of the muscles along his jaw line, and guessed that he wasn't going to put up with too many more of her flippant replies. "Ms. Evans, the Consortium is willing to drop all charges against you if you will testify that Derek Tagawa hijacked your ship, murdered two GDF pilots, and engaged in various acts of coercion, extortion, and mayhem, up to and including the bodily injury of one of our most valuable operatives."

Mayhem? she thought. *That's a new one.* But she only tilted her head to one side, then said, "How is Mr. Waite?"

"You can ask him that yourself," the general responded smoothly, a malicious glint in his dark eyes.

Although she hadn't seen him give any signal, the door opened, and Conrad Waite stepped in, looking somewhat out of place in an impeccably tailored dark gray suit, something far more suited to the tony boutiques and shops of Lakeshore Drive where she'd seen him last than the wilds of Hunan Province. Her gaze flicked to his hands, which showed no sign of the havoc Derek had wreaked. Obviously, the Consortium had spared no expense to get its operative back in fighting trim.

He stopped and stood next to the general, face impassive, but she could see the cold, hungry gleam in his steel-gray eyes, and an uneasy sensation began to churn in the pit of her stomach.

Somehow she managed to force a smile onto her lips and said, "Hi, Conrad. You're looking well."

"No thanks to your boyfriend—" he began with a barely concealed sneer, but the general raised a hand, and Waite subsided.

"It's really very simple, Ms. Evans," the general said, tone so impersonal he might as well have been discussing the weather. "Either you sign an affidavit saying that Derek Tagawa was guilty of all the acts I described earlier—which, in addition to the original murder sentence, will guarantee that he'll be kept in solitary confinement on Titan for the rest of his days—or I'll give you to Mr. Waite here. He expressed an interest in you, said you two had some unfinished business."

That cold, uneasy sensation in her stomach solidified into a lump of ice. She understood all too well what the wolf-like glitter in Conrad Waite's eyes meant. Yes, she supposed he did think they had unfinished business. He'd wanted her, and Derek had intervened. But she couldn't let them see her fear, couldn't let them guess at how the blood in her veins seemed to have suddenly turned to liquid nitrogen, or how she was very, very glad she hadn't eaten anything lately, as she was certain that otherwise she would have thrown up.

"You can't do that," she retorted. "Whatever crimes you might think me guilty of, I'm still a citizen of the Consortium, and that means I have certain rights—one of which, I'm pretty sure, is not being handed off to one of your goons like some war prize."

The general smiled, and Cassidy wished he hadn't. It was empty, cold, like the rictus grin of a skeleton. "Yes, you are a citizen of the Consortium, but you are also in the Zone, which is currently under martial law, and therefore not subject to the usual civil codes in effect in other parts of the planet. My word is law here, and I can do whatever I like. As can he, with my blessing."

At those words, Waite stepped away from the general's side, came closer to the chair where Cassidy sat, her hands still bound. He bent down, his breath hot against her neck as he whispered, "I hope you don't recant. They'll lock Tagawa up forever anyway, no matter what you say, but that way the general can give you to me in good conscience."

Despite her best efforts, a shiver worked its way down her spine. "I sort of doubt he has a conscience. And I know you sure as hell don't."

He chuckled, then straightened and sent a knowing look in the general's direction. "She's not going to give up Tagawa, sir. I can take her off your hands now—"

"Don't be so impatient," the general broke in, looking annoyed. "Really, Ms. Evans, it will do you no good to defend a criminal like Dr. Tagawa. He was fairly caught, and his current crimes only compound what he was already guilty of."

"He was only guilty of trying to do the right thing," Cassidy snapped. "Something you obviously know nothing about."

For a second or two, he didn't respond, only stood there and gazed at her with eyes as cold and black as those of an Iradian sand snake she'd once seen in a traveling exhibit in Luna City. Then he gave the briefest nod. "She's all yours, Waite," he said dismissively, turning toward the door before pressing his thumb against the biometric lock and then leaving her alone with Conrad Waite.

She pushed herself up from the chair, not even sure of what she was doing, only knowing that she was not going to remain sitting there passively while the hit man reached out to take her. It was an empty gesture, because he was close enough that he simply lifted a hand and grasped her by the arm, pulling her closer to him, so close she could catch a trace of the expensive aftershave he wore. Something clean and brisk, so unlike him.

"Oh, yeah, they work fine now," he said, apparently noticing her shocked glance downward at the fingers that held her in an iron grip. "Six hours with my hands stuck in a bonesetter. Do you have any idea how much that hurts?"

A shake of the head, the only thing she could manage in that moment. Terror seemed to have seized her by the throat in a hold just as crushing as the one Conrad Waite currently had on her arm.

"It hurts…quite a bit," he told her. "But, despite what you're thinking, I don't hurt women…unless I'm being paid to do so. Lucky for you, or I'd take every second of pain out of your hide." He paused, and she felt his lips brush against her hair, even as every muscle in her body tensed in revulsion. "What I will do is make sure you forget all about Derek Tagawa."

He shifted, and she could tell he was coming in to kiss her, and oh, God, she'd suffered that once, but she knew she wouldn't be able to again, would rather die than let him touch her. Her hands were bound, though, and even if she managed to knee him in the groin, what would that get her? The door was thumb-locked; maybe if she somehow incapacitated Waite, she could use his finger to get the door to open. But he was a trained killer, and she was only a freighter pilot. He'd stop her before she got anywhere close enough to hurt him.

I'm sorry, Derek, she thought. *You should've hooked up with a merc or an assassin or someone who actually knew what she was doing—*

Even as that despairing thought passed through her mind, and even as Waite's face grew closer, those hard gray eyes locked on hers, seeming to see her desperation and revel in it, the building shook, and then shook again.

"What the—" he began, just as a third quake rocked its way through the structure.

That time, Cassidy thought she'd heard a distant explosion just before the building trembled. "Feels like some kind of attack," she said, taking advantage of his momentary discomposure to step away from him. "Who have you guys pissed off lately?"

He shot her an angry look. "That's impossible. No one would dare attack this facility."

The building shook again. "Then I guess whoever is shooting at you has a different definition of the word 'impossible,' than you do, because that sure felt like a pulse cannon. Or something."

Not bothering to reply, he grasped her by the arm and went to open the door, pressing a furious thumb against the scanner before hauling her out into the hallway. Wherever she was, it felt like a military compound of some sort—cold gray walls and floors, harsh overhead lighting. Men and women in uniform were rushing all around them, clearly intent on mounting some kind of defense of the installation.

Conrad Waite ignored them, however, hauling her in the opposite direction from where most of the soldiers appeared to be headed.

"Where are we going?" she asked, not sure if she really wanted to know the answer.

"Hangar," was his brief response, and her blood ran cold once again. It seemed clear that he wasn't too worried about pitching in to help fight off the attackers, whoever they might be. No, he apparently just wanted to get out of there with his prize intact.

She stumbled along with him, hoping in that moment that if she couldn't be with Derek, then the people shooting at the base would at least score a direct hit on the section of the building she was in. Better to be buried in rubble than to end up being Conrad Waite's sex toy.

But then she felt him pull up, even as he drew a pistol from the waistband of his trousers, and looked to see where he was staring. A lone man stood in the center of the hallway, a very large pulse rifle pointed at Waite's head. Aside from the gun, this newcomer didn't look particularly intimidating—he was of middle height, swarthy, neither attractive nor unattractive. Something in his dark eyes told her he was no one to mess with, however.

"Stand still," he said, tone so neutral she couldn't really tell what his intentions might be, and before she could do anything else, before Waite could start to take aim, the pulse rifle fired once. The hit man's grip on her arm abruptly loosened, and he went flying backward, a smoking hole dead in the center of his forehead.

"What—"

"No time for that," the stranger said. "Come on."

The world seemed to be spinning faster and faster around her. "Where—"

"Someplace safe." A certain glint entered those hard, dark eyes, and he added, "This is a rescue, Ms. Evans. Don't screw it up with questions."

She had no idea what was going on, but she knew one thing—this man had just saved her from Conrad Waite. Therefore, going with him seemed a far better alternative than anything else she could think of right then.

Without replying, she stepped away from Waite's corpse, then followed the stranger as he turned and jogged down the corridor, heading where, she had no idea.

So far, they hadn't hurt him too badly. A few kicks to the abdomen after he was first captured, a couple more blows to the head for good measure after he was shackled to a chair. After that, though, they left him in this square, gray room, alone with his worry.

There had been no mention of Cassidy, and so he didn't know what had happened to her. Had she gotten away? Was she captured? Dead?

No. He refused to entertain that possibility. She'd already proven herself sharp and able to adapt quickly in a volatile situation, so no matter what might have happened, he made himself assume that she was all right. Otherwise, he thought he might go crazy, trying to figure out what was happening to her right now.

They'd taken the camera, of course, and his handheld and fake I.D. and everything else he had on him. That hadn't worried him too much, since the recording he'd taken in the processing plant had already been safely uploaded to their benefactor. What he planned to do with it, Derek didn't know for sure. Merely sending it to the top news agencies wouldn't do much good. They were all tightly controlled by the Consortium and would never air such damning images. No, their unknown sponsor must have some other kind of plan, although what, he couldn't begin to guess.

As to what his captors they planned to do with him… well, that didn't take a rocket scientist—or an atmospheric one, for that matter—to figure out. If he were lucky, he'd be sent back to Titan. If he were unlucky, there would be some kind of "accident" between here and there, and his body would end up being shoved out an airlock. Either way, his future didn't look too appealing.

But he could live with that if he at least knew Cassidy was all right. He'd understood the risks involved in coming here, and had accepted them in the name of exposing the Consortium's dirty laundry, but Cassidy wasn't as emotionally invested in that as he was. She'd come because she wanted to support him.

Because she loved him.

He didn't know what he'd done to deserve that love, but he couldn't deny it, either. And that was what made this situation all the more horrible to him. She'd loved him, and trusted him, and that had gotten her…what?

Not knowing was always the worst.

His hands were tightly shackled behind him, and he could feel his fingers beginning to go numb from lack of circulation. Maybe that was a good thing. If all of him went similarly numb, then maybe some of the pain he was now feeling would go away.

The room where he was being held was completely silent except for the faint hum of the air circulators.

So when a distant *boom!* reverberated throughout the building, he heard it clearly.

What the hell?

That explosion was followed by another, then another. Derek twisted in his chair, but couldn't do much with his arms bound behind him and his ankles attached to the chair's legs. All he could do was sit there, heart pounding, wondering what in the world was going on. An attack, clearly, but by whom?

A sizzling, crackling noise, and the door exploded inward. Through the swirling smoke stepped probably the last thing Derek had expected to see—an enormous Stacian, fully two meters tall, a pulse pistol in either hand. His copper-colored gaze fell on Derek at once, and he spoke into a wrist-mounted comm. "Found him. He's shackled."

A woman's voice emerged from the comm. "The laser cutter should do it."

"Copy that."

The Stacian approached Derek, gave him a ferocious grin, and said, "Afternoon, Dr. Tagawa. You should probably hold still for the next minute."

Another explosion jolted the building. Roughly a million questions crowded Derek's brain, but he decided right now it was probably best to go with the flow. "I'll do my best."

The alien extracted a silvery device from the pouch at his belt and set to work. The sharp, tinny scent of super-heated metal arose from the shackles, and a few seconds after that, Derek heard a metallic clank as they fell to the floor. Flexing his fingers, he lifted his hands, shaking his arms to get the blood going. At the same time, the Stacian knelt and cut through the shackle on Derek's right leg, and then his left. Afterward, he thrust his massive frame to a standing position once more, then said, "Time to go."

"Are you with—" He let the words break off, since saying "benefactor" or "sponsor" in these circumstances sounded a little foolish.

But the alien seemed to understand, saying, "Yes, I'm giving her a hand. She wants to talk to you. But we need to get out of here. Now."

Her. So their benefactor was a woman. Derek wondered if that had been her voice issuing from the Stacian's wrist-mounted comm. He supposed he'd find out soon enough—if they made it out of here alive.

No time for stealth. The alien tossed Derek one of his pistols, then pulled a third gun out of the holster strapped to his leg. "If it moves, shoot it," he said briefly before heading out the door.

Those instructions seemed simple enough. Derek followed the Stacian, who was moving at a not-quite run down the corridor. A burst from each of his pistols, and the two soldiers who had just rounded a corner slumped to the ground. The alien never even broke stride. Clearly, he'd had experience with this sort of thing before.

Their surroundings were unfamiliar. Definitely not the GARP facility. Maybe a section of the processing plant taken over by GDF personnel? An entirely separate base? Derek couldn't tell, and right then he supposed it didn't matter too much. The important thing was getting out of here…wherever "here" might be.

"Cassidy Evans?" he panted. He would've said he was in decent shape, but that Stacian had long legs.

"Safe," the alien replied. "One of my associates already has her."

That news seemed to lend him an additional burst of energy, and so, as they jogged to the right and went down another hallway, Derek hardly even blinked when they came upon another group of soldiers, four this time. They didn't even have time to get off a shot before a barrage of pulse bolts from his and the Stacian's guns mowed them down.

"Not a bad shot, Dr. Tagawa," the Stacian said, with a ferocious baring of his teeth.

"Thanks," Derek replied, feeling a grin of his own stretch at his mouth.

At the end of the hallway was a set of doors that now stood open. Part of the reason they hadn't closed automatically to keep out the tainted air was that a number of bodies lay piled there, acting as effective door stops. In the center of the carnage stood a grim-faced man, a pulse rifle cradled in his hands.

"She's aboard already," the stranger said, calmly as if he were discussing what he'd had for breakfast that day. "Let's go."

Aboard? Derek wondered. He didn't stop for questions, though, only followed the strange man and the Stacian toward, of all things, a Sirocco-class transport, the hatch open but no gangplank deployed. As he ran, he took a quick look around. They were definitely still at the processing facility, at a wing that jutted out from one side. Then he heard another explosion rock the base, and thought he saw a sleek arrowhead-shaped craft circle the plant before heading up into the murky sky.

"We're out," the strange man said into his own wrist-mounted comm. "Jerem, provide cover, but you can stop the bombardment."

The Stacian lingered at the open hatch, obviously waiting for Derek to go in first. As he clambered aboard, he thought he heard the incongruous sound of a boy's voice emerging from the stranger's comm.

"Come on, Dad—just one more strafing run. This is fun!"

"I said stop, and I mean it."

"Fine," came the reply.

The stranger caught Derek staring at him and shrugged. "Kids."

And then they were all aboard, the Stacian pulling himself inside and closing the hatch, even as Derek felt a pair of arms go around him and give him a fierce hug.

"You're safe!" Cassidy exclaimed, pulling him against her so tightly that he had to work to force some air into his lungs. "They said you would be, but—"

"I'm fine," he said, kissing the top of her head, inhaling the sweet scent of her hair. She felt so very real in that moment, real and alive and unharmed, standing here in his arms as the ship lifted off and accelerated away, moving so fast that he staggered a bit to retain his balance.

Then, realizing they had a somewhat incongruous audience consisting of a Stacian and a man who had to be mercenary of some kind, Derek released her gently and glanced over at the other two occupants of the cabin. "So...." he began, and then stopped, not knowing exactly what to say. *Thank you...and who are you, precisely?*

"So," said a new voice, one that belonged to a woman who was now emerging from the cockpit and making her way into the luxurious little craft's main passenger compartment, "I'm guessing you have a lot of questions, Dr. Tagawa, Ms. Evans."

"A few," the two of them replied in unison, and then stopped and looked at one another in some amusement.

"That's understandable," the woman said. "Please, take a seat." She flicked a glance over at the swarthy stranger, the merc. "Jerem?"

"Fine," the man replied. "A bit put out that he couldn't keep dropping ordnance on the base, but...."

"Typical." She smiled, then returned her attention to Derek and Cassidy. He guessed she was somewhere around his age, maybe a year or two younger. Attractive, with that long dark red hair and smoky green eyes. "My name is Miala Thorn, and that's my husband Eryk."

Somehow Derek managed to keep his eyes from widening. Even cloistered academics like himself had heard of the notorious Eryk Thorn. No wonder the man had come across as a mercenary—he was the mercenary's mercenary. Nothing had been heard of from him for several years, and the Consortium had boasted that he'd been caught and imprisoned, but obviously that was just another of the lies they'd cooked up for public consumption.

Derek nodded, and Cassidy said, "It's very nice to meet you, and...." Her gaze strayed to the Stacian, who had propped himself up next to the hatch.

"Rast sen Drenthan," he replied. "My wife would come out to meet you, but as she's busy piloting this ship, that'll have to wait."

Wife? This whole thing was getting stranger and stranger.

Miala Thorn seemed to note his confusion, and said, "I'll get to the explanations in a minute, but first I want you to see something." She tilted her chin up toward the vid-screen that was mounted in one wall of the passenger compartment, and Derek saw her lift her handheld and point it at the screen. It came to life, showing the video he'd taken inside the processing plant, now overlaid by narration in a crisp feminine voice that he realized belonged to Miala herself.

"...It is vital that the citizens of the Consortium understand the depths of the lies their government has told them about the disposition of the victims of the Cloud. Rather than being treated with the respect they deserve, those victims are being harvested, mined for any valuable items they might still have within their bodies, and then processed so the elements within their corpses can be used for fertilizer and any other uses the Consortium deems valuable."

Derek glanced over at Miala. "That's...amazing."

"Oh, it gets better," she said, still smiling. The screen blanked for a fraction of a second, then went on to show another channel with the same footage...then another... then another. "I took over all the satellite feeds. You can't see anything else. Not your favorite vid-drama, not a low-g football match...nothing. And anyone who watches those things on their handhelds...they'll all be seeing the same thing as well." Her smile widened, sending green lights dancing in her eyes. "I have a feeling the Consortium is going to be answering a lot of questions in the near future."

"But...why?" Cassidy asked. "That is, I—we—really appreciate what you've done for us, but why us in particular? Why this case?"

"Because of me," said another woman, now just stepping out of the cockpit, but stopping by the entrance, in case she needed to go back in and handle something quickly. She had dark hair pulled back away from the fine bones of her face, and very deep blue eyes. Oddly, something about her seemed almost familiar, as if Derek seen her somewhere before. But that had to be a mistake. When would he have ever met a woman like her, someone who piloted a Sirocco-class starship and was apparently married to a Stacian?

"Or rather, because of Liam," she added. "Liam Jannholm. I'm Lira, his older sister. When I found out what had happened to Theo—" Breaking off, she gave a grim shake of her head. "Of course I was shocked at first. But then when I looked into it further, something didn't smell right to me. I tried talking to Liam about it, but he didn't want to have anything to do with me, let alone listen to what I might have to say about his husband's death."

"But why wouldn't he talk to you?" Cassidy inquired, then hesitated, as if worried that she was getting too personal in her questions.

But Lira only smiled, and that was when Derek recalled where he'd seen her. A holo-portrait on Liam's desk, showing her in the dark gray uniform of a GDF officer, captain's stars shining on her collar. Well, she didn't appear to be in the GDF now, that was for sure.

The Stacian, Rast sen Drenthan, shifted slightly and said, a wry tone to his deep voice, "Lira's family did not precisely approve of her...choices."

Well, Derek could see why some families might have a slight issue with one of their children marrying a Stacian. Being at almost-war for nearly a hundred years tended to have that sort of an effect on people.

"Oh, yes, I'm definitely the black sheep," Lira said cheerfully. "My sister will still talk to me on the sly, but Liam always did have his head up his ass."

Miala Thorn's mouth quirked. "So Lira came to me with her concerns, and I started doing some investigating on my own. I'm not too bad at poking into databases and getting the information I need."

There was an understatement. "I see," Derek commented, his tone neutral.

"And I saw what was really going on, and sent along some information to members of the underground. They took care of actually helping you get off Titan." Her expression turned serious, and she pointed her hand-held at the vid-screen, turning off the images of countless bodies on their grim journey to being "processed." She went on, "I am sorry about the leak on Europa. I'm still trying to figure out what exactly happened there."

"It's all right," Derek said, and Cassidy nodded. "We survived."

"Barely, and only because of your own resourcefulness. At any rate, I've been keeping watch and assisting as I could. The truth needs to come out. The citizens of the Consortium need to know precisely what sort of government they're supporting."

Glancing from her to the others in the passenger compartment, Derek saw equally grim expressions on her compatriots...grim, but determined. "And your stake in all this?"

"Let's just say we know what it's like to run afoul of the Consortium," Eryk Thorn said. "They've been trying to catch up with us for years, but luckily their people aren't quite as good as they think they are."

No, Derek kind of doubted that. This small group of people made quite the formidable army all on their own.

"You might not have gotten caught at all," Lira said, her expression shifting to an irritation her next words explained. "Except Liam was being rotated back to the GARP facility, and saw Ms. Evans leaving the supply depot. Apparently the authorities had notified Liam of Dr. Tagawa's return to Gaia, and told him to keep an eye out for his former compatriot and the woman who appeared to be traveling with him. So Liam made contact and said he had a possible sighting, and that put everyone on heightened alert. The only real break you caught was that the surveillance cameras near the pipeline where you entered the base were down. It took them a bit to catch up with you...and then it took us a bit to catch up with them, if you take my meaning."

"It's all right," Cassidy said, although the smile she offered appeared a bit shaky. "You did catch up with us, which is the important thing."

Derek wondered exactly what had happened to her during her brief captivity, but he would have to ask her about that later. "So...what now?" he asked.

Miala tilted her head, seeming to consider him. "Normally, I'd say that was up to you, but since you've now managed to piss off the entire Consortium government…"

"…we don't have a lot of options," Derek finished for her. That was putting it mildly. They'd be hunted in every sector controlled by the Consortium, which meant a large portion of the galaxy was now off-limits to them.

It was something he and Cassidy had discussed briefly, but only in passing, a contingency they hoped they'd never have to implement. Could he ask this of her, to come into exile with him, to the one place he thought they might be safe?

She must have seen the question in his eyes, because she nodded and then slipped her hand into his. "It's all right," she said softly. "I always did want to see Eridani."

TWENTY-ONE

MAIR LENNIS, PRESIDENT OF THE PLANETARY COUNCIL, was an older Eridani male, his hair now pale lavender with age, his skin an even paler lavender than his hair. But he held himself straight and tall as he greeted Cassidy and Derek, telling them they would be granted sanctuary on his world and in the sectors controlled by the Eridani Hegemony.

"We here on Eridani...and on many other worlds... understand the sacrifices you have made to ensure that the truth will not be buried," he said in his calm, soft voice. "Arrangements have been made for you to make your home here in Teliir, but if you should find anything not to your liking...."

He let the words trail off, and Cassidy said, "I'm sure it will all be wonderful, Mr. President. We can't thank you enough for allowing us to claim asylum here."

A smile. "I would say it is nothing, but I know for you it is far more than that." He took her hand and bowed over it, and although she'd somehow thought his skin would be cool, it was actually warm, warmer than her own. "A vehicle is waiting to take you to your new home. If there is anything you require, send word directly to my secretary, and he will see that the matter is addressed."

She stammered her thanks, and Derek added his own, saying he was sure they wouldn't need anything else, that the president—and, by extension, the rest of the government—had already done so much for them.

Then that same secretary, a younger Eridani man, his hair vivid purple, guided them out of the gleaming high-rise that housed the president and his staff, and on into an aircar, this one driven by a mech so shiny it looked as if it had just come off the factory floor that week. The unfamiliar streets of Teliir began to slip by, all gleaming glass and steel and other metals Cassidy couldn't even put a name to. Everything was clean and bright, and so very unlike the few glimpses she'd had of Gaia. Here, the sky was pale purple, the sunlight faintly tinged with blue.

Very beautiful…but very alien.

They hadn't said much on the trip to Eridani. Once Lira Jannholm had piloted her Sirocco-class ship safely away from Gaia, they'd headed to Triton, where they rendezvoused with another, older ship, this one piloted by Miala and Eryk Thorn's son, who didn't appear to be a day over fourteen. Cassidy had wondered at his parents allowing him to take on such a dangerous task as bombarding the GDF wing of the processing plant, and then flying on to Triton alone. A few minutes in Jerem's company, however, was enough to convince her that Miala and Eryk knew exactly what they were doing… and so did their son.

On Triton they'd said their goodbyes and given their thanks, and Lira and Rast took Cassidy and Derek the rest of the way to Eridani, a journey of some fifteen hours through the shifting, shimmering non-colors of subspace, something she'd never seen before. It had been some hours before she'd allow herself to doze on the divan in the passenger compartment of Lira's ship, head pillowed on Derek's shoulder. And then they'd come to Eridani.

It was clear that Miala had sent word ahead, for Cassidy and Derek were welcomed without question. At the time Cassidy wasn't sure what to make of that, except it was clear that the Eridanis, for all their talk of mutual cooperation and understanding, enjoyed seeing the Consortium's shortcomings revealed in all their glory.

Now she and Derek were alone in the house that had been given to them, a modest villa-style structure on the outskirts of Teliir. She had no experience of acreage or any terrestrial units of measurement, but the place seemed to have hugely extensive lands, with no sign of neighbors on any side. Alien trees in shades of purple and blue and dark, dark red shaded the grounds, through which an actual stream meandered, bordered on either side by silvery-gray sand. Everything seemed to have been attended to, from personal hygiene products in the bathrooms to wardrobes stocked with clothing to the full refrigeration unit in the kitchen.

Hand in hand, they'd walked over the property, still silent, still trying to take it all in. Or at least, that was what Cassidy was doing. She didn't know if she wanted to guess what might be going through Derek's mind, what he thought of this completely new life they'd been given.

Finally they returned to the large central room that functioned as a sort of combination living area/dining room, all tastefully furnished in shades of purple-tinged blues and grays, the dining section separated from the living area by what appeared to be a free-falling cascade of water, one that disappeared into a bed of gray rocks and then, by some hidden miracle, was pumped back into the ceiling to start the process all over again. So much water, such an extravagant use of it. It was something she could never have imagined, but she had a feeling she'd be facing much more of that in the days to come.

"So…." she said at length.

He turned to her, took her hands in his. The faintest beginnings of a smile touched his lips, brought some warmth to his dark eyes. "So…I'm thinking this definitely beats a cell in MaxSec."

"Or the *Avalon*," she agreed.

"Or pretty much any place I've ever lived."

Something inside her seemed to ease slightly then. "So…you're okay with all this?"

"I think I am." Still holding her hands, he brought one to his lips and kissed her fingers gently. "On the trip here, I thought about what I was leaving behind—my family, my home world, my career. But in a sense, I'd left them behind when I was sent to Titan. I felt pretty sure I wouldn't see any of them ever again. I'd already said my farewells." His dark eyes caught hers, held, and she made herself remain that way, her gaze fixed on his. "When I was captured back there, when I thought I was either going to be sent back to MaxSec or killed outright, I wasn't thinking about any of that. I was only thinking about you, whether you were safe, whether you'd managed to get away. That tells me I know what's important." He paused, and she held her breath, thinking there was no way he was going to say what she desperately hoped he would. "What's important is *you*, Cassidy. *Us*. We make quite a team, don't you think?"

"I think so," she managed and then he was kissing her, mouth finding hers with an urgency and need that told her he had no regrets, only wanted what she wanted, which was the two of them together, no matter what happened.

He scooped her up then, and she laughed out loud, clinging to him as he took her to the master suite, which was decorated in soft blues accented by the same deep crimson of the trees she'd spotted outside. There he laid her down on the bed, and she reached up and pulled him to her, mouths coming together once again even as they wrestled with the unfamiliar fasteners and construction of the Eridani clothing they wore. At last, though, they were naked, flesh pressed to flesh as they erased the worry and doubt and fear of the last few days in a joining that told them this was right, that this was where they were meant to be…and who they were meant to be with.

Afterward, Cassidy dozed a little, and awoke to see Derek coming toward her with a tray of exotic-looking food, beautifully shaped fruit in shades of purple and crimson, pale loaves of bread, a bottle of purple-hued wine.

"I thought you might be a little hungry," he said, setting the tray down on the bed next to her.

She was, but hungrier still for his presence, as if the lovemaking of earlier had only served to whet her appetite. Well, to be fair, they hadn't been able to be together nearly as much as she would have liked, considering all the running around they'd had to do to avoid being killed. And now, watching him as he settled himself next to her, chest still bare, although he'd put on a pair of loose-fitting dark pants—well, she could feel the heat rise in her once again, and knew this simple meal was only a refueling stop before they went on to more important things.

He'd opened the wine in the kitchen, it seemed, since he tilted it immediately into one of the glasses on the tray, a beautiful goblet with the faintest hint of iridescent lavender moving over its surface, and handed the glass to her. As she waited, he poured some for himself, then paused, looking at her. She'd pulled the sheet up to hide some of her nakedness, but the upper curve of her breasts was still visible, and she saw a fire to match her own rekindle in his gaze.

But then he raised his glass. "I'm not even sure what we should toast, but with everything we've been through, it seems as if we should make some sort of gesture."

She had to agree. Tilting her head to one side, she took him in, from the beautiful almond-shaped dark eyes to the broad shoulders and the fine, sensitive hands. No, she'd never been with anyone like him…and now that they were together, she couldn't imagine being with anyone else. They'd have to make their way in this world, because she knew he wasn't the sort of person to sit idle, but they could worry about that later. For now, they had each other, and that was enough.

Holding his gaze, she said, "To the universe, for bringing you to me."

"To the universe," he repeated softly. "And the most amazing woman in it."

They drank then, sipping the cool, delicate Eridani wine, and after that fed each other the unfamiliar fruit, tasting and teasing and deciding which they liked best.

Afterward they made love, while new and strange constellations crossed over the skylight above the bed. Those stars were the last thing she saw before she fell asleep, and she smiled.

It was all new and foreign, but Derek was here, and that meant she was home.

THE END